"Cheers to Maggie Davis for lifting everyone's spirits! . . . [*Hustle, Sweet Love*'s] crackling good humor will leave you in stitches."

Rave Reviews

"*Hustle, Sweet Love* is funny, sexy, and wholesome. It should be read with a good tanning lotion . . . it's hot enough to give you sunburn in the dead of winter!"

Romantic Times

No Holds Barred . . .

"My hair, please," he said thickly, trying to disengage her paralyzed clutch.

"Are you going to make love to me?" she croaked. "Right away," he promised, taking her mouth with an eager roughness.

"You're driving me crazy," he breathed into her neck. "I have a plane to catch. We'd better get—we'd better go to bed."

"What?" she cried, knowing she'd lost her mind there for a moment.

He looked down at her impassively. "You said you wanted to hurry."

"I did not." She jerked violently when he pulled the fragile scrap of her black bikini panties down her legs.

Lacy looked down at herself. "That's outrageous," she breathed. She had on strappy black sandals, black embroidered stockings, a black satin garter belt and nothing else. "You're crazy," she protested weakly.

"I'm surprising myself," he admitted. "But I have a feeling this is going to be an evening to remember.

"To think I found you," he murmured against her cheek, "hustling in a bar."

Hustle, Sweet Love

HUSTLE, SWEET LOVE

Maggie Davis

PaperJacks LTD.

TORONTO   NEW YORK

AN ORIGINAL

PaperJacks

HUSTLE, SWEET LOVE

PaperJacks LTD.

330 STEELCASE RD. E., MARKHAM, ONT. L3R 2M1
210 FIFTH AVE., NEW YORK, N.Y. 10010

First edition published December 1988

10 9 8 7 6 5 4 3 2 1

ISBN 0-7701-0922-5

1

"How much?" the little fat man in the sequin-decorated beanie asked breathlessly.

His wide eyes traveled upward from Lacy's non-stop legs, in black embroidered stockings, to her tiny waist and temptingly revealed breasts, and his gaze locked, jammed, and couldn't move.

"That is," he said, obviously awe-struck, "if your schedule isn't all filled up for tonight."

Good grief, Lacy thought—whirling around on her bar stool to face the group of conventioneers in matching sequin-decorated beanies who were avidly watching—*it's the dress*!

She had floated into the hotel bar in a daze of happiness to order a split of champagne and celebrate the most wonderful thing that had happened to her in a long time: getting a new job as fashion writer for *Fad* magazine. She was still wearing the black Claude

Montana that she'd modeled on the runway in the hotel ballroom for the Western States Fashion Wholesalers' show.

The Montana number was the wildest of the wild, something not really intended for Tulsa, Oklahoma; it was only included in the fashion show to top off the finale. The Montana was made of black silk crepe with exaggeratedly padded shoulders and the neckline plunging to the waist. It was also slit up the front from the hem almost to the crotch in a style more suited to New York or the more far-out boutiques of Rodeo Drive. The fillip for the wholesalers' fashion show—guaranteed to bring gasps of delight—were embroidered black-on-black silk stockings attached to an equally scandalous black satin garter belt that managed to reveal a naked pearly strip of Lacy's delectable inner thigh. That is, unless Lacy had her knees together and demurely pointed to the wooden panel of the bar. Which she'd had until a few minutes ago, when she'd thoughtlessly crossed her legs and attracted fat little Mr. Beanie.

The Claude Montana was the latest "tarty" look from Paris. It had knocked 'em dead, dress wholesalers and retail-store buyers alike, when Lacy had pranced down the hotel-ballroom runway in it, her smoky-blond hair teased and sprayed into a fantastic curly cloud around her head. At five feet nine inches, she'd carried the whole thing magnificently. The show's coordinator had agreed that only Lacy Kingston, with her face and figure virtually a clone of top models Cheryl Tiegs and Christie Brinkley, could wear the Claude Montana black crepe extravaganza and not have it turn into a vulgar disaster. With Lacy's All-American Girl body, brilliant green eyes and wide, mobile mouth, she was provocative, wanton, and had impeccable class.

That is, except in the old-West-style bar called the Grand Saloon. Mr. Sequin Beanie and his friends seemed to have been so impressed with Paris's *haut monde* "tarty look" they had taken her for a real tart!

Lacy was famous for her zany sense of humor, but she felt a very real twinge of irritation. Hookers often passed themselves off as models; she'd run into that more than once when telling people what she did for a living. Which was one reason she wanted to get out of her present line of work. Being gorgeous and outwardly sophisticated didn't really mean that one was that way to the core, even in the competitive fashion business known as the rag trade. At twenty-three, Lacy had definitely grown somewhat cynical, as she fended off passes from wholesalers, retailers and fashion photographers. Right now, she told herself, she had a right to celebrate her new job without being pestered. She'd waited for years to be a fashion writer. She'd earned her quiet little split of champagne; ordinarily she'd never touch a drop of alcohol because it could do the most horrible things to the complexion, like robbing it of precious moisture and causing wrinkles. Now here, she thought, staring at him, was Mr. Beanie People, wanting to know how much of her evening time he could buy!

Good grief, Lacy thought, what a nerd! How could she get rid of him?

Lacy's devilish sense of humor stirred restlessly. She'd had a split of champagne on a stomach that had had breakfast but no lunch or dinner. Some perverse demon, at that moment, seized her tongue.

Lacy scooped up her smoky-blond teased curls with one hand and shot Mr. Beanie a look from under her fake inch-long model's eyelashes that should have melted his shoelaces.

"It'll cost you, honey," Lacy said in her best imitation of Marlene Dietrich in the classic 1930s movie *The Blue Angel*.

The little man in the red hat seemed to tremble visibly. "How much?" he asked hoarsely.

Lacy also did a good imitation of Mae West in her famous old movie with Cary Grant called *She Done Him Wrong*. She stared at the little man, fighting down the urge to giggle. She didn't want to kill him outright.

She had no idea what price hookers were asking either in New York—where she'd just come from—or in Tulsa. She looked over Mr. Beanie's head and saw the bar's patrons were nearly all men, a seemingly affluent lot in expensively tailored Western-style clothes. At the moment they all seemed to be looking at her.

The same reckless devil prodded Lacy again. "Fifteen hundred dollars," she said throatily.

She never knew where the words had come from; they just seemed to jump out of the air. Lacy lifted the almost empty champagne glass to her lips and watched the little man literally stagger backward.

"All night?" he sputtered. "Gotta be all night at that price!"

Ugh, Lacy thought, watching him. She was realizing that she hadn't the faintest idea of what a big-time, worldclass hooker would do to earn fifteen hundred dollars. In spite of her sophisticated veneer and the Claude Montana, Lacy was still a well-brought-up lawyer's daughter from Long Island.

Mr. Beanie was dumbfounded, too. As he tottered away to report back to his friends, Lacy turned back to the bar. The next time, she promised herself, she'd watch what she was wearing when she bolted out of fashion-show dressing rooms to celebrate. *Fifteen hundred dollars*? Of all the sums she could have named, why that?

She supposed she knew the answer. Underneath her lacquered, professional beauty, Lacy was a girl who'd had only one disastrous sexual experience, in the front seat of a Buick convertible at age seventeen, and she'd been running ever since. Fifteen hundred dollars seemed like the right figure to keep away short fat men in sequined beanies looking for hookers, that was all.

She finished the last of the champagne in the bottom of her glass, studying her reflection in the bar mirror behind the lighted liquor bottles. She had to admit the dress was really awful, but she'd gotten used to wearing crazy, shocking clothes, because of her basic, hard-to-hide All-American Girl image. Lacy studied her hair. The dark-blond curls springing out from her face in wanton, teased, high-fashion were too much, she thought morosely. It was going to take her a full hour to wash out the hair spray and setting gel. Nobody appreciated all the trouble that went into professional modeling; it would take another hour to cream her face, because her skin had a tendency to acne when exposed to the West's hard water. It would be midnight, even as tired as she was, before she could finally creep into bed. Thankfully, the show moved on to Scottsdale, Arizona, then New York and oh, glory—her job on *Fad* magazine! She was really going to be a writer, she thought, mentally pinching herself to be sure it was true.

"I'll buy," a low, quiet, very male voice said.

Lacy lifted her inch-long fake lashes slowly. She'd forgotten what the subject was. "Hmmm?" she murmured abstractedly.

Whoever he was, he was tall. So tall that Lacy, five feet nine and tall even sitting down, had to look up. Six feet four or more, her mind registered. Dark hair expensively styled—at least a forty-dollar haircut—framed a taut, authoritative, good-looking face with a strong jaw, high cheekbones and a determined slash of a hard mouth. And what a body! Her eyes passed up and down it quickly, noting that he was not only tall but wide. The last time Lacy had seen a physique like that was at the circus. The broad-shouldered *V* that tapered to hard, slim hips and long, muscled legs belonged to a circus aerialist—big chest, big biceps and forearms, strong, tough-looking hands.

Lacy felt a very peculiar tingling all the way down to the pit of her stomach. There was nothing about this stunning man that reminded one of a circus. He was encased in a magnificently tailored tuxedo, with black tie and a conservative starched white shirt. A big, very expensive Rolex gold watch rode a wrist lightly speckled with fine black hairs. A gold ring with a fine blue-white diamond adorned a finger on the same hand. The exposed French cuff had a square cuff link, expensive and tasteful.

Wow, Lacy thought weakly. What a lot of power, what a lot of carefully stated authority! He looked about thirty-six or -seven, she judged as she lifted her eyes slowly and met patiently waiting, powerful gray ones, like a poker player's. There was a distinct shock as that look connected with hers; his eyes seemed to be wired for 220 rather alarming volts.

"What?" Lacy said between suddenly stiff lips.

"I said you're on," he told her quietly.

"Urk!" It was all the response Lacy could allow herself. She knew he wasn't referring to buying her a drink.

"I assume it *is* all night," he added smoothly.

One of his large hands, the one with the gold ring on it, grasped Lacy's arm lightly but firmly in the soft flesh above her elbow. His movement was intended to politely guide her from the bar stool, but to Lacy the grip was as inexorable as a pair of handcuffs.

She didn't need a computer printout at that moment to know that the towering hunk in the tuxedo had overheard her conversation with Mr. Sequin Beanie and was taking her up on it. She had to do something clever and intelligent. And quick! Lacy wet her lips. The gray eyes followed the movement with a sudden, powerful interest. "I'm all booked up," Lacy said helplessly.

Why, she wondered with a sort of horror, did her mind keep feeding her all these wrong lines tonight? She didn't know where they were coming from! Obviously the gray, commanding eyes didn't believe her. His next words proved it.

"I don't think so," he said. "You wouldn't be sitting here in the bar at this hour if you were."

Help, Mother, I'm being hustled by the Mob! Lacy's inner voice wailed as she stared at him. He did look something like the Mob, except that he was actually too tasteful. The Mob would have a bigger diamond ring. *Two* bigger diamond rings?

She had to get out of this somehow, Lacy knew. She was being mistaken for a hooker by perhaps a member of the Mob with a body like a six-foot-four circus aerialist in a perfectly tailored Savile Row tuxedo.

"No credit cards or checks," the devil in Lacy's tongue said smartly. The devil thought that would take care of it, but it didn't.

"Cash," the low, even voice replied.

The eyes like the Antarctic Ocean flowing under ice dropped to Lacy's black strappy sandals with their four-inch heels, went carefully up her legs in their embroidered black-on-black silk stockings to the entrancingly pearly strip of thigh and then to Lacy's admirably slender waist, to the nearly vulgar cleavage saved by her truly lovely breasts, to her blush-stained throat and finally to her face.

The look was one that should have raised Lacy's blood pressure a notch in spontaneous fury—calmly calculating, the look of a sharp, perceptive buyer trained in stock manipulations, blackjack games or even bank embezzlements. Thoroughly appraising. Obviously very, very interested.

His free hand reached into the perfectly cut tuxedo jacket and drew out a handsome English leather wallet and laid it on the bar. He moved a little closer so that his big body blocked the view. Only the bartender in his red jacket a few feet away could see what was going on. Then the long, tanned fingers flipped open the wallet so that Lacy could see an array of fifty- and one-hundred-dollar bills packed in it. Just as quickly, the fingers flipped the wallet shut again and put it back in the inside pocket of the black tuxedo.

It looked, Lacy dithered, like he was carrying literally thousands of dollars! Her heart was pounding so, she feared it would do devastating things to the precarious Claude Montana cleavage. Like jump out and land on the bar next to the champagne bottle. "I can't," she heard herself say.

That was right, she *couldn't*. Newly employed fashion writers for *Fad* magazine were very vulnerable. The circus aerialist who looked somewhat like a large black panther thought she was a hooker. What was it going to take to make him go away?

"I'm waiting for a very important—client," Lacy hissed. She thought that was the right word. "Now beat it."

The Antarctic-gray eyes rejected that, too. "Shall we go?" he said, exerting a little pressure on her elbow.

Lacy clung to the edge of the Western-style bar with one desperate hand. "There's been a misunderstanding," she babbled. *Why not let him have it? Why not the truth?* "Actually, I'm a model!"

The moment the words were out of her mouth Lacy knew it was another mistake. He'd heard that one, too. She saw the corners of his mouth turn up, then his gray eyes lifted, leveling on the bartender, who was now pretending to be polishing glasses.

"There's a city ordinance against soliciting in hotels." His voice was expressionless, unyielding. "Bill, the bartender there, will confirm that."

Lacy swiveled on the stool and saw the bartender nodding. She'd blown it, she thought frantically. She could just see the item in the *New York Daily News*: "Lacy Kingston, former New York fashion model and would-be *Fad* magazine reporter, was arrested in a Tulsa, Oklahoma, hotel bar last night for—"

SOLICITING?

"Who are you?" Lacy squeaked, in the grip of sudden, mindless terror. "A cop?"

Policeman! her inner voice screamed instantly. Say, *policeman*, dummy! Or law-enforcement officer. Anything but *cop*!

"Let's get out of the bar, shall we?" the inexorable voice was saying.

Lacy's knees buckled as she slid from the bar stool, and it wasn't because of the champagne she'd been drinking. She'd been in worse spots before—though at the moment she couldn't think of any. Pass it off with a few laughs, she tried to tell herself. Remember the time she'd punched out Peter Dorsey, the great fashion photographer, and blown the contract he'd offered her just because she wouldn't go to bed with him? Remember the I. Magnin buyer just last week? Remember—

None of them looked like this sleek, powerful Mob-type banker in his tux who was nearly dragging her by the arm away from the bar! Now they were sprinting across the lobby at a fast clip. Lacy saw two bellboys spring to open the elevator doors as though she and her escort were VIPs.

The lobby was no place to scream for help. On the other hand, if he was a cop, this didn't look like the way to the paddy wagon, either.

They were almost at the elevator. Lacy dug her four-inch heels into the lobby carpet and skidded to a stop.

"I forgot my purse," she cried, looking up at the dark head that bent to her attentively. "I have to go back to the bar!"

"It's on your arm." Strong fingers tightened around her elbow, guiding her inside the elevator. The bellboys rushed to guard the doors as they closed.

"I wasn't soliciting," Lacy cried. She tried to get her arm out of that deadening grip. "Besides, the hotel won't allow you to—"

"I know what the hotel allows and what it doesn't," he said as the elevator began its ascent.

Lacy slumped against the side of the elevator. "How?" she whispered.

He looked up to study the blinking lights over the doors. "Because I control enough of the hotel stock to say."

OK, now they were in an elevator, she told herself, numbly fighting down panic. She needed a game plan. But at the moment she was going to have to settle for going along with what was happening, to wait for the doors to open on the next floor and then to run like crazy. Even if she was a little dizzy with champagne, she bet she could beat him in a foot race if she took off the ludicrous heels. On the other hand, she really felt like throwing herself down on the floor of the elevator and crying hysterically.

Lacy stared at the right shoulder of the black tuxedo towering beside her. It looked as monolithic and unshakable as the granite hills of South Dakota. The jaw, the handsome, hard-cheekboned face didn't look like a lot of laughs. Neither did the firmly set mouth, with its slight indent at the corner that would have been a nice, shallow dimple on anybody else.

There he stood, six feet four of muscle and purposeful concentration, looking at the floor-indicator lights.

He obviously heard Lacy take a loud, sobbing breath, because he turned to her. "Don't crouch down like that," he said. "I'm not going to hurt you. In contrast to some of your other clients, I suppose." He studied her with a slight frown. "You really are extraordinarily . . . beautiful, for this sort of life." The eyes became rather steely. "You charge for it, of course."

"Glurg," Lacy breathed. She wanted to draw herself up and match him steely look for steely look, but she found all she could do was cower. Just as he said.

"Ah," he said, suddenly remembering. "The money."

The wallet came out again. Lacy watched, mesmerized, as tanned fingers opened the black silk purse still hanging by the strap from her shoulder. They counted off one-hundred-dollar bills. One. Two. Three— At one point he lifted gray eyes to see her watching, and the corners of his mouth turned down. He took the wad of bills and shoved them abruptly into her purse and snapped it shut.

Where, Lacy thought wildly, was the game plan that was going to rescue her from this? She was getting paid in advance for something she was definitely *not* going to do!

"Be calm," he told her as she trembled. "The money's yours. There'll be nothing kinky, nothing rough."

Kinky? Rough? Lacy felt as though she were going to faint. How am I going to get out of this without landing in the newspapers? her inner voice wailed.

He watched her with a faintly inquiring expression. "You haven't been doing this long, have you?" he observed.

"Too long, actually," Lacy gritted, feeling weak.

He suddenly moved to put both his big hands on her shoulders, pulling her to him slightly to look down at her. Lacy couldn't move. The elevator slowed, purred to a stop, but the doors did not open.

The hallway, she thought frantically as she stared up at him. She would make a break for it. There were always fire stairs in a hotel. She could outrun him going downstairs. Even if he did look like a professional athlete. She braced herself to leap out into the corridor at the first move.

The elevator doors, however, remained shut. The tall man held her with one hand and reached over her shoulder to push a combination number on a bank of buttons to release the computer lock. With a lurch, the elevator started up again. The top button said, PENTHOUSE.

Penthouse?

There were several long, terrible seconds while Lacy tried to realize there would be no hotel corridor, no fire stairs. *Penthouse?* The only way out of something like that was by parachute! The elevator came to a stop, and the doors pulled back.

Oh, God, she saw it really was a penthouse! It was not a hotel corridor but an elegant, small foyer decorated in smoked-glass panels, abstract paintings and chrome chairs against deep chocolate-brown carpeting. She saw a vast room in beige and black and brown, wrapped around by large windows that showed a spangled panorama of lights that was Tulsa, Oklahoma, at night.

"Here we are," he said, taking her by the arm again.

Lacy allowed him to steer her into the vast room. She could only think hysterically of escape.

And there was none.

2

"I believe you were drinking Dom Perignon," he said pleasantly. "I'll call down for some."

"No champagne!" Lacy cried shrilly. Where she was now, in the penthouse, was just as bizarre as a wallet jammed full of one-hundred-dollar bills. The room was *luxurious*! Then there was the fantastic Rolex watch, the tasteful blue-white diamond ring and the fabulous Bulgari cuff links. It was impossible not to think that she might end up with her feet encased in a block of concrete.

It had to be a dream. Or a movie, Lacy told herself. She knew she'd fallen asleep during an in-flight movie on her way back to New York, and all this was percolating through her dream-filled unconscious!

The big male body in the perfect tuxedo had gone to a panel of switches behind a glass and wood bar at the end of the room. As he pushed a switch, an incredibly lush version of "Lara's Theme," from *Dr. Zhivago*, filled the room right up to its vast, wraparound windows. Quadraphonic sound, Lacy thought weakly. It went with everything else. Now, as never before, she had to think of something, and quick!

"Perhaps you'd like something else to drink." He lifted a bottle of Scotch from under the bar, uncapped it and threw some ice into a glass. His eyes never left her as he poured himself a drink.

Lacy couldn't control a shudder. This was coming right down to the line, and whatever it was, she didn't need a map to tell her it was very dangerous—not only to her totally inexperienced body and her new job with *Fad* but to something else, too. The weird, devastating quiver deep in her flesh returned when he looked at her, like a hot tidal wave coursing through and tightening the most extraordinary muscles, in the most extraordinary places. She'd never felt anything like it before.

Stop that! Lacy told herself sharply. You're in hot water, stupid! Stop thinking all these things just because some totally gorgeous strange man is looking at you. See if there's a terrace you can leap from—like they do on *Magnum, P.I.*

She watched him put his drink down abruptly. He started toward her, moving with such effortless grace that it left her breathless. Lacy readied herself to deliver a karate chop. Strangely she didn't scream when he took her firmly by the hand and pulled her to him. It was the moment for the karate chop, but she couldn't do it.

"Shall we dance?" he said in his low, faintly husky voice.

Dance? Her thoughts did a series of flip-flops. DANCE? Now he was going to put those tremendously powerful-looking arms around her and hold her close?

He felt her uncontrollable shaking as he pulled her to him. "You're very tense," he murmured. "Just relax."

The strong, powerful arms that embraced her didn't help any. He looked down at her, his hard, chiseled banker-gambler's features impassive.

"If it makes you feel any better," he said, "I'd like you to know I appreciate really beautiful things. It's a passion of mine. And you are"— the appraising gray eyes moved over Lacy's face, studying her piquant, narrow nose, the arch of her brows, the eyelids with their burden of heavy, fake model's eyelashes and finally her wide, quivering All-American Girl mouth— "unbelievably lovely. Even in that ridiculous get-up."

She gathered he didn't like the fabulously expensive Claude Montana. Before she could protest, he put one hand decorously in the middle of her back, seized her fingers with the other hand and whirled her away in a waltz.

They moved across the thickly carpeted room to *Dr. Zhivago*'s liquid three-quarter time, Lacy's stiletto heels occasionally snagging in the deep pile of the carpet. She danced stiffly, pressed against his powerful body, her head spinning helplessly. The black windows of night-time reflected their images as they slow-danced: a tall, magnetically handsome stranger in the superb black shape of his tuxedo, Lacy an outrageous vision of loveliness with her cloud of smoky-blond curls, her slender, long-legged body.

Like most big men, he was light on his feet, an excellent dancer, even though he was so big and rock solid, it felt like being held against Mount Rushmore. Lacy's nostrils filled with the aroma of expensive men's cologne, soap, starched Egyptian cotton shirt front and the faint, cleanly pungent scent of his skin. He was dangerously strong; he almost lifted her from her feet with no effort at all when they turned. And Mount Rushmore, Lacy found with rising panic, was very aroused. Talk about virile. She couldn't miss it, pressed against him like that.

She was trying to ignore the evidence of his interest, leaning away from him tactfully, when he murmured in her ear, "What did you say your name was?"

Don't tell him, was her immediate reaction. You've got to get out of here before anything more happens. "Jane Doe," Lacy blurted. It was just another of those remarks that came rushing out of nowhere. The evening had been filled with them.

Dr. Zhivago beat on for a few more bars. "That makes me," he said sardonically, "John Smith, I believe."

That did it. There she was, being mistaken for a hooker by an aerialist who doubled for Mount Rushmore and who might or might not be a member of the Mob! What had gotten into her, anyway? Red-alert buzzers went into action. Then he suddenly bent his dark head, and the next thing she knew his mouth softly covered hers.

The feel of it was incredible. It was not only national red alert, it was total, sensual wipeout! She was stunned as his warm, firm mouth moved over hers with dazzling gentleness. *Gentle*? she wondered.

Her body jerked like a puppet's, falling into his arms. Even more gently, his kiss deepened.

"Open your mouth," he murmured against her lips.

It was as though she had no will of her own. She gasped as his tongue caressed her teeth, trailing urgent fire. Then, as Lacy gave a little sob of amazement, he took the sweetness of her opened mouth.

Zounds! *Zap*! *Bam*! *Powie*! Lights, sparks, fireworks, went off behind Lacy's eyes. Her feet would not move. It was impossible to escape. She'd never been kissed like that before in her life. She felt herself clinging to Mount Rushmore, with her fingers digging into his perfect tuxedo jacket. What kind of man was this who could slow-dance a hooker so magnificently and then kiss like this? she wondered, dazzled. Tenderly? Gently? With all that incredible *bam*! *zap*! *powie*! et cetera? For a *hooker*?

Lacy opened dazed eyes and looked straight into the gray expanse of the now-boiling Antarctic Ocean. "You're unbelievable," he was murmuring. Mesmerized, Lacy watched as the gray eyes bored into hers, seeking answers to as yet unasked questions. "You look so . . . untouched."

Right the first time. *Untouched*! That was the key word for the day. And she was going to stay that way. She must be out of her mind to let him even hold her like this! "I, uh . . . I'll take that drink now," Lacy croaked. Anything to get out of his arms. "Make it ginger ale or a Coke, please."

He didn't release her. Mount Rushmore was far too absorbed in what he was doing. He held her even closer, fingers splayed and softly rubbing through the silk of her dress. He said, his mouth caressing her hair, "It's time we got out of these clothes."

She tore herself free and bounced back from him. Actually, Lacy leaped back from him, executing a fancy, totally spontaneous pirouette that nearly landed her on the floor.

"I don't take my clothes off!" she yelped. "Never!"

She looked around frantically for the exit, the fire stairs, parachutes, the air force—anything.

He was already shrugging out of his tuxedo jacket. He draped it over one corner of the bar. "You don't take off your clothes," he repeated, watching her.

"No, I don't take off my clothes," Lacy cried hysterically. There must be some way out of the penthouse, there had to be. She didn't see anything that remotely resembled a door to a kitchen, or even the bathroom. "It's my specialty," she babbled. "I do everything with my clothes on!"

He thought that over, strong, tanned hands planted on narrow hips, his stony features obviously giving it some consideration. Finally he said, "I think I'll pass on that one. Your clothes, please."

Now what?

"Ah," she cried, suddenly inspired. A game plan had formed after all!

All she had to do was get Mount Rushmore in some helpless position, knock him out somehow. Render him immobile so she could rush for the elevator, take it to the lobby and then get out of Tulsa, Oklahoma, quick. From the airport she could call some of the models in the show and tell them she was shipping the Claude Montana back. Forget Scottsdale, Arizona. She could ask them to clear out her hotel room and send her clothes back to New York.

With an unthinking gesture, Lacy threw her silky mane of curls back with one hand and held it, elbow raised, to the back of her head. The profile of her throat, her shoulders and provocatively exposed breasts was instantly outlined. It was the wrong move, she saw immediately. The gray eyes had gone a deep, stormy color.

Aha! She suddenly knew what she could do. She had to approach the fierce black panther fearlessly, stroke him into submission and then hit him over the head with the nearest heavy lamp. But definitely not give him an opportunity to get her into the clutches of his dynamite kisses anymore. The mystery of those had nearly done her in.

Lacy looked around. All the lighting, unfortunately, was recessed in the beige ceiling. There were no lamps. She looked at the big, muscular body apprehensively. Even the famous right to the jaw that had decked Peter Dorsey, New York's most celebrated lecher-photographer, looked as though it would just bounce off that one.

She suddenly had a brilliant idea. "But I don't mind undressing *you*," she cried with totally false enthusiasm. "Let me help!"

But instead of advancing sinuously, seductively, as she'd planned, in her desperation she practically threw herself at him like a jet-propelled missile, her heels snagging in the carpet to make it an especially erratic launch. He staggered slightly as she zeroed home, grabbing at his shirt front.

"Yes, let me," Lacy cried. "It's my—"

"Specialty," he finished for her. He stood perfectly still, looking down at her with a quizzical expression.

"Yes, how did you know?" she cried.

He allowed her shaking fingers to loosen the tuxedo's black tie and pull it away. As Lacy stood with the black silk scrap of the tie in her hand, she couldn't see anything but a broad, never-ending chest. *Big* and *virile*, her rattling thoughts registered. For a woman who had emphatically avoided being interested in men since she was seventeen, Lacy was being assailed by a wave of awfully troubling but thoroughly interesting feelings.

She swallowed, hard. Watch what you're doing, her inner voice warned her. Black panthers pounce.

"Mmmmmm," Lacy murmured, acting her part, but adding a few shaky *mmmmm*s inadvertently. She made her fingers spread out across the crisp white cotton chest and found something there that went, *Thud, thud*. The sound did something terrible to her. She was so frightened she could hardly think.

Her fingers scrambled across the shirt buttons. She wanted him to stop breathing and being so warm under her hands and going, *Thud, thud*, like that, because he was going to hate what was coming next.

The game plan called for her to get his shirt unbuttoned and then yank it down over those big, powerful, muscular arms and entangle him in it so that he couldn't move while she ran for the elevator. In order to get his shirt unbuttoned right, she discovered she had to pull it out of the neat black trousers.

Very carefully, Lacy dropped her hands to the tabs of the evening suspenders buttoned to the waistband of the black tuxedo trousers. As she touched him, though, he put his big hands over hers. Not stopping her, just covering her hands while he searched her face.

"What is it?" Lacy quavered, trying not to look.

"I want you to stop being so frightened," he said. "You're really too lovely not to be . . ." He hesitated. "Not to be treated well. Do you understand?"

"Y-yes," Lacy jittered. She understood all too well. That's why she had to get out of there.

To her horror, when her hands unfastened his suspenders and gingerly pulled the zipper of his fly down enough to get his shirt out, his hips were so narrow that his trousers sort of slithered slowly down around his knees.

Lacy stared. Her fashion-trained mind registered: sculpted Gianni Versace briefs, raw Italian silk in a gold-beige color, with interwoven self-supporting spandex, suggested list price, $95.00. Available at better men's stores in New York, Palm Beach, Dallas-Fort Worth and Beverly Hills. Semi-transparent. Lacy couldn't believe what she saw. Mount Rushmore was enormous all over.

With a muffled cry, Lacy grabbed the shirt to yank it over his arms. She dragged on it, leaning her weight on the cloth, hauling the shirt down to his wrists, so he couldn't lift his hands, swathed in strong, tight Egyptian cotton.

She had a sudden, crazy desire to weep. It was like putting your favorite tiger to sleep at the vet's. All she needed now was the heavy lamp.

Lacy staggered out of harm's way. But he only stood looking down at his entrapped arms and hands quite carefully, his legs encumbered by the dropped trousers around his knees. While she panted in terror, he lifted his dark head, eyes gone quite cool.

"I'm really not," he said carefully, his arms still trapped, "into bondage or anything like that."

With a loud scream, Lacy threw herself across the room, almost falling headlong before she reached the foyer and the elevator.

"Please," she howled, punching the button, "open up!" She heard the sound of the cage rising. When she turned to look over her shoulder, she saw him still standing where she'd left him, watching her calmly. Then she saw him hunch his powerful shoulders and heard the distinct sound of ripping cloth. *Rrrrrrrrrp.* The whole back of the shirt just gave way. She lunged inside. He was unfastening the gold cuff links to pull the shirt off when the elevator doors closed.

Lacy sagged against the wall of the elevator in dry-eyed fright. She was free, she was home safe. She wasn't a fifteen-hundred-dollar all-night hooker anymore! Only—

Good grief! She still had the money!

She still carried the little black peau de soie silk handbag over her shoulder. She'd never taken it off!

Lacy grabbed at the small purse and opened it. A roll of one-hundred-dollar bills popped up in it just as the elevator came to a stop at the twentieth floor.

The doors didn't open. Lacy stared at the panel of buttons, clutching the fifteen hundred dollars in cash in her fist. The computer lock to make it go down into the hotel, she realized numbly. She didn't have the combination!

"Aaagh!" Lacy cried in violent despair.

The next moment there was a jolt, and the elevator began to rise.

"Oh, no," she wailed, knowing where it was going. He was pressing the button to bring it back up! She was going to faint. It couldn't end like this! She was going to suffocate, her heart was racing so.

"Help," she whispered as the doors opened.

He stood there. He had taken off his shirt and his impeccably tailored evening trousers and his elasticized hose and his polished black oxfords. All he had on his sleek, powerful body were the Gianni Versace self-supporting spandex raw-silk briefs. Semi-transparent, Lacy noted, shaking uncontrollably. And a perfect flat gold chain around his neck, the Rolex gold watch on his wrist, the diamond ring on his finger. He wore a look of icy reserve as he surveyed the roll of bills clutched in Lacy's hand.

Her fee, Lacy realized, staring down at it. She'd followed her game plan, tied him up and leaped into the elevator with fifteen hundred dollars. *A scam.* From the look in his eyes she could see he knew what the word meant, too.

He was holding a bar glass in his hand.

"I fixed your ginger ale," he said.

3

"It's not what you think it is," Lacy cried. "I don't want your money! I'm not even a hustler. I'm really a model!"

"Of course," he said. His hand seized her fingers and placed them around the glass of ginger ale. "Here's your drink. I'm not going to call the cops, so just relax."

"You aren't?" she squeaked.

"No." He released her arm. "We have an arrangement for the evening, and I'd like to get on with it. I appreciate," he said evenly, "that this must be a tough way for you to make a living, operating a scam. Obviously either you make big money or you're desperate."

"I'm desperate," Lacy whispered. She couldn't take her eyes from the long fingers and neatly manicured nails. Even his hands looked very sexy and assured.

The gray eyes were on her face searchingly. "Do you operate this setup alone, or do you have a partner? Some sort of lover? Pimp?"

Partner? Pimp? Things were just getting worse, rapidly. Now she was not only a hooker, she was a con artist—a bandit!

"I work alone," she said. Maybe if he thought she was just a poor working girl, he wouldn't send her out of there with her feet in concrete. "I support my orphaned mother. And a brother. In a wheelchair." He just didn't know how desperate she was.

He cocked an eyebrow at her. "Your mother's orphaned?"

"We never know who our parents are in our family," she said, trying to make it all hang together.

"Ah," he said, raising both eyebrows. "I see."

He looked wryly thoughtful as he raised his hand. His touch was gentle, inquisitive. One finger wrapped around a glistening curl, then released it.

"Amazing," he murmured. Very slowly his big hand dropped to the smooth column of her throat, his palm resting against Lacy's wildly beating pulse. His fingers held her throat lightly.

Lacy closed her eyes. It was incredible, but the *zap! bam! powie!* was back. She should be screaming by now, but all he had to do was touch her, and this happened instead!

"Do it quick," she whispered, expecting the worst. She preferred that big, powerful hand to just snap her neck instead of strangling her slowly.

He gave her a strange look. "As you wish. But there's no need to rush, is there?"

Lacy opened her eyes, wide. On the other hand, if he wasn't going to exact his revenge there on the spot, there was still the matter of delivering fifteen hundred dollars' worth of something she knew practically nothing about.

"I give refunds," she said, without hope.

"Keep the money," he murmured, looking down appreciatively at her wide, soft mouth. "I'm not going to haggle."

Lacy tilted her head back expectantly. He was probably going to kiss her again. Which, she found, was not so terrible after all. Not when compared with leaping out windows or being transported to the Tulsa garbage dump in concrete.

But instead of kissing her, his hand found the zipper in the back of the Claude Montana and slowly pulled it down. The black crepe slid across her skin, the sleeves slipping down. There hadn't been room under the dress for a bra. Lacy quickly clutched her full white breasts with both hands.

"You don't usually have to come across, do you? That's not surprising," he murmured. "Don't cringe, let me look at you."

Lacy lifted her chin defiantly. She would have thought her skin would crawl under that probing gray-eyed gaze. But instead, for the second time that evening, she felt another blush rising in her face.

"My God," he muttered almost to himself, "you're too incredibly beautiful to be doing this sort of thing."

She was frozen as his hard, warm hands slid down her bare back, pushing her dress over her hips and to the floor. She heard him take a quick, in-drawn breath.

"But you do come dressed for it," he murmured appreciatively.

Oh, God, the garter belt! Lacy thought, too late. That awful black satin garter belt that held up the provocative black stockings. Outrageous on the runway, pure disaster *here*!

"Do you know what you look like in that thing?" he said hoarsely.

Lacy moaned. Under the sudden leaping fire in those gray eyes, her naked breasts broke into responsive tingles. Why did she feel she wanted those big tanned hands on her, stroking and caressing her? The garter belt felt as though it were crawling down her stomach. Under the silky black embroidery her legs shivered in anticipation.

"You'll have to kill me first," she gritted.

"On the contrary." All the coiling power of the black panther had returned. He raked her with desirous eyes. "Don't be afraid. I assure you, you won't do anything you don't want to."

Nothing she didn't want to do? The man was a dangerous, egotistical lunatic! Nobody ever said anything like that, Lacy was sure, to a hustler in their whole lives!

"Take that!" Lacy yelled. She hit him hard with an edge-of-the-hand karate chop on his brown column of a neck where it joined his massive shoulder. Her fingers went numb instantly.

Maybe she forgot to yell, "Hah!" she thought, dazed. The way they taught in karate class.

"Don't hurt yourself," he murmured, his lips nuzzling her hair.

She raised her leg to knee him in the groin, but he caught it easily. Lacy stook on one leg, helplessly, wondering what to do.

"Jane," he said tentatively. "Jane—Janey, let's not be rough."

"My name's not Jane!" she yelled, trying to get her black-stockinged leg back.

"It is now," he reminded her. His thumb stroked her knee softly. "You have the most magnificent legs I've ever seen."

Suddenly he released her. She was quickly enveloped in his arms, pressed hard against his chest, his mouth dropping down to seize and nibble the warm, tender skin of her throat. The urgent feel of his lips sent instant shock waves into Lacy's body. She was helpless as his demanding mouth moved to a sensitive spot under her ear, tasting it, his breath touching her hair, then to the silky skin of her shoulder and up again to the line of her chin. His mouth stopped there, leaving Lacy gasping, waiting for more. She opened her eyes wide.

So this was what it was like to have an obviously experienced, ardent, aroused man make love to you, Lacy thought, stunned. It was terrible; it was wonderful; it was totally mind destroying!

He murmured against the corner of her lips, "You're so fantastically beautiful. All over."

"Uh," Lacy said, her mind gone crazy.

His other hand was caressing the smooth, tight flesh over her ribs, sliding under her arms, stroking with his thumb. With excruciating slowness, a finger traced the heavy fullness of her breast.

Why didn't he just go ahead and kiss her, maul her, ravish her and get it over with? she thought with a sob. Instead of all this horribly tantalizing stuff? She gasped again as his head bent, and she clutched at his thick, nicely styled hair with both hands. Then she felt his hot mouth seize a delicate, shrinking, rosy nipple that instantly tightened to a hard bud of pained excitement. She almost screamed. Did he know no man had ever done this to her before? Couldn't he tell? He was sending ruthless fountains of fire through her body, and there was a sudden, alarming ache in her groin. She heard herself making loud, sobbing noises. She was practically climbing all over him.

"My hair, please," he said thickly, trying to disengage her paralyzed clutch.

Lacy met those gray eyes, wild-eyed. "Are you going to make love to me?" she croaked. It was more of a plea than a question.

"Right away," he promised, taking her mouth with an eager roughness.

"You're driving me crazy," he breathed into her neck. "I—" He seemed to shake himself. Then he lifted his hand behind her back and looked at his gold Rolex watch. "I have a plane to catch at seven-thirty," he said somewhat hoarsely. "We'd better get—we'd better go on to bed."

His words dragged Lacy back to sanity. "What?" she cried. She tried to pry herself away from his big body, knowing she'd lost her mind there for a moment.

He looked down at her impassively. "You said you wanted to hurry."

"I did not!" Where had the game plan gone, anyway? He had wiped everything out of her mind with those crazy, wild kisses!

She wrenched herself out of his arms and tried to stamp away, dazed but indignant, with naked breasts, quivering body and long legs in black embroidered stockings.

"You're not going anywhere like that," he growled deep in his throat. He followed after her quickly, bent and with a smooth motion lifted her in his arms. "Bed is better."

"Put me down!" Lacy howled.

He paid no attention. The bedroom, apparently, was a sharp right from the foyer. He carried her to it with long, determined strides.

"I'm going to sue you!" she shrieked as he let her slide from his arms down the full length of his body.

"And I'll charge you with soliciting and attempted robbery. You don't mind if I keep this on, do you?" He held both her hands in an easy grip as he bent to open the fasteners on the garter belt.

"What are you doing?" she cried.

She jerked violently when he pulled the fragile scrap of her black bikini panties down her legs. Then he refastened the snaps on the garter belt, leaving it and the black stockings.

Lacy looked down at herself. "That's outrageous," she breathed. She had on strappy black sandals, black embroidered stockings, a black satin garter belt and nothing else.

He cocked a dark eyebrow at her. "Outrageous and lovely. It suits you."

"You're crazy," she protested weakly.

"I'm surprising myself," he admitted. He slid his hands around her waist and pulled her to him. "But I have a feeling this is going to be an evening to remember. To think I found you," he murmured against her cheek, "hustling in a bar."

Yes, well, she supposed stranger things had happened. She found his mouth with her own, eager for the wild sensation of his dynamite kisses.

His hands pressed against her inner thighs, making them open to him. Then his fingers were unaccountably searching out the damp, throbbing core of her flesh, making her body arch toward him.

"Oh, oh, oh," Lacy quavered. Nothing like this had ever existed before. She was surrendering completely to him without a thought for the consequences.

She couldn't protest when he picked her up in his arms and advanced a few steps to a tremendous bed covered with a black velvet spread. He came down on it over her, his heavy, hard body pressing all along the writhing, yearning length of hers, holding her under him.

"You want this, don't you?" he muttered, lifting himself away from her for a moment to peel off his clinging briefs.

Lacy stared up at the handsome face above her. Yes! No! It was too late to tell him about that disastrous experience on senior-prom night in the Buick convertible. And that she was really afraid of men. And that she might be frigid. She found she didn't care. This was the most terrible night of her whole life.

"Yes," Lacy said helplessly.

"You're so responsive," he said raggedly. "God, you can't be faking this!"

"Mmmmm," Lacy answered, trying to hold his hard, good-looking face between both hands so he'd kiss her again. His kisses were fabulous. That was no fake. It was—

"I—oh!" Lacy cried in alarm as absolute reality thrust somewhat painfully against her and took possession. She hadn't thought it would be like the one and only first time. "We don't fit!"

"Yes, we do—relax," he told her. "Don't be frightened. I'm not going to hurt you."

"Yeow!" Lacy cried wildly. She was wrong—it was nothing like she remembered. The shuddering black panther had her in his paws, clenching in a savage rhythm that was sending skyrockets through her body. And worse, she was going absolutely mad, making all sorts of loud, lustful sounds as that inexorable force choked out its own impassioned pleas for her to take it easy, then urged her to do just the opposite.

A frenzied Mount Rushmore overwhelmed Lacy, descended all over her like an earthquake, boulders tumbling, trees giving way. A hot, ravenous mouth dragged volcanic bursts of her fire into his destroying lips. At the very center of the seismic uproar, Lacy trembled with the earthshaking pleasure that was driving into her, enveloping her, lifting her to a shattering peak where she melted into streams of flame, molten lava and exploding sparks. At her ecstatic cry of discovery, Mount Rushmore literally blew apart.

Then an avalanche rumbled down on top of her and buried her beneath it.

It was a remarkably long time before the cosmos put itself back together again. "I can't breathe," Lacy murmured stoically after a few minutes. And after she had pulled a strand of tangled hair from her swollen mouth.

"I'm sorry," he said hoarsely. He raised himself at once on his elbows and looked down at her, his eyes a stunned, opaque slate color. He cleared his throat.

"That was . . . quite an experience," he managed.

They stared at each other.

"Me, too," Lacy said with quivering sincerity. Their bodies, still pressed together, were covered with a satiny sheen of damp. And he was still gasping.

The black panther's taut, handsome features continued to study her upturned face searchingly. Then he shook his dark head. "I can't believe," he said between gasps, "that you do this for a living."

Lacy's eyes opened wide. "Why?" she whispered, dreading the answer.

His expression was more than a little baffled. "Because," he said with an effort, "you put so much into it."

Lacy bit her lips. Did that mean he hadn't seen through her total lack of experience? And the fact that she hadn't the vaguest idea of what one did to earn fifteen hundred dollars? Good grief, did that mean he was *satisfied* with the transaction?

She was suddenly and incongruously pleased. Just as quickly she felt a deep pang at how awful it was to put a price on anything so wonderful. Lacy was certainly no judge of these things, but Mount Rushmore had been fantastic, tender, impassioned—Wow, her dazed mind added, you can say that again—and generally stupendous. And she had discovered her own latent passion as a result.

She had a feeling that there was even more to it than that. Because the circus aerialist and the black panther and Mount Rushmore and the Mob banker-gambler were all of them, she guessed, rather special, rather supermarvelous for any woman lucky enough to fall into their hands. She wouldn't be surprised if they had known a lot of women.

That, for some reason, made her feel so depressed she almost wanted to cry. He really didn't look like a compulsive woman chaser, she thought, examining that hard, chiseled face that was so intently studying hers. She could see women chasing him, rather than the other way around. Strands of his dark, curling hair fell over his forehead, dripping small beads of perspiration into his eyebrows and thick, tangled black eyelashes. She could see the firm line of his mouth was definitely softened, definitely blurred from all that wild, hungry kissing. He looked rather sweet.

Impulsively, Lacy reached up to touch his mouth with the tips of her fingers. He bent his head quickly to kiss them lightly, softly. She felt a terrible, unfamiliar ache rising in her throat.

"I want you again," he murmured.

"Again?" She opened her eyes wide. That seemed impossible after what they'd just done.

"Again." The note of authority had crept back into his voice. "We have the rest of the night, remember."

Oh, *that*. "Ah—you have a plane to catch," she said, staring at him.

"Let me worry about that," he said, burying his lips in her hair.

Lacy clasped her hands around the hard column of his neck that was sweat-slick with lovemaking and drew his head down to her.

She wanted to find out something as she lifted her mouth to him eagerly. And that was whether a deliberate search for all the *zap! bam! powie!* would make it all spring to life again. It did. She heard him make a growling sound of pleasure deep in his throat. She couldn't help remembering the hoarse, exultant cry he'd given when Mount Rushmore had exploded, spewing rockets and fountains of flame. And she felt a curl of heated sensation answering in the depths of her own flesh.

Still locked in the expanding wildness of their kiss, Lacy let her fingers explore his thick, sweaty hair and the places behind his right ear. She felt his strong frame shudder under her touch. When her hand dropped to the satiny creases of his neck, he trembled again. She had a certain power, she realized, fascinated.

"Mmmmmmmm," Lacy murmured, thinking how marvelous this all was.

In answer, he dug his lips into her throat, lavishing her wet skin with small, biting kisses. Then he nibbled his way down her shoulder and into the warm, sensitive spot inside her elbow, making her squirm with the electric feel of his tongue against the nerve points it found. Both his hands held her arms, gently imprisoning her, keeping her still while his mouth went on to circle and caress her aching breasts. When Lacy moaned, she thought she heard him say something.

"I beg your pardon?" Lacy breathed.

"I said," he murmured, his voice muffled against all her creamy softness, "I'm damned if I can believe any of this."

4

It was easy to leave the penthouse after all.

While the black panther was taking his shower in preparation for his 7:30 a.m. flight and singing an old Beatles song, "Yesterday," in a slightly off-key baritone, Lacy found the door to an unused-looking kitchenette, the door to the hotel service area behind it, crept down the steps to the floor below and took the elevator to the lobby.

There was no need to hang around any longer, even though he'd telephoned down for room service to deliver an elaborate breakfast for two, including champagne. And even though he had said he wanted to talk to her as soon as she got dressed. There was, Lacy knew unhappily, simply nothing for them to talk about.

And so you see, she told herself later that morning on a TWA flight going back to New York, he would never know, and neither would anybody else, that she'd spent the night as a successful hustler in a penthouse in Tulsa, Oklahoma. Even her friends, who all knew she was totally zany, would never believe that one!

Worse, she still had the money. She'd been so frantic to get away while he was showering that she had only managed to get partly zipped up the back, clutching her strappy sandals to her chest to tiptoe through the rooms.

Forgetting to leave the money behind was the last straw, Lacy told herself. No wonder she was so horribly depressed through the remaining mists of her slight champagne hangover.

It was more than just depressed—considering that Mount Rushmore was only the second man she'd made love with in her whole life, and she didn't even know his name. To make it worse, he'd been convinced she was a hooker—you'd think a massive guilty psychological trauma would settle on her mind and wipe out the whole episode, like amnesia.

Instead, she was finding that all the men she saw in Tulsa's busy air terminal and on Pan Am's 737 to New York looked strangely like malnourished refugee midgets from a war zone, compared with the great hunk she'd just left. When Lacy gazed out of the jetliner's window, all she could see was the reflection of those storm-gray eyes looking down at her from that hard, virile face, reminding her of what it was like to be held in his arms. And all those stupendous earthquakes of passion, which she was positive were not your ordinary, everyday earthquakes of passion at all. At least not the kinds she'd been offered in the past.

She found herself visualizing the sleek, beautiful body, with its gold neck chain, its big gold Rolex watch, until she was totally distracted and the plane's copilot came back to sit on the arm of Lacy's cabin-class seat and strike up a conversation and try to arrange a date with her. Which pilots or copilots usually tried to do when they saw her, especially on Pan Am, although Presidential, with all those smooth D.C.-area types, was worse.

Mount Rushmore has a wife, dummy, Lacy tried to convince herself, finally getting rid of the essentially unappealing copilot and curling up in her seat to get some sleep.

But she couldn't sleep.

Stop it, she fretted. Mount Rushmore has a wife and at least three beautiful children in Tulsa and an expensive house in the suburbs within commuting distance of his job as banker-gambler for the Mob, and everything else that goes with it. Like vacations in Europe, she thought with a lump in her throat, traveling by Concorde or the QE II, with every woman in sight hungering after him. And naturally a sixty-foot power cruiser and his own Lear jet, since he was apparently in his midthirties and obviously not living at poverty level. He'd certainly have earned it all by now. And at least three or four mistresses, she knew with terrible despair, the way he makes love.

You're just exhausted and you've had a bizarre experience, she rationalized. Try to forget it.

She really hadn't had much sleep. When the alarm clock had gone off in the penthouse, she'd opened her eyes to find that he was already awake, resting on one elbow beside her and looking down at her with the most curious, intent expression on his face. And of course he'd wanted her again, even though Lacy didn't really think anyone could make love that many times. Still, he had been carefully slow and tender, perhaps just as tired as she was, his dark hair tousled, rousing her very gently one last time. And perhaps because it was the last time, it had been more devastatingly sweet, more wildly fervent than all the rest.

"Take your shower," he had murmured when the last earthquake had subsided. He held her closely and trailed kisses down the side of her face and into her throat as he said huskily, "And I'll order the world's biggest breakfast. We have to talk about this."

Lacy had known even then, still lying with his arms around her, that there was simply nothing for them to talk about. He wouldn't believe her—he hadn't believed her from the beginning that she wasn't a hooker, and she knew there was nothing, really, that she could tell him to make him change his mind. It was fate, miserable fate, and she had to be resigned to it. Besides, with all that all-night lovemaking, she was so physically exhausted she could hardly think. And so she had crept out of the apartment while he was still loudly singing, "Yesterday, all my troubles seemed so far away," in the shower.

She was never going to sleep again, Lacy knew despairingly, unless she could manage to forget the whole thing. She sat up straight in her seat and waved down the Pan Am flight attendant. She had to stop thinking about creeping out of the penthouse in Tulsa, Oklahoma, before dawn, leaving some part of her strange, just-discovered passionate emotions behind. Otherwise, she was going to drive herself into a nervous breakdown.

"I'll have a martini," Lacy told the flight attendant, even though it wasn't even lunch time and she was well aware of the moisture-robbing effects of alcohol on the complexion and the real threat of thousands of wrinkles. "Make it a double," she choked, closing her eyes.

Lacy started work at *Fad* magazine a week later on a Monday, reporting to the editorial offices in the Fad Publishing Group's skyscraper on Madison Avenue. After the lesson she'd learned on Basic Image and what had happened in Tulsa, she chose her outfit carefully, appearing before the managing editor, Gloria Farnham, at 9:00 a.m. in a crisp Geoffrey Beene navy shantung suit with a gray and white striped shirtwaist, navy string tie and matching navy kid gloves and shoes and purse. Her smoky-blond curls were drawn up in a severe topknot, with only a few errant strands escaping to fall gracefully over her temples and the creamy nape of her neck.

Managing editor Farnham, who was wearing an Emanuel Ungaro sheath, took one approving look and said, "Very nice, sweetie, you're on Seventh Avenue-garment-house assignments, anyway," and took Lacy into a large, chaotic room that was the *Fad* magazine heartland.

So this is the magazine business, Lacy told herself with a rush of excitement. She followed the elegant figure of the managing editor through acres of close-packed desks that seemed to cover the entire ninth floor of the Fad Publishing Group building. It was a busy place even early in the morning, with ringing telephones and both male and female figures hunched in front of computer terminals amid a clutter of styrofoam cups and Danish pastries.

Lacy could see working for *Fad* was obviously going to be a thousand times better than runway modeling in hotels and convention centers across the United States. Now, at last, she was a member of the fourth estate, a journalist, something more than a body for wholesalers to hang clothes on, a part of the whole mysterious power of the Written Word. Even if in this particular case it confined itself mostly to beauty care and women's fashions.

She took a deep breath, backing up out of a cul-de-sac of promotion displays she had blundered into and hurrying after the managing editor. This was it. Her chosen career. Excitement. Creativity. Ideas. She hoped she never had to hear another model's discussion on the advantages of using adhesive tape under the bust line when there was no room to wear a wired bra, and what was the best cover-up for a large, determined hickey, as long as she lived.

"Oh, it's you," a small, darkly pretty but very harried-looking woman intoned as the managing editor stepped into her glass-partitioned cubicle. She quickly put her hand over the receiver. "Whatever it is you want, Gloria, we did it yesterday, but we can't find it. But someone's looking for it, OK?"

"Don't be silly, sweetie," the managing editor responded with a vague, silvery laugh. "This is Stacy Kingsley—she did those articles for *Women's Wear Daily*, remember? It's just absolutely marvelous to have her with us. Now, darling, you've got to find her a desk."

"No, I don't remember," the assistant editor said, staring at Lacy over the stacks of back issues of

Vogue, Bazaar, Mademoiselle and *Glamour* that spilled over her desk and onto the floor. She kept her hand clamped over the telephone receiver but not tightly enough to smother the faint conversational noises that emanated from it. "God, Gloria, are we doing a photo shoot here in the office? And if so, what for? Take her away—I can't do anything with her right now!"

"Jamie, sweetie, she's a *junior fashion writer*, not a model anymore. You're going to put her on New York dress assignments with the rest of your juniors."

"Oh, my God," the harried woman said under her breath, "not another one." The assistant editor, without taking her hand from the receiver, lifted her elbow and used it to point awkwardly to the edge of her desk. "Find a place to sit, will you, Stacy? I'll be with you in a minute."

"It's Lacy," Lacy murmured, trying to keep in mind all the wonderful things about her new profession. "Lacy Kingston."

"Have fun," managing editor Gloria Farnham said, drifting away out of the crowded glass cubicle, oblivious to the pile of *Elle* and *Harper's Bazaar* magazines that fell to the floor behind her.

The assistant editor watched the retreating figure of the managing editor with weary eyes. "Gloria the Space Queen," she muttered. "But she's great reading off cards at board meetings. She makes everything sound like she did it all by herself."

"I'm really excited about working here," Lacy began politely.

"Are you still there?" the assistant editor said, turning her attention back to the telephone. "Philip, listen to me—don't touch your brother's chicken pox. They're sacred, do you hear? No, I don't care if he told you they itched. They're *his* chicken pox—just let Terry and the doctor take care of them, OK?'' There was a brief pause as the faint noises answered on the other end. ''Right, and the same thing applies to your video games. Even Terry understands that. At least I thought he understood it before I left this morning.'' The assistant editor groaned, using her free hand to cradle her forehead. ''Philip, just try to hold things together until six o'clock, will you? I promise you I won't be late. I'll be there by the time Dr. Who gets the Tardis out of the time warp. I'll watch it with you. Guaranteed.''

When the assistant editor hung up, she pushed a pile of magazine proofs out of the way and gave Lacy an apologetic smile. ''My youngest has chicken pox, and my oldest is baby-sitting. My sitter is out sick because she's the one who gave him the chicken pox in the first place. It's been hell for two days.'' Her tired brown eyes traveled quickly over Lacy, who was perched on the corner of her desk amid the stacks of magazines. ''Good Lord, brains *and* beauty this time —you double threats slay me! What's wrong with fashion modeling—did they have a surplus of Christie Brinkley look-alikes this year?''

''Ah, well, no—yes,'' Lacy managed, blushing. ''But actually, I *did* lose a Playtex bra ad once because they said I looked too much like Cheryl Tiegs.''

The assistant editor snorted. ''That's a liability? The rag trade is a crazy business.'' Her brown eyes flickered over Lacy's face. ''Heavens, you look like you were put together to music! It's unbelievable.''

"Actually," Lacy said uneasily, wanting to drop the subject, "my bottom's a little too big. Somebody always mentions it.

"I really want to write," she added. "I'm serious about that."

The other woman had to laugh. It was a nice, friendly laugh that immediately made her look younger and much prettier. "Ah, model talk! I never met a model yet who didn't think she was rather ugly—it's a professional disease. I bet your boyfriend doesn't complain," she observed dryly. "Your bottom looks pretty gorgeous to me."

Lacy froze. There was no reason, at that moment, for what happened in Tulsa to rise up in her mind vividly, but it did. She had a distinct recollection of the black panther's tender, appreciative caresses in the very place they were talking about. It was going to haunt her forever, she knew with an inward shudder; that long night of fantastic lovemaking was burned into her brain.

"Sorry about that," the assistant editor said quickly. "I struck a nerve, didn't I? It's a man, isn't it? Did you get out of modeling to forget him? Did the bastard do something rotten to you, kid?" she asked sympathetically. "Or was the jerk just married?"

"Oh, no," Lacy choked. She tried to pull herself together and knew she was blushing madly. Other women had romantic love affairs that broke their hearts. She was stuck with a story about being mistaken for a hustler in a downtown Tulsa, Oklahoma, hotel. "I'm really—well, yes, I'm trying to forget it," she said truthfully.

The assistant editor sighed. "You've come to the

right place, kid, believe me. We've got four junior writers now and only one permanent job slot, so you can work yourself to death while competing—how's that?'' When she saw Lacy's weak smile, she went on, ''The money is lousy, and dress manufacturers never like anything you write about their clothes. You'll be exhausted, your feet will hurt, your makeup will smear, and your hair will come down in the rain. When you finish a good story, nobody will notice. Only six months later Gloria will come back and want to know why you're in such a slump when you were so great when you started. You see that snake pit out there, don't you?'' she said, nodding in the direction of *Fad* magazine's editorial room. ''The company makes its money renting out the rest of the building and cramming us in here. Our circulation's off thirty percent, and we've been operating in the red for more than two years, with *Vogue* and *Bazaar* beating our time mainly because we refuse to admit they're even out there. I'm Jamie Hatworth, and you report to me. I'm assignments editor, as well as four million other things around this place, and my kids have forgotten they have a mother. Well, almost.'' She began to rummage around her paper-littered desk looking for something. ''Can you really write, Stacy—Lacy?'' she wanted to know. ''More importantly, can you work like a dog? You're going to be doing stuff for a section called Fashion Updates. It's short features about manufacturers and wholesalers. You'll hate it. Now, after all this, aren't you getting a headache? Don't you want to sneak out and freshen up your makeup? Don't you want to quit right now and walk out of here?''

''Yes, yes, yes,'' Lacy said quickly, beginning to catch on. She grinned. This was more like it. ''And no, no, no, to the last three. It sounds exciting, honestly it does. I really like the rag trade. I just wanted to get out of modeling, that's all. Besides, I'm getting pretty old."

"You're practically dying of it," the other woman said dryly. "Wait until you're all of twenty-five.

"Now," she said, handing Lacy a typewritten sheet, "here's a list of dress houses the junior writers are working on. And because you're such a nice kid, I've given you all the turkeys nobody's heard from in years. What you have to do this week is bring me two hundred words on each of them and why we should do a story in Fashion Updates." She craned forward to look down the edge of the sheet. "Some of them may be dead," she murmured. "It's an old list of Gloria's."

"Oh, thank you," Lacy cried with enthusiasm. "I want to tell you how much I appreciate this. I'll do a good job, you'll see."

"You're incredible," the other woman said. "God, I feel like a baby killer!"

"Just show me my desk," Lacy told her, "and I'll get to work."

"Oh, yes, the desk." Jamie Hatworth frowned. "Actually we haven't been able to find a free desk around here in years. But there's a utility table over in the art department the junior writers are sharing. You'll love it."

"It's OK," Lacy said in a rush. "I'll work anywhere. After four years of journalism school and modeling, I just can't believe this is finally happening."

The assistant editor groaned. "Wait, don't run away," she ordered as Lacy slid down from her perch on the corner of the desk, "there's more. The company cafeteria closed in August, but you can brown-bag it in the ladies' lounge if you don't mind standing up while you eat—it gets pretty crowded in the john. You won't get your paycheck for about three weeks because the personnel department's out with bubonic plague. They don't say they are, but at the rate they process your paper work, it's the same thing. And don't forget to make out a weekly petty-cash voucher for bus tokens. Taking cabs to your assignments is a no-no even with two sprained ankles, but *Fad* does pick up the bill for public transit.''

"Good," Lacy said determinedly. "I don't mind riding the bus at all.''

"You're giving me a neurosis,'' the assistant editor moaned. "Please close the door when you go out. I don't want Gloria to come back with any more of you. Chicken pox is ruining my life as it is.''

5

She'd gotten carried away, Lacy realized, somewhat depressed, as she sat cross-legged on a stack of dress boxes in the Thirty-second Street loft of Fishman Brothers Frocks and Superior Sportswear a few days later. She had had this weird conviction that everything was going to turn out better—and look what had happened!

Poor Mr. Fishman's clothes were really bad, she thought, resting her chin on her hand—there was no other word to describe them. Of course, if she had to model his spring line for customers, she wouldn't have anything to say about it. But she was on the other side of the fence now as a *Fad* magazine writer, and she could say that Fishman Brothers Frocks were a bomb, even though poor Mr. Fishman had dragged out nearly every piece in his spring line for her inspection.

Lacy had to admit that nearly everything her boss, assistant editor Jamie Hatworth, had said about a junior fashion writer's job was true, although she'd assumed at the time that the assistant editor was only trying to be funny. The list Jamie had given her of Seventh Avenue dress houses actually did include several elusive firms whose owners had gone out of business, were unavailable, missing or presumed dead. She'd spent weary hours trying to find the entrances to abandoned-looking loft buildings, back staircases and freight elevators to the sinister depths of some of New York's oldest garment factories. Just getting into these places was a major achievement—only to discover the name on her list was a company that either had never been heard of by current tenants or had shut its doors shortly after World War II. *Fad* magazine's back files, Lacy couldn't help concluding, were a little out of date.

Not only that, but since it had rained for the past two days, Lacy's usually neat and lovely pale-blond hair was straggly and wet and most of her makeup had worn off. Her soggy feet were definitely beginning to ache. Fashion writing had one thing in common with runway modeling. It was tough on the body.

Mr. Fishman, a large, unlit cigar in his mouth, held up yet another creation in mega-red and eye-popping orange and looked at her hopefully.

I have to take responsibility for my own actions, Lacy thought, studying the dress. Her mother and father, who had seen a fearlessly headstrong streak in each of their three beautiful daughters, had tried to deal with it patiently, lovingly and with the omniscient wisdom of several volumes of Dr. Spock. But

Dr. Spock, the Kingston parents had reluctantly concluded, had never known siblings like the free-spirited, independent Kingston girls of East Hampton, Long Island.

Lacy tried to smile encouragingly at Mr. Irving Fishman, but she couldn't help thinking whoever had designed his spring junior dress line must have been colorblind. She vaguely remembered Mr. Fishman saying his son-in-law, a former unsuccessful portrait photographer in Queens, was trying his hand at it, encouraged by his wife, Mr. Fishman's daughter, who was a very successful obstetrician. Fishman Brothers Frocks and Superior Sportswear was obviously heavily into family.

"They're very strong hues," Lacy said diplomatically. She felt she should contribute something, since Mr. Fishman was looking so doubtful himself. The number the dress manufacturer was holding up, a chartreuse and grape acrylic satin, made for a curiously unsettling effect on the viewer. Like seasickness.

"Hughes?" Mr. Fishman rumbled from the depths of his cigar-ash-sprinkled shirt front. "I'm not familiar with his work. No, this is a Birnbaum, a Leonard Birnbaum. Frankly he should have stuck to taking class pictures of kiddies in P.S. 28, Queens, and never mind that my *meshuganeh* daughter Rosalie thinks he's another Picasso. A Picasso I don't need. What I need is a good cloak and suit man." Mr. Fishman took the cigar out of his mouth and stood staring at the satin creation. "It's his green and purple period, she tells me," he said, wincing. "My wife says we should be lucky Birnbaum didn't go into house painting."

Lacy frowned at the frock being held at arm's length by Mr. Fishman. In spite of the horrendous colors the junior dresses' basic lines were quite good, many of them bias cuts in the popular skimpy 1930s style, all daring kneecap length with the exception of a few ultrachic designs that hung to midcalf.

Hey, Lacy thought, suddenly inspired. She could never resist a genuine hit-on-the-head creative idea. Maybe Fishman Brothers' dresses weren't tacky *enough*! "Mr. Fishman, why don't you go for the Palladium disco crowd trend? You know, split skirts, a few bugle beads and all that. Tacky to the maximum! What you've got here is definitely not Sears, Roebuck or J. C. Penney, now is it?"

"My best markets," Mr. Fishman groaned. "Why should I turn my back on Sears after all these years? I'm looking at a disaster."

"But there are other markets," Lacy insisted. It wasn't her job to be a fashion consultant to Fishman Brothers; if nothing else, it was a conflict of interest. As a reporter for one of the oldest rag-trade magazines, she could actually, if she wanted to, do a fairly truthful job on Fishman Brothers Frocks and Superior Sportswear and write up their awful spring dresses objectively. And ruin their whole line. But Lacy wasn't made that way.

"I'm thinking maybe beads," Lacy said, falling into the language of dress wholesaling. "I'm thinking maybe Schapiarelli beads of the 1940s, which would go smashingly with those Joan Crawford padded shoulders.

"So you jump the trimmings price to maybe twenty or thirty percent of wholesale," she went on judiciously, "who cares? Actually a markup that big in the disco market is an incentive. There's nothing like overpricing to stimulate interest.''

"Nineteen forties beads?" Mr. Fishman murmured thoughtfully. "I got a nephew in trimmings and notions on Fourteenth Street with shelves of 1940s beads he should get rid of if he should be so lucky.''

"Wow—antiques," Lacy said, her eyes sparkling. "Really? That's a gold mine if he's got that many old beads. You ought to think about it."

"Around the neck," Mr. Fishman said, thinking about it. "I could see glass beads around the neck, why not? Over on Broadway and Times Square they are making photographs of movie stars on the fronts of T-shirts with sequins in them. If sequins, why not my nephew's beautiful annual-tax-loss beads? Like nice scenic views of Niagara Falls maybe, and even heads of celebrities in lovely sparklers."

"You mean," Lacy said, awed, "photo reproductions of the heads of famous people on the front of your dresses filled in with beads?" Even she wasn't capable of such a gigantic leap of inspiration. Her eyes were drawn to the purple, orange, green and red satin dresses on their hangers. "You've seen it," she murmured. "You've seen . . . *tacky-max*. You know what it is!"

"I have observed a few things in my time, darling," Mr. Fishman said modestly. "Frankly, I never thought of disco dresses for Fishman Brothers. But then before this, I wasn't desperate. A nice phrase, 'tacky-max.'" He looked thoughtful. "You're a genius, my dear. Please accept my heartfelt thanks for your wonderfully creative ideas." Mr. Fishman took his cigar out of his mouth quickly to lift Lacy's hand and kiss it in a very gallant way. "You're such an extraordinarily gorgeous and intelligent young lady, I don't know why you're *schlepping* up and down Seventh Avenue in the rain and cold doing this work for some magazine when you could be married to maybe a nice doctor in Connecticut and have several lovely children by now. If I had a son, I would be honored to introduce you to him. You wouldn't consider maybe modeling for my cousin in Denver, would you? He could use some help with a ski line he has out there."

"Not a chance," Lacy told him, "but you're very sweet to ask, Mr. Fishman. I'm a writer now, I hope never to go back into modeling.

"Listen," she cried, hit by another sudden inspiration. "If your whole new design change works out, well, you're going to be needing some promotion." She was thinking of all those fashion shows she'd done so many times at places like the Pierre and the Waldorf-Astoria. "You might have something really big here."

"Promotion?" Mr. Fishman said, looking vaguely surprised. "You mean such as tea-time showings at selected hotels in the Catskills, like Grossinger's? We did it once, my lovely young lady, and believe me, Fishman Brothers died from hunger. Everybody was out playing golf. Nobody wanted to look at sportswear modeling while eating little lox sandwiches and *goyisheh* tea with milk in it. Six people showed up for the fashion show. It cost a fortune. It was a bomb."

Lacy shook her head. Several ideas were forming in her mind all at once, and she was having a hard time keeping them sorted out. One was that the heads of celebrities, like famous rock stars, embellished with glass beads on the front of wildly colored disco dresses was a brainstorm. Especially if some promotion person could get the celebrities to approve their autograph-type signatures under their likenesses, for a royalty. Lacy could just visualize the Palladium's strobe lighting system hitting a packed dance floor full of wildly gyrating bodies, ninety percent of them wearing chartreuse and grape acrylic satins with laser-like reproductions of Michael Jackson and Prince on their chests. It was the ultimate in tacky-max! It was terrible enough to be sensational!

Lacy swallowed, hard. Promotion was not her business; she'd just started a new career in fashion writing. But she could see where she'd have a thousand wonderful ideas if she was in it.

"If the disco line turns out the way I think it will," she said, sliding down from the stack of dress boxes in Fishman Brothers' loft, "you ought to be able to promote it right up to the sky, Mr. Fishman."

"You do it, my beautiful genius young lady," the dress manufacturer said promptly. "Quit this difficult writing job you have now and do promotion for Fishman Brothers. As an added incentive, I'll introduce you to my wife's nephew by marriage, a handsome young millionaire who is an orthodontist in West Orange, New Jersey, and he's only thirty-two yet."

"Mr. Fishman," Lacy said, smiling, "you're making me an offer I can't refuse, but I have to. I haven't been working on my new job for even a week yet—give me time! But I will promise you one thing. I'll do my best to write a story on your disco dress line if you'll let me see what you do with the beads."

"Next week," Mr. Fishman promised, seizing her hand to squeeze it fondly. "The workroom will have a couple of demo models together, you should see it the moment it's done, I give you my word on it.

"You're an angel," he shouted after Lacy as she let herself out by way of the ancient open freight elevator that took her from Fishman Brothers into the biting autumn wind of midtown Manhattan.

Lacy took a deep breath as she pulled the collar of her Norma Kamali flight jacket up around her ears. It was Friday, and Fishman Brothers Frocks and Superior Sportswear had been the last on her list of most unpromising fashion interviews, but somehow at the eleventh hour she'd struck gold.

Of course, she was working on leads for stories that would only make the back pages of *Fad* if they got in at all. And she was still competing madly with the four other junior fashion writers for the one permanent job slot. But things were looking better!

It was already early-autumn dark when Lacy got home, dumping her soggy shoes just inside the door of her apartment and padding to the kitchen in her stocking feet. By the time she had taken her dinner of sprouts, tomatoes and cottage cheese, which she'd prepared that morning, out of the refrigerator, she'd used her free hand to shrug off her flight jacket and pull her black silk tailored shirt out of her slacks to hang free comfortably. It was let-down time.

She ran her fingers through her still-damp hair. After her first week at *Fad* she felt as though she could spend the whole weekend just lying in a bubble bath with her eyes closed, listening to the stereo play Chuck Mangione.

Sitting at the kitchen table, Lacy kept her eyes fixed on a large full-color advertising poster that hung on the wall opposite. The thirty-six-inch-long glossy print prepared for a long-dead ad-agency account showed a tall, almost-skinny nymph with a cascade of wheat-fair hair, her gently curving hips tilted to support one hand at her crisp silk waistline, her other hand raised to airily clasp a Virginia Slims cigarette. The blue taffeta dance dress Lacy wore was perfection, its tight, rippling folds and ruffles dipping to expose her bare left shoulder, then swathing her body from her delicately full breasts to a burst of short skirt in two overlapping deep ruffles that ended just above her knees. The tilt of the head to one side, the impish gleam in light-filled green eyes, the sheath of hair blown into a glittering aureole by a large electric fan stationed just off camera, all projected the frenetic verve that cigarette ads were into that year.

That was the old Lacy Kingston pizazz, she thought, remembering that they'd been playing a Sister Sledge number that day in the studio on the powerful stereo. She had reacted to the wild, throbbing music and low voice of the photographer urging her to "sparkle, Lacy, sparkle—blow my mind—give me that look again, baby, you're dynamite, give me that Lacy Kingston delivery!" The camera had advanced *zzzt, zzzt, zzzt*, recording an almost unbelievably entrancing vision, catching her poses, dancing, her mercurial changes of expression—all the tricks of the fashion-modeling trade she'd learned in her teens.

That had also been the same day she'd slugged Peter Dorsey. New York's most lecherous photographer had pestered her all morning and then tried to slip his hand down the front of her dress with the excuse he was trying to adjust it. Lacy had fallen back on the tae kwan do karate lessons she'd taken all through junior high school and had feinted, chopped and counter-chopped. Peter Dorsey had gone down in a tangle of Nikons and Pentaflexes. With, his insurance company later claimed, two loosened front teeth and a damaged septum.

The photo proofs had never gotten into the hands of the advertising agency for Virginia Slims. Lacy's lawyer father had handled the lawsuit by Peter Dorsey, which had claimed, among other things, that Lacy had been too young and inexperienced to take photographic direction and that she had misunderstood Peter Dorsey's moves and intent that day when she modeled in his studio.

It had been a real downer professionally for a rising young model to have to settle the lawsuit out of court on her father's advice, using up her savings and borrowing money to meet the judgment and to accept publicly the worst implications of what the suit had accused her—that she was temperamental, unprofessional and uncooperative. Few top notch photographers could afford the time from their busy schedules to have both their noses and their front teeth anchored against possible assaults; it had been nearly a year and a half before Lacy had worked again, and when she did, she only got jobs from agencies that booked trade shows and runway modeling.

Now, thank goodness, all that was behind her. In spite of its problems, Lacy was certain that fashion writing was going to be her most rewarding profession.

Lacy went to put the kettle on for a cup of tea, reaching up into the kitchen cabinet for her container of Red Zinger tea. She flipped open the top and started to pour what she thought was Red Zinger into the pot, and a large roll of fifty- and one-hundred-dollar bills popped out as though they had fermented inside.

If she hadn't been so tired, she would have given a healthy shriek of exasperation. There it was again, Lacy told herself. All that money. Thirteen hundred dollars of it, since she'd taken some out for the rent, that haunted her like an ax murder. A used Red Zinger-herbal-tea box was no place to keep the roll of bills, but she was afraid to put the money in her checking account. Her father had once had a client who'd been putting strange money into his bank account without telling the Internal Revenue Service, and now he was serving time in the federal penitentiary in Atlanta. Lacy shuddered. If she put it into *her* bank account, she was sure she'd need to declare it, too. How? Under what category—*earnings*? Every time she thought about it, she felt sick. If she had to forget anything that morning in Tulsa, why couldn't it have been her silk stockings or the tarty black garter belt? Why did she have to forget to leave the *money* behind?

Also, she didn't know the slightest thing about the black panther, including his name, so she couldn't even return it to him by mail! Seeing the bills again brought back all sorts of things Lacy wanted to forget. Like his tuxedo shirt holding his arms captive, his trousers down around his knees in the penthouse, looking rather fascinated and puzzled. And looking so beautiful in bed with his hair all sweaty and tightly curled, his stupendous muscular arms holding her gently, eyes like molten silver. And everything else,

Lacy moaned, close to inexplicable tears. When she was about sixty or seventy years old, maybe she would manage to forget it.

She was stuffing the roll of bills back into the tea box when she heard a hammering on the front door of her apartment. With a sigh, Lacy put the Red Zinger back on the shelf over the sink and went to see who it was.

When she opened the door, the tall, beautiful redheaded vision of Candy O'Neill, another model with the Leonard Thornton agency who lived just down the hall, was holding the leash of her large, ferocious-looking Doberman, Baron Ratthausen of Morged-Schalfstein. At least that was the dog's pedigreed name. No one ever called him anything but Sicky-Poo, because he was so neurotic, he was the only attack Doberman who threw up on people. Lacy took a cautious step backward.

"Watch it, will you, Candy?" she told her friend quickly. "I just got my rugs shampooed."

"Oh, Lacy," Candy began at once in her throaty, redheaded voice, "I've got a really heavy date tonight, and would it be too much of a favor to ask you to babysit Sicky-Poo?" At the look on Lacy's face, she went on quickly, "Dr. Magruder, Sicky-Poo's canine psychiatrist, says he's ninety percent socially rehabilitated—he's stopped eating the bottom off curtains and hardly any carpet these days."

"I don't know," Lacy said doubtfully. Candy O'Neill was a good friend, and they swapped favors as well as each other's clothes occasionally, especially for modeling assignments. But Candy's gangling, half-grown Doberman was a major baby-sitting job. Even when Sicky-Poo wasn't giving in to a faulty passive-aggressive mechanism, according to his shrink, he had a disconcerting habit of hiding under the bed and alternately snarling and moaning. To be around anything that mixed-up was pretty unnerving.

Lacy tried to think of several convincing excuses. "Can I beg out, Candy?" she tried. "I really just finished cleaning my apartment, I'm maxed out after my first week on a new job and, ah, you know how Sicky-Poo reacts if he gets to feeling aggressive. Really—he's sweet, but he's almost too much to handle."

"Ahr couldn't agree moah," a booming voice said from the hallway behind the redheaded Thornton model. "He ruined my L.L. Bean Top Siders the first time I met Candycane."

"*Candycane*?" Lacy said, giving her friend a startled look.

"Oh, that's Pottsy, my date," Candy explained, shoving the reluctant Doberman inside Lacy's front door. "His real name's Harrison Salstonstall Potts the fourth." As a large hand extended itself over the model's shoulder, Candy went on, "Pottsy's got a suit on tonight—I want us to make the movie without having to do the Fantastic cleaner and sponge bit again."

"Chahrmed," the voice in the hallway said, shaking Lacy's hand firmly.

Lacy held onto Sicky-Poo's collar, able to make out the general shape of the man behind Candy. Her friend went on a little breathlessly, "Leonard Thornton scouted Pottsy himself at the Yale-Harvard game. I think Pottsy was tight end for Harvard, and Leonard couldn't resist him. Actually, Pottsy has an M.B.A. but right now he's a male model."

Male model, Lacy thought, putting one leg over the Doberman's back to keep him from lunging out the door in the direction of Harrison Salstonstall Potts IV. A male model was always a large negative as far as dates were concerned. The gorgeous hunks that made their living posing for *GQ* and the macho Jockey-underwear ads in *Playboy* were impossible, demanding peacocks; you couldn't get their attention even in the dark of a movie theater—they were usually secretly combing their hair. Male model from *Harvard*? The bulk of Harrison Salstonstall Potts IV stepped cautiously into the light. Her eyes traveled upward from massive male legs attired in very Ivy League slacks to a chest in the same J. Press corduroy covering and finally to a face that was carved in stunning, genial Old Colonial lines. Harrison Salstonstall Potts IV looked as though he had just accepted Betsy Ross's flag on behalf of the Continental Congress. He was impressively beautiful, if one liked thick, unruly chestnut hair with an impossibly healthy sheen to it, bright-blue eyes and a large, patrician mouth that curved up ingratiatingly. As it was doing now.

"Dahgs can be trained properly, even in invah-ranments like New York," the Ivy League hunk said in an accent in which every nasal vowel dropped from his lips like a freeze-dried Boston baked bean. "That's what I keep telling deah Candycane."

"Yes, no," Lacy replied as the Doberman, activated by the sounds of Back Bay aristocracy, alternated vicious snarls with a distinct retching noise. "Candy, I don't know that I'm up to all this," she pleaded. "That is, I'm going to be awfully busy tonight.

"I have to—I have to—I have to work up a promotion for a dress manufacturer," she cried, inspired. "Why don't you and Pottsy just take Sicky-Poo for a walk down Broadway?"

"Promotion?" the massive date said interestedly, throwing caution to the winds to step even closer. "My mahster's degree focused on public relations, actuahlly."

"My goodness, Lacy, are you doing P.R. now?" the model asked. "I thought you just got a job on *Fad* magazine."

"I did, I have," Lacy puffed, holding a convulsing Sicky-Poo down with her knee. "Actually, I'm not doing publicity for Mr. Fishman. I'm, ah, looking for someone to take his account. What he needs is, uh, a fashion promotion at a restaurant or hotel," Lacy managed, moving her foot out from under Sicky-Poo's unattractively slavering jaws. "Yes, well, maybe a press party. Mr. Fishman's got a really promising line of disco dresses."

Before Lacy could insist that Candy take her Doberman back to her own apartment before he had a complete mental and physical collapse brought on, apparently, by proximity to Harvard's male model, those booming accents observed, "Press potties ahr my true métier, deah lady."

"He doesn't have a budget," Lacy cried. Her life was too complicated for male models with a master's in public relations. Just once she was going to let trouble pass her by. "It's OK if Sicky-Poo stays the night," Lacy tried to say as the Doberman dropped to the floor, exhausted, and rolled over on his back. "Just pick him up in the morning."

It was too late. Harvard's gift to masculine beauty, giant economy size, stuck a hand that could cradle a football helmet as easily as a jellybean against her door to hold it open. "Deah lady," his elegant consonants trumpeted, "a budget's no problem. Not when a genuiahn creative experience is involved. Do the brothers Fishman have an address where Ahr could reach them?"

"No budget," Lacy cried. Sicky-Poo closed his eyes, all four legs extended and gave a convincing imitation of a death rattle. "Oh, Candy, you and your damned dog . . . No money," she said more loudly, looking Harrison Salstonstall Potts IV straight in his bright-blue eyes. "I mean, you probably won't get paid. Do you hear me?"

His genial Revolutionary countenance beamed down at her. "Loud and cleah, sweet lady," the Boston accents responded. "Fortunahtly, Ahr have a small independent income."

6

By modest independent income, Harvard's gift to public relations meant about $130 million dollars largely held in trust by the Bank of Boston. So Harrison Salstonstall Potts IV, Lacy realized, really could afford to regard his degree in public relations as a "genuahn creative experience." Even so, she was stunned to hear a few days later that Pottsy had been to see Irving Fishman and that Fishman Brothers Frocks and Superior Sportswear had given him their account for an almost no-budget promotion for their new disco-dress line.

"What did your crazy date promise poor Mr. Fishman?" Lacy wailed to her friend. "Don't you know I'm not supposed to be doing this sort of thing? I'm not supposed to be giving fashion advice—I'm a magazine writer. I'm not supposed to be turning flaky millionaire male models loose on anybody I'm interviewing! It's going to get me fired.''

"Pottsy wouldn't let a thing like that happen," the redheaded model said reprovingly. "He could always buy the magazine. Next to public relations, Pottsy is really serious about being a publisher. He even has a novel he's working on.''

"Publisher? Novel?" Lacy replied with a faint scream. "Now I know I'm in trouble!"

The next morning Lacy hurried to Jamie Hatworth's office to reveal the whole story about advising Fishman Brothers on their disco-dress line and how Harrison Salstonstall Potts happened to get involved it it. To Lacy's vast relief, the assistant editor put her baby sitter on "hold" to listen quite sympathetically.

"He's got to be the weirdest public relations man I've ever heard of," Lacy confessed, glad to find a shoulder to lean on, even if it was that of her immediate boss. "I don't want to lose my job, it means more to me than I can tell you." Honesty compelled her to add, "But I *did* start this whole thing. Some days I think I must be genetically defective, the way I keep opening my mouth when I'm not supposed to.''

"You haven't lost your job," the small, pretty assistant editor assured her. "What weirdo did what, kid? Start from the beginning.''

"I mean," Lacy moaned, "a male model who lives in a loft in SoHo with two crazy artists and poses for them in his spare time instead of paying rent? And who's supposed to be a millionaire only the only places he takes Candy on a date are to the Museum of Natural History on free-admission days and down to

Grand Central Station to watch the stock-market reports on the big screen? You've got to be kidding!''

"No, I know Boston," Jamie Hatworth said thoughtfully. "But go on."

"It's all my fault Pottsy's involved in this," Lacy said, feeling she could give way to a considerable store of subliminal guilt. The memory of what had happened just a few weeks ago in a certain bar in a certain hotel in the West as a result of her talent for saying the first thing that came into her head was still horribly clear. "Sometimes I think I need to join some antiassertiveness class somewhere," she moaned. "One where they teach you to be so uncommunicative and withdrawn you're practically in a coma."

Jamie Hatworth only smiled. "So you were the one who came up with the bright idea for Irving Fishman's new disco-dress line? We received a ton of press releases about it this morning. OK, worse things have been done around here." She paused. "I'd tell you what, but I don't want to encourage you."

Lacy moaned again, uncomforted. "I know it was a sort of breach of professional ethics for me to give any sort of fashion consulting advice, but the way Mr. Fishman was headed with all those green and purple satin dresses, I just got carried away. And then I just happened to remember what public-relations people did when they got stuck with turkeys. They give a big promotion party—you know, a lavish buffet and invite the media, with gorgeous models in skimpy clothes handing out press releases. But I didn't mean that Harrison Salstonstall Potts ought to do it!

"Actually," Lacy said, holding her head in her hands as she propped her elbows on Jamie Hatworth's desk among the March proofs of *Fad* magazine, "I thought that when Pottsy went to see Mr. Fishman to solicit his account that would be the end of it. But unfortunately Mr. Fishman remembered seeing Pottsy play tight end for Harvard several years ago, and now he thinks I'm a genius for having found him!"

"It does sound a little complicated," the assistant editor agreed. "So your friend the Thornton model has this free-lance public-relations man she's seeing, and he went over to Irving Fishman to get Fishman Brothers' promotion account? And in addition to your talking Irving Fishman info a disco-dress line, he also bought the idea of a big promotion from, ah, the Harvard weirdo?"

"It seemed like a good idea at the time," Lacy shuddered. "I mean, I've done plenty of public-relations shows. I used to be the girl who came out in a tiger-stripe bikini at stockholders' meetings carrying the flow charts of profit-and-loss statements. And I've done plenty of sales rallies at the Atlantic City Bunny Club when I needed the money, wearing those corsets and the bunny ears and reciting poems about positive mental attitude and selling the sizzle, not the steak. But I've never seen anybody like Pottsy," she admitted. "He works for practically nothing because he thinks public relations is so 'creative'!"

Jamie Hatworth was staring at Lacy with a more than usually thoughtful expression. "Can I ask you something, kid?" she said suddenly. "Do you ever date?"

"No," Lacy said, with a quick, inadvertent

grimace. It was a subject she wanted to stay away from. "I really don't need any more distractions, honestly. I'm very career oriented. Why?"

The other woman shrugged. "Just asking. Maybe wondering where all this . . . energy . . . comes from." Jamie Hatworth made some notations on the month's assignment sheets in front of her. "I kind of like it," she murmured, scratching her head with her pencil. "There might be a story in it, especially if there's going to be a fashion show. The press and electronic media will be there, won't they?"

"Oh, yes," Lacy affirmed, not sure what Potts Productions had arranged but aware of certain sketchy plans Candy had relayed. "I'm sure they've all been invited."

"Well, who knows?" Jamie Hatworth sighed. "Maybe we could use something strange at *Fad* for a change. They used to call it 'originality' in the old days." She picked up *Fad* magazine's assignment sheet for the month and marked it, "Fishman Brothers—Kingsley," without looking up.

"You mean you want me to keep covering it?" Lacy breathed. "You mean go through the whole Potts Promotions disco-dress launching for Fishman Brothers Frocks and Superior Sportswear and *everything*?"

"Why not?" Jamie Hatworth said, picking up the telephone receiver to reconnect with her sitter. "It's more than any of the other junior fashion writers have going for them right now, isn't it?"

The real impact of the assistant editor's remark hit Lacy about fifteen minutes later, when she had settled down at the clutter of the utility table in the art department the junior fashion writers shared to a rewrite of Swiss knit-top ski boots.

She was *competitive*, Lacy realized, staring at the words she had just written on the lighted screen of the computer terminal about knitted tops keeping the snow out of your Swiss-made equipment. After only a few weeks she was holding her own with the other four junior fashion writers. And they were all trying out for the one permanent job slot!

They were an interesting group, Lacy had found, and easy to know, mostly due to the fact that when they sat down to work at the same time at the makeshift table jammed into the art department, their elbows bumped. And of course they had to wait their turn at the terminal. It didn't take long before they'd introduced themselves.

Ariana Lockworth was an art-history major from Wellesley who was working in fashion reporting, she told them, to finish her research on the meaning of historical and sociological influences on the changing styles in women's clothing.

"You mean like bustles and flapper hats?" Lacy had said interestedly. "Did that sort of reflect how women felt about themselves in those days?"

"Only peripherally." Ariana was tall, bony, and had a gloomy expression. "But it reflected how society felt about *them*. Today we're into an overt decadence," she said, eyeing Lacy's pink denim bustier over a black cotton turtleneck, "that emphasizes breasts, nudity, legs and modern woman's neurotic craving for accessibility.

"That," she added hollowly, "goes far to downgrade their worth."

"I see what you mean," Lacy murmured thoughtfully. The part about decadence she could certainly agree with; she could hardly forget the terrible tarty Claude Montana cocktail dress and the effect it had had in Tulsa.

Nancy and Clorinda were two other members of the junior fashion writer's group. Nancy was a former model who'd burned out doing bit parts in movie videos, especially massed chorus effects with the Bee Gees, and Clorinda was an out-of-work jazz singer.

"Jazz is coming back," the soignée black girl said a trifle belligerently. "It will replace all this dung about rap rock."

"I never thought jazz had gone away," Lacy said, puzzled. "It's all my dad listens to."

Everybody hated the fifth member of their group, Keith, a good-looking athletic type who wore black suits and red suspenders. And who had just recently come into publishing after his glorious career on Wall Street had been cut off prematurely by the stock-market crashes.

"Don't mind me, girls," Keith said smugly to everyone, "I'm not really competing. I'm a management trainee."

They knew Keith was telling the truth. While the four women scrambled and competed for the one open junior-writer job, Keith was headed for the top and management levels. Where, Nancy had pointed out, the boys are.

This new break, then, was more than Lacy had ever hoped for; she had to keep pinching herself to see if she was dreaming. With an exclusive story on a successful Fishman Brothers promotion of their new disco dress, she had a chance to do a virtuoso piece of writing that could win a lead slot in the front of the magazine in some future spring issue of *Fad*. And after the editorial staff had gone bananas over her piece, Lacy daydreamed, managing editor Gloria Farnham would naturally submit it to the annual York Dress Design Institute Award for fashion reporting. She would get first prize and a bid from *Vogue* to join Condé Nast Publications. Or *The New York Times*. Anything was possible, she told herself deliriously.

On the crest of such wishful thinking, it was more than a little horrifying to find that Harrison Salstonstall Potts IV was planning a Potts Promotions extravaganza and fashion show at a nightclub on Forty-seventh Street off Broadway formerly called the Spearmint Patch that had been known in decades past, before lawsuits and bankruptcy disputes, as the home of the twist. Now renamed the Zebra Lounge.

"No, no, you need the Waldorf-Astoria," Lacy desperately tried to explain, remembering her own rather difficult days as a promotion-shows model. "Or the New York Hilton is good. You prepare a guest list of all the buyers from the big department-store chains, as well as all the newspapers and New York television stations, and get well-known guest artists, like Mel Torme and Lainie Kazan, to donate their time. It takes weeks of organization and there are things like mailing lists—"

"Undoubtedly, deah dreamboat," Pottsy trumpeted genially, "but what Ahr have in mind, since the brothers Fishman are relying on sheer artistic creativity and not limitless promotional funding, is a trendy, lighthotted preview in natural envahrahnments.''

"What natural envahrahnments?" Lacy cried. "I can't understand the way you talk. You mean, you're going to do it all on freebies?''

"Moah or less, moah or less. Thursday naht at the Zebra Lounge is not to be sniffed at, deah lady, even when one considers the owner is a personal friend of mine. And my modeling compatriots, the best-looking men in New York, if I do say so myself, have contributed generously to the guest list. Mah mastah plan is to display the brothers Fishman's excellent creations in the *haut monde* of select café society, featuring *le dernier cri* of their fashion wholesalers' genius. Then we will wait for the demands of the press to overwhelm us with cries for moah. And as for guest artists,'' he said, patting Lacy's head, ''my roommate, a fellow of the Art Students League, has issued open invitations to the upper school, which will attend. We have virtually an ironclad commitment that Tiny Tim and his All-Girl Ukulele Orchestra will donate their time following the runway revealments.''

"You're mad, mad,'' Lacy groaned, genuinely horror struck. Unfortunately she wasn't able to convince even Candy, who had been assigned to round up teenage models for the show from a yoga school in Bayonne, New Jersey, partly owned by Potts Industries of Marblehead, Massachusetts.

"Please listen to reason,'' Lacy begged her friend. "Nobody can do a dress-promotion fashion show on freebies, not even your nutty date. You can't bus a totally inexperienced group of girls into Manhattan to model in a fashion show without any rehearsal. You can't have a fashion show on a Thursday night in a disco off Times Square that nobody's ever heard of! I don't think Mr. Fishman's even got his demo dresses sewn. He has gotten the copyrights for the celebrity likenesses though," she added as an afterthought. "This is *my* story—the one that's going to make me famous," Lacy wailed. "Unless that lunatic from Boston kills it completely!"

The redheaded Thornton model just sighed. "Actually, I think it's going to work out all right," Candy O'Neill tried to assure her. "I leave it all up to Pottsy. He says, 'Just pray it doesn't rain.'"

Thursday night, however, as Candy and Lacy made their way downtown in a yellow cab with arm loads of boxes of Fishman Brothers new Disco Queen dress line, midtown Manhattan was awash in a northeast storm that had swept even the Theater District bare of crowds. Harrison Salstonstall Potts was waiting for them in front of the Zebra Lounge with an umbrella and a large smile on his indestructible Revolutionary countenance.

"Bring the costumes, deah lovelies," Pottsy shouted as they spilled from the cab and into the entrance. "Mah low-budget mastahpiece has just begun!"

"Oh, no," Lacy breathed, staring up at the sign over the entrance advertising the Peptic Ulcers punk-rock band. The horrid sound that emerged from the Zebra Lounge penetrated even the storm's loud roar. "Disco—not this!" she tried to explain as Pottsy swept them inside. "Little hats, chic black net stockings," she breathed as a wall of sound assaulted them in a tunnel-like entrance painted pale pink and studded with sequins. "Not punk rockers! You need Billy Joel, Barbra Streisand, Victoria Principal—"

A tall man with a pale face wearing horn-rimmed glasses emerged from a jammed wall of bodies in what was undoubtedly the biggest crowd inside anywhere in the Times Square area that rainy night. "I'm Leonard Birnbaum," he shouted hoarsely before a crowd of youths with shaved heads and safety pins in their noses surged out of the crowd and swept him away. "My clothes!" he screamed. "My art!"

For a brief moment, Lacy shut her eyes. She had a fleeting thought that if perhaps she willed herself somewhere hard enough, whatever good fairy there was left in the universe would reach down into the screaming, surging uproar of the Zebra Lounge and lift her gently away. To someplace like Butte, Montana, or New Delhi, India. Because the agonized figure, she distinctly remembered, was Mr. Irving Fishman's photographer-dress-designer son-in-law from Queens.

Even Candy O'Neill, struggling with the disco-dress boxes for the fashion show, was beginning to look noticeably pale. Candy's face turned positively chalky as the hulking form of Harvard's public-relations man bent and shouted something before he left them to make his way through the wall of bodies to the bandstand.

"Something terrible has just happened," the redheaded model tried to scream over the riveting sounds of "Take My Body." "What Pottsy just told me."

Lacy shook her head, able to see Candy's lips moving but not hear her frantic words. She felt as though she couldn't move from the sight of the truly incredible crowd that had been assembled in the pink plaster spaces of the lounge's main room and that had been, according to Pottsy, prevailed upon to attend by half the male models in the city. It wasn't hard to recognize such well-known faces as the nationally famous talk-show host trying to hide behind a sequined plaster partition, the former governor of New York State and a U.S. Army general in civilian clothes. It was virtually impossible to ignore most of the starting lineup of the Jets, several stars from the New York Rangers, the alternate chorus from the Radio City Rockettes, most of the upper school of the Art Students League and the regular patrons of the Zebra Lounge in chrome-plated bicycle chains, Mohawk coiffures of various colors and leather knee boots with giant spurs. She couldn't see anything that remotely resembled tacky, trendy, enchantingly neon-colored disco outfits in all the milling, screaming mob that filled the Zebra.

"I said," Candy shrieked, her mouth close to Lacy's ear, "Pottsy tells me the models from the yoga school didn't show up!"

The next morning it was quite unnecessary to carry extra copies of *The New York Times* and the *New York Daily News* into *Fad* magazine's editorial room. As Lacy passed from the elevator area into makeup and copy editing, there were already half a dozen writers collected around both newspapers, fascinated with their front pages.

When Lacy reached Jamie Hatworth's office, the assistant editor looked up and said blandly as she studied her own *New York Daily News*, "There was good television coverage on the *Today* show this morning, too. But I got the impression the TV news teams only got there after the fire started. Is that you?'' the editor asked, pointing to the front page of the *Daily News*, where a rather indistinct but ravishingly long-legged figure in a revealing satin dress decorated with the head of Elton John in bugle beads across the front followed in the footsteps of two firemen. They were carrying out the thrashing body of a punk rocker in leather tights and a hangman's mask from the pink-sequined maw of the Zebra Lounge.

"I'm hoping and praying nobody recognizes me," Lacy whispered, throwing the extra copies of the newspapers she'd brought into Jamie's overflowing wastepaper basket, vastly relieved that she was not, apparently, going to be fired on first sight.

"Actually," Lacy said, "I can explain everything. I'm so tired. I haven't been to bed at all because I had to shower and wash the smoke and soot out of my hair. But then nobody warned me that the fashion show was supposed to end with a sound and light display by the Fishman Brothers' designer, Mr. Birnbaum. That's how the fire started."

"It's probably the most extensive news coverage I've ever seen of a Seventh Avenue dress line," the assistant editor said. "Maybe this Boston P.R. man is a genius after all. Did you notice that the Russians have offered to let us inspect their missiles, and the *Times* has moved that story onto page two, inside, so they could carry that great photograph of a Rockette carrying out Joe Namath with all the smoke and flames behind them?"

"That was my friend Candy, not a Rockette," Lacy pointed out, "and I hope you notice she's wearing Fishman Brothers Disco Queen in a princess cut.

Actually, Candy was on the stage when the sound and light show shorted out, which happened, the firemen said, because of all the rain and the roof was leaking. Nobody was hurt," Lacy said with a faint shudder, "but when I got home I just started shaking, thinking about all those people jammed in there like that."

"You were *modeling*?" Jamie Hatworth said, raising her eyebrows. "Is that why you were wearing Irving Fishman's disco dress in the *Daily News* photograph?"

Lacy eased herself tiredly into a chair after having swept a pile of back issues of *Marie-France* onto the floor. "Well, you see," she went on, lightly massaging her aching, sleepless head with the tips of her fingers, "none of the girls from the yoga school Pottsy owns showed up to model the clothes because their bus driver didn't want to make the trip from Bayonne in the storm. And that left just Candy and me. I couldn't really let Candy do it alone, now could I? Not just one poor model in front of all that howling mob with that punk-rock band, and then Mr. Birnbaum's sound and light show he was going to start up for the grand finale. It was *my* story," Lacy said, drawing herself up with as much pride as she could muster after a hectic, sleepless, twenty-four hours. "Actually," she admitted, "nobody was paying much attention until the sparks started cascading all over the stage when the wiring for the light show shorted out. The whole place really loved it, you know how people in New York are. They were clapping and yelling until, of course, they realized the Zebra Lounge was actually on fire. *The New York Times* reporters," Lacy sighed, "and the *Daily News* didn't come until the fire engines arrived. So *The*

Village Voice and *Rolling Stone* have the only eyewitness coverage from inside. I was so busy trying to get people turned in the right direction to go out the fire-exit doors in the back instead of the front, which was jammed up, that I didn't notice the television-news crews had arrived."

"Fantastic," the assistant editor muttered. "Absolutely fantastic. I haven't seen media coverage on *Today* and *Good Morning America* like that since the last Iranian hostage situation. Irving Fishman will be ecstatic. The Harvard nut case's reputation is made in public relations.

"Although," the small pretty woman said, looking up and smiling wryly, "it sounds like you and your girlfriend did most of the work."

"Poor Candy," Lacy said with genuine regret. "This hasn't been too great for her, after all the work she put into Pottsy's promotion. Because after the electrical connections under the roof were shorting out and just making the most spectacular fountains of blue and red flames, these two figures came sort of creeping out where, ah . . . "

To her embarrassment, Lacy found herself blushing. "Well, Pottsy was making out with the girl singer from the punk-rock band in this crawl space under the stage when the floorboards started to smoke. I was on the runway showing a Fishman Brothers Tacky-Max number in a sort of a mauve-plum color. When I turned around, there was this totally *nude* figure of Pottsy in front of me. I hate to say this, but all those weird people thought it was part of the fashion show, and it just blew them away. They were screaming and applauding and yelling for more, and then, of course, just as Pottsy was running around trying to get his pants on, the fire department came and plowed right through the dance floor with this enormous canvas hose.''

"And your friend?'' Jamie wanted to know, holding a finger to her brow in a gesture that effectively hid her face.

"Never wants to see Pottsy again,'' Lacy said with a sigh. "Candy has definitely had it with Harvard.''

"Well,'' the other woman said, stroking her eyelids as though they pained her, "it's not, strictly speaking, a *Fad* fashion story. But I think Gloria might just go with it. I'd approach it as an exclusive eyewitness account but definitely not as if you were participating in any way. Like actually modeling Irving Fishman's clothes. Although at this point, I don't think anybody really cares.''

"You mean you want it?'' Lacy said in a low, strained voice. "You mean you really want it? You want me to write . . . all this after all? You mean it's not a total . . . disaster?''

"It all depends on your first draft,'' the assistant editor said, closing her eyes.

In spite of her headache and her sleeplessness, Lacy managed a raggedly brilliant All-American Girl smile. "Believe me, Jamie, I can promise you I'll never get involved in public relations again. I never liked it to begin with, anyway. What I want,'' she added fervently, "is just to settle down to the peace and quiet we usually have around here.''

7

But peace and quiet was not to be.

Two days later, as the staff of *Fad* magazine filed into their vast, overcrowded editorial room, managing editor Gloria Farnham, wearing a truly spectacular Ted Lapidus ultrasuede poncho and matching slacks, met them with a vaguely pained smile.

"Well, sweeties," she called out over their early-morning editorial racket, "I hate to tell you this, but today's schedules are going to come absolutely unglued, so don't do anything important!" As the magazine staff stopped what they were doing and turned to her, she went on, "Well, actually, what's happened is—the new owners have called an employees' meeting."

After a moment's shocked silence someone in the crowd cried, "*New owners?*"

"Just read your announcements," Gloria said, looking around her. "My God, where are the new announcements about the employees' meeting, anyway? Well, when you find them, don't forget to assemble in the auditorium in half an hour."

It was Jamie Hatworth who found the stack of neatly typed announcements under the art department's morning delivery of coffee and Danish. "I don't think I can cope with this," she cried. "People were saying we'd been sold out to a conglomerate, and I refused to believe them. But it's true! Look at this."

Mike, the layout artist, finally read the announcements aloud for those who didn't get their copies.

"There will be an important employees' meeting at 9:30 a.m. in the large assembly room on the twelfth floor today to introduce Fad Publishing Group's new corporate owners. Please attend."

No one waited for nine-thirty to arrive. They all filed silently out to the elevators. In the hallway, Lacy murmured to Jamie Hatworth that perhaps the new owners would do something about getting the junior writers their desks.

"Don't push it," the editor said out of the corner of her mouth. "We may not be needing desks by five o'clock."

The large auditorium for the Fad Publishing Group on the twelfth floor was rapidly filling up by the time Lacy, Jamie Hatworth and the layout artist arrived. They had to take whatever seats they could find together, which turned out to be the less desirable ones on the extreme left and in the fifth row, right under the podium. Too close, the layout artist observed, for what was going to happen.

"What's going to happen?" Jamie Hatworth asked under her breath. "Do we get a cigarette and a blindfold? Steak and lobster for our last meal?"

"Actually these are the conglomerate guys," the layout artist said in a low voice as they slid into their seats. "The brass *over* the Fad Publishing brass is coming to look us over. From the scuttlebutt I heard this morning, this conglomerate crowd who bought us out are tigers, wolves from Wall Street that are hooked into several California banks." He twisted his body in his seat as if to sniff the air. "Do I smell fear in here? Half this crowd knows they won't be here in six months. Not with hardnoses like Michael Echevarria."

The layout artist produced a rolled-up copy of *People* magazine and passed it across Jamie Hatworth's lap to Lacy. "Read it and weep," he said sotto voce. "It's a profile of our new masters."

As Lacy opened the copy of *People*, there was a stir in the auditorium. The buzz of conversation died out as half a dozen men in business suits came on stage and grouped around the podium.

It was true, Lacy could see, the figures on the stage all looked rather wolfish, with their trim bodies, their hard-jawed faces, all wearing three-piece Brooks Brothers-style suits in dark gray or charcoal pin stripes. The "Wall Street wolves" were neat, compact, deadly. Except for a man who was two or three inches taller than the rest and who wore a continental-cut fine black Italian silk-and-worsted suit that fit his powerful, *V*-shaped frame like vinyl.

The group of executives parted respectfully as the tall man stepped to the podium and laid down a sheet of notes. He lifted his expensively styled dark head and viewed the assembled *Fad* employees through eyes that said he was all too accustomed to corporate takeovers. His shirt was white silk and the French cuffs that showed a fraction of an inch above his strong, tanned wrists were graced with heavy gold cuff links. He wore a plainly stated, exquisite blue-white diamond set in yellow gold on his left hand.

"Michael Echevarria," the layout artist muttered, reaching over the assistant editor to poke a finger at the copy of *People* magazine in Lacy's lap. "Father Basque, mother Irish, raised in an orphanage, used to be dock hand, stable boy at Belmont. Also construction worker, real-estate tycoon, moved in on the stock market like Ghengis Khan three years ago at age thirty-four."

"*Glurk*," Lacy said, staring.

"Good morning," the smooth, quiet voice of the black panther said to the assembled employees of the Fad Publishing Group. "I am Michael Echevarria, president and chairman of the board of Echevarria Enterprises, Incorporated, to which your company now belongs." He bent his handsome dark head to look down at the page of notes. "I know most of you will be interested to hear that there will be no personnel changes at any level of *Fad* magazine and its affiliates for a period of three months.

"That," he said, "should take care of the majority of your questions."

"Bastard," a male voice said quite clearly behind Lacy.

The cold gray eyes flickered over the first few rows as though the comment had been heard and noted. "However," the president and chairman of the board of Echevarria Enterprises went on, "I'm here to announce that there will be an ongoing evaluation of all jobs during this period by the Echevarria management team"—here he made a slight jabbing motion with his hand to indicate the executives around him—"represented on the platform this morning. Fad's new vice-president of administration, George Hanley, will give you details of how the evaluations will work shortly."

He continued to make a rather cursory study of the first few rows of auditorium seats, not referring to his page of notes now, as though what he had to say was, in the light of all the companies he had taken over, fairly routine.

Lacy felt the grip of her first stunned paralysis fading away, to be replaced with a familiar tidal wave of panic.

It was he! This sleek, towering presence in the fine Italian suit was not Michael Echevarria, president and chairman of the board of whatever he'd said, but the whole bizarre experience of that night in the penthouse in Tulsa in the flesh! It was the black panther and Mount Rushmore and the circus aerialist, sole owners and proprietors of all that *zap! bam! powie!* and other phenomena! And the man who still thought Lacy Kingston was a hustler!

With the full realization of who it was up there, Lacy began to slide her long, slender model's body down in the seat, putting her legs with some difficulty under the row in front in order to get as low as possible and out of sight. She managed to get her shaking hand over her eyes, thumb and forefinger to her temples, as though overcome by some powerful thought she had to consider. Like how she was going to get out of the large auditorium on the twelfth floor

of the Fad Building in the next few minutes. She
needed a hat to pull down over her face. She needed a
pair of sunglasses for a disguise. She needed to turn
into the White Rabbit and jump down the nearest
rabbit hole.

Actually what she needed to do, she thought over
waves of terror, was something practical. Like get
down on her hands and knees and crawl over the legs
of the staffers from *Fad* until she got to the aisle,
where she could just wriggle away on her stomach to
the auditorium doors. Because her mind was screaming that the man on the stage who had just taken over
Fad magazine was the man in Tulsa who had pur-
chased her all-night time as a hustler. And she still
had his fifteen hundred dollars!

"This means," the cool, authoritative voice continued, "that all Fad Publishing Group jobs will, in
the next few months, be subjected to intensive study,
with the goal of recommending revision or replace-
ment of personnel if necessary. In the same three-
month period—"

Lacy was practically horizontal in her seat by this
time, her heart pounding, one hand holding the *People* magazine over her head in what she hoped was a
casual manner in order to hide the distinctive, telltale
color of her smoky-blond hair. She had to eliminate
the hair. She clamped her eyes shut. She had to eliminate the sight of her emerald eyes. Which he would
undoubtedly remember looking up at him so dazedly
and willingly when he had taken her in his arms and
made such wonderful, passionate love to her in the
penthouse that night.

"What *are* you doing?" Jamie Hatworth hissed as
Lacy slid even lower.

Glung! went the auditorium seat, snapping into the up position as Lacy slid too far, lost her center of gravity and dropped into space. She found herself sitting on carpet-covered concrete, trapped with the seat at her back and her long, nonstop legs under the row of seats in front of her.

"—this will help assess current nonefficient procedures," the president and chairman of the board of Echevarria Enterprises finished. His dark head swiveled in the direction of the suddenly loud and disruptive sound of one of *Fad* magazine's junior writers sliding out of her seat and hitting the floor.

There was a moment of prolonged silence.

"Hey, kid, are you all right?" the layout artist cried, getting out of his seat and stepping over Jamie Hatworth to help.

Someone a few rows back said loudly, "Did she faint?"

"Shouldn't we all?" another voice drawled from the other side of the auditorium.

Since Lacy's legs would not cooperate, the layout artist and advertising man on Lacy's right were having a difficult time dragging her out from under the row of seats. The ad man held Lacy awkwardly under her arms, her elbows at right angles, while the layout artist rather enthusiastically ran his hands down Lacy's thighs to her knees and gave them a helpful tug. Between the two of them they finally got a flushed, disheveled Lacy to her feet.

Which was the last place she wanted to be, standing up alone and facing the stage.

The president and chairman of the board had observed the rescue operation in the left row of auditorium seats with a stony expression. Now his cool, assessing stare took in Lacy, first as an employee who had managed to interrupt him in the middle of a sentence, then, as his gaze passed over Lacy's elegantly slender figure in her Geoffrey Beene suit, with the growing interest of a man who could not help but be impressed with a ravishingly beautiful young woman. Even one who had just fallen flat on her fanny.

As the silence dragged on, the chairman's thoughtful look lingered on the topknot of Lacy's distinctive hair and the strands of dark-blond curls beginning to unravel around her cheeks and ears. Even more slowly and thoughtfully his look dropped to Lacy's wide emerald eyes and then to her mouth, which was hanging open, helpless and speechless. In the few seconds it took for recognition to register, the gray eyes turned dark, black pupils dilating in sudden shock. Then there was an Antarctic blast of something indescribable.

For a long moment they stared at each other.

Without taking his probing gaze from Lacy, whose knees were giving way, allowing her to sink back down slowly into her seat, the president and chairman of the board raised his hand commandingly, index finger crooked, to the group of executives standing behind him. A young man in a charcoal pin-striped suit rushed to the black panther's elbow. The chairman murmured something to him, not turning his head, his eyes still fixed on Lacy. The pin-striped executive immediately left the stage.

"I would now like to introduce," Michael Echevarria said in the same cool, uninflected voice, "a man you will get to know very well in coming weeks, Fad's new vice-president of administration, transferred from our corporation to yours, Mr. George Hanley."

Another hard-faced executive took the podium while the pantherish figure of the conglomerate head strode quickly from the stage.

What Mr. Hanley, Fad's new vice-president of administration, had to say to the assembled *Fad* employees Lacy never knew. She sat where she was, immobilized and nonfunctioning, not even hearing Jamie Hatworth's anxious whispers prodding her, only thinking about what she was going to do now that she was out of another job. It was probably even too late to make contact with the Western States Wholesalers for their spring tour. Not to mention that the show coordinator *had* been rather nasty about the return, via priority mail, of the somewhat-worse-for-wear black crepe Claude Montana.

When the last of the speakers on the stage had filed out of the auditorium, Lacy was not surprised to see the Echevarria executive in his pin stripes bending over her. "Miss Kingman," the conglomerate wolf said. He was muscular and keenly self-important. But he couldn't resist an appreciative look as Lacy bent to examine the runs in her stockings where they'd caught on the rows of the seat in front when she fell. "That's your name, isn't it—Miss Tracy Kingman?"

They'd gotten to Gloria Farnham, Lacy thought, groaning. All it took was that crooked finger from the chairman of the board and his corporation executives had scurried off to find out who she was.

When Lacy nodded, not bothering to correct him, the corporate wolf went on, "Mr. Echevarria would like to see you in the office of the publisher, Miss Kingman, as soon as possible."

There it was, she told herself. The blow had fallen. Now she was being summoned by the new owner of

Fad Publishing Group to explain how she had jumped from one place and profession in Tulsa to another in New York so quickly. When anyone in their right mind would know no explanation was possible.

Lacy got to her feet with the resigned air of a felon who has just been ordered to the warden's office. He hadn't believed her before. She had no hope of being able to explain her way out of this, either.

8

Unfortunately, Keith got on the elevator with Lacy. Before she could punch UP, the *Fad* management trainee had punched the down button. Keith's coat jacket was open, his tie was loosened, and he was pale, as though he were recovering from a great shock. He looked as unhappy as Lacy felt.

"Please, I really have to go upstairs," Lacy said weakly as the elevator cage started down. "I've been summoned to the executive offices."

"Well, I'm leaving," he told her. "You'll just have to wait."

"Leaving?" For a moment Lacy was distracted from her own troubles; Keith, their ex-millionaire Wall Streeter who was always so condescending with the other junior writers couldn't be quitting, she told herself. "You mean like—leaving permanently?"

He turned to look at her scornfully. "Well, you don't expect me to stay *here*, do you? With Michael Echevarria—'*El Lobo*' himself?"

"*El Lobo*?" Lacy gasped.

Keith looked even more condescending. "It means 'the wolf.' Of Wall Street, of course. His reputation's not as questionable as Ivan Boesky's," he went on. "I mean, nobody's charged Echevarria with anything illegal. He's just a basher. His specialty is bashing stocks, corporations, brokers—anything that gets in his way."

He looked at her with suddenly narrowed eyes. "He's called you to his office, hasn't he? I saw what happened in the auditorium. You better not go. I hear he's the same way with women."

"W-with women?" Lacy stammered as the elevator doors opened and they stepped out into the Fad Publishing Group Building's lobby. "You—you don't mean he 'bashes' them, too?"

"Who knows?" Keith said ominously. "It would certainly be in character."

"But what's bashing?" Lacy said frantically as she tried to keep up with him crossing the lobby. "Do you mean psychological or—" She shuddered. "You can't mean anything like physical abuse!"

They went through the Fad Publishing Building's swinging doors, and then they were on the sidewalk. Keith stood with one foot on the curb to hail passing cabs.

"Bashing is an attitude, my dear," he shouted over the mid-Manhattan traffic. "I once saw Michael Echevarria grab a broker by his tie and push him into a computer and screw up an hour's trading. He got a buddy of mine fired for talking to his girlfriend on the telephone about good stocks to buy.

"He's *El Lobo*, all right," Keith said, jumping into a cab that had just drawn up. "I wouldn't work for him if you gave me fifty percent of *Fad* magazine's stock."

Lacy shuddered. It sounded bad enough. She bent to the cab's open window. "But, Keith, isn't talking to your girlfriend about what stocks to buy illegal?"

Their former management trainee pointed to the *People* magazine Lacy was still clutching. "Read about him," he shouted as the cab pulled away. "But don't let him get near you!"

9

The gold on the heavy plate-glass doors said simply, PUBLISHER and under that, FAD MAGAZINE GROUP. Beyond the executive secretary's lushly furnished area there was another door of carved Norwegian oak, and beyond that was the *Fad* publisher's office with Sheraton and Hepplewhite wing chairs, a Persian rug and green-silk-damask-draped windows that overlooked the corner of New York's Madison Avenue and Thirty-seventh Street. Seated behind a huge Second Empire mahogany desk in the borrowed office was the black panther from Echevarria Enterprises, Inc., reading something from a file folder spread before him. He did not look up when Lacy came in.

He looked even bigger, even more powerfully broad shouldered sitting down, if that was possible, she thought with a sudden leap of her wildly thudding heart. His hair was a little rumpled, as though he had just run his fingers through it several times in the privacy of the publisher's office, but otherwise from what she could see of it and the angle of his jaw, his high-cheekboned face registered a familiar icy reserve.

"Sit down," he told her, not looking up.

Lacy stayed on her feet.

"Tell me what you're doing here," he said smoothly as he studied another sheet from the file folder.

Lacy lifted her chin. "I really am a model," she declared, wanting to be employed but wanting to go down fighting, too. "That is, I *was* a model. Now I'm a junior fashion writer." Even as she spoke, she knew it sounded terribly unconvincing.

"Is your name really Kingston? Adelaide Lacy Kingston?" He set the paper aside and began on another. "That's not another alias, is it?"

It looked like her job résumé, Lacy thought, craning. "I was named for my grandmother, actually."

If it was her job résumé, then it was her personnel file he had in front of him. Lacy could guess what frantic effort must have gone into pulling her file in *Fad*'s personnel office, what rushing around and hysteria there must have been to find it. She'd only been there a few weeks and she already knew about personnel's chronic problems.

"You started this month as a writer?" he said from behind the paper. "That's quick work. Did you have a friend on the staff who got you the job? Someone you, ah, did a few favors for in return? What's his name?"

"What?" Lacy said, incredulous.

"His name, please." Now he lifted his head and those all-too-familiar Antarctic-gray eyes met Lacy's with all the crushing impact of a moving concrete truck.

Oh, wow, she thought weakly, did this always happen? When a man you'd been to bed with looked at you, did you always remember suddenly and with such hot, devastating reaction what it was like to have his arms around you, his naked beautiful body holding you and his hard mouth kissing the corners of your lips? Just barely, tenderly brushing them?

"Stop that," his cold, furious voice said.

Lacy gulped. Whatever her face had been registering, it must have been her own version of 220 sizzling volts. While his expression had hardened with an ice coating of black fury.

"I'll give you your money back!" Lacy blurted. She'd already spent part of it on the rent, but not much. "I'll—write you a check!"

He looked as though he could grind, chew up and swallow ragged pieces of automobiles, she thought, fascinated, as she watched his teeth clamp together.

"I really am a model," Lacy squeaked. Her throat had gone dry. "I even had one year as the L'Oreal Girl, before I got my B.A. in English from NYU."

"You were out of work for fifteen months," the cold voice chopped her off. "It's there in your résumé. And it's well known what models do to suplement their incomes. Tell me the name of the man who got you your job here."

"*Some* models!" she protested. "A few models maybe, not all of them!"

"What did you live on for a year and a half?"

"My earnings!" Lacy yelled.

Wrong line again, she knew immediately. "And unemployment!" It was too late. "Listen, I really need this job," she pleaded. "I'm a fashion writer—I submitted all my clippings when I applied here at *Fad*. I'm a darned good one!"

"You free-lanced a couple of times for *Women's Wear Daily*, that was all," he said, lifting a clipping from her file folder to study it.

"I'm good, or *Fad* wouldn't have hired me!"

"Tell me his name," he persisted.

For a moment she could only stare her fury. "Hollings J. Blackhammer!"

She saw his tanned, strong fingers reach for a note pad on the desk and a pencil. "What does he do at *Fad*?" he said in a tone like ice floes grinding together.

"How do I know?" she flung back. "I just made him up!"

There was a small snapping noise as the pencil in his fingers broke in two. He stared down at the polished expanse of the *Fad* publisher's desk with a stony expression. "Your contract with *Fad* prohibits moonlighting," he said with the control of limitless rage, "in any, uh, conflicting activity. I suggest you read it again."

"Moonlighting? Is that what you thought I was doing in Tulsa?" Lacy cried, appalled. "*Moonlighting*? I was modeling in a wholesalers' show!"

He tapped a finger ominously on the polished surface of the desk. "I imagine you made substantially more with your sideline," he rasped, "than you did with modeling."

"You're not serious!" Lacy cried, knowing that he was.

"*Fad* does not need," he said, his grim lips hardly moving, "employees with this sort of . . . conflicting vocation. I'm sure I don't have to explain to you the reasons why."

Lacy continued to stare at him. Obviously he was absolutely convinced that she was some sort of part-time—

She realized, with genuine horror, that on the basis of the evidence there wasn't much else he could think. There she'd been in Tulsa—and here she was *now*. Due to a horrible stroke of miscalculation, she still had his money, and he thought she was capable of supplementing her junior fashion writer's salary (which of course wasn't permanent yet) the way—he also thought—she'd been doing in Tulsa.

"I tried to get rid of you," she blurted, "I told you I was all booked up!" Inwardly, Lacy groaned. It was happening all over again, the weird, demon-ridden words just came spilling out. "You're the one," she tried again, "who practically dragged me out of the bar and wouldn't let me explain! Drat, it was all sup-posed to be a joke!" She took a deep breath. "Listen —did I act like—what you're trying to tell me I acted like? Don't try to mix me up, you know what I mean! It's all your fault," she quavered, "you and all those crazy, wild—"

Kisses, Lacy was going to say. But she stopped abruptly.

There he sat, insulting her with every word that he uttered, obviously hating her, and himself, for what had happened. The way he was acting, she'd die before she'd tell him that she'd lost her head in Tulsa. That for the first time his sensuous, magnificent love-making had aroused her own passionate nature and left her shaken and confused and unable to forget the experience. Or the man.

She was astonished to hear him say suddenly, in a low, vibrant growl, "Why did you walk out when I told you I wanted you to stay? I had something to say to you."

"Walk out where?" Lacy said, baffled, thinking of the auditorium.

"You know very well where," he ground out. "You know what I'm talking about. In Tulsa."

Oh, *that*. Suddenly she could not meet those probing gray eyes. She couldn't explain about that morning in the penthouse, not now. It brought back an aching sense of guilt, and embarrassment. Besides, there couldn't possibly be any explanations: he had the sort of mind that made him believe, even now, that she had some sort of influential friend at *Fad* who'd helped get her a job.

"Look, I need this job," she pleaded. "You *can't* take it away from me! I worked so damned hard to get it!"

Oops—wrong move again, she saw as the muscle in his jaw froze. What she'd meant was she'd spent eight months job hunting, sandwiching it in between modeling assignments and traveling, submitting her few free-lance articles to practically any fashion publication that would look at her stuff and trying desperately to get into print. Not what his face was showing.

"Echevarria Enterprises," he said, looking stonily down at the surface of the desk again, "has announced all editorial personnel will continue in their present jobs for the next three months. The magazine doesn't need a panic right now about who's going to be terminated and who's going to stay. It needs to get on a moneymaking basis without any further unnecessary" —he bit down on the word—"disruptions." He reached for a note pad on the polished mahogany and drew it toward him. "If you continue to be employed here, there has to be some guarantee that you won't have a negative impact on the job environment."

What was he saying? Negative impact? "What am I," Lacy cried, "some sort of acid rain or something? I can't believe this!"

The gray eyes glittered. "Disruptions," he snarled, "being here. Using your obvious . . . 'appeal' . . . to get special jobs, special treatment."

"Are you kidding?" Lacy gasped. "You mean, you think I'm going to be hooking here on the job at *Fad*?"

"I haven't accused you of that," he scowled. "On a purely business basis, I have to accept your explanation that what happened in Tu—in your recent past was your idea of a joke. That *is* your explanation, isn't it, that you were suddenly overcome with a desire to be humorous?

"Whatever your motivation," he went on before he could answer, "it's not going to happen again. Not at my magazine, anyway. I intend to see there's some control maintained over your sense of . . . fun."

"Oh, dirty," Lacy breathed, staring at him. She got the message this time. "That's really low, you know."

"Therefore, during the three-month period of job re-evaluation, it's going to be necessary to protect the work environment here and keep personnel on a stable, efficient basis, so I intend to intervene personally. That is, I want an agreement with you that there's an exclusive demand not only on your on-time but your off-time activities, too. It is," he finished, "purely precautionary."

For a moment, Lacy couldn't believe what she'd just heard. "You're going to make a demand on my *what*?"

"There's a lot at stake in any takeover, and corporate stability is top priority during the initial shaking-out process," he said grimly. "I can't afford to let you complicate the status of a particularly sensitive acquisition."

"I don't believe this," Lacy cried. "In the first place, I can't be sure what you're talking about!"

"The methodology is already established—we can take it from there. I can make space for you," he continued, picking up a pencil from the tooled English-leather holder on the desk and drawing the note pad before him, "on Fridays. You will have a weekly appointment to meet me at my East Side condominium here in New York. Let's say early evening sometime, as soon after work as is feasible."

"Methodology?" She stared at him. "Is that what you call it? I thought you said it was moonlighting. Or my weird sense of humor!"

"Only Friday nights are available," he informed her, "as I spend my weekends out of town."

"This is completely crazy." She took a deep breath. "Did you say you're, ah, going to supervise my free time? To protect your *company*?"

"Sufficient free time," he said, not looking up. "I haven't got room on my schedule for all of it."

"That's insulting," Lacy yelled. "It's probably downright illegal!"

"On the contrary," he shot back, "conducting your . . . unauthorized activities . . . while you're employed here, is a violation of your contract with *Fad*. That's what's illegal." The pencil in the tanned fingers began to draw heavy parallel slashes on the white surface of the note-pad paper. "I'm demanding total exclusivity," he said, scribbling dollar signs next to them. "Otherwise, the whole thing's a waste of my time."

"Your time? I'm not even sure what we're talking about!" Lacy stared at that set, handsome face, thinking it seemed impossible that this was the man who had held her in his arms and loved her so passionately and tenderly for one whole fantastic night. And yet it was, she thought, feeling almost tearful. What made him think she wouldn't show up for a Friday-night date with him just because she *wanted* to? And without all this garbage about corporate stability and protecting the work environment?

In the next moment, Lacy regretted her weakness. Whatever he was offering had really taken her off guard, but that didn't mean she was absolutely lacking in integrity, in self-respect. "That's blackmail," she cried, coming to her senses. "That's all it is, you're *blackmailing* me!"

"Call it job insurance," he said smoothly.

"I'm a writer—a *writer*, do you hear me?" Lacy found herself suddenly breathless as those furious eyes met hers. She was so distracted by the effect of his hard-bitten, incredibly sensuous face, even the faint virile smell of the shower soap that he used, that she felt her indignation leaking out of her like air from a punctured bicycle tire. Quick, Lacy told herself, he may be fantastic looking, but remember, this man is ruthless, cruel and unfair. And obviously all too willing to believe you're something you're not. He's probably severely neurotic.

He didn't look severely neurotic, she thought. He looked dangerously, sexily irresistible. Even scowling.

She was struck with the vengeful thought that she ought to agree to the stupid idea if only to get him to stop haunting her dreams. Once she gave him enough rope to demonstrate thoroughly what a total rat he was, it would wipe him from her subconscious forever.

"Do you mean," Lacy hooted, "that you'd go to all this trouble, that you'd actually *blackmail* me, just to get me to go to bed with you on Friday nights?"

Their eyes locked, her emerald glare pinning his gray, chilling gaze. "Is that your interpretation, Miss Kingston?" He lifted a dark, sardonic eyebrow. "I said we'd meet on Friday nights. That could mean dinner, the theater, nothing more than that in some social circles."

"Not in mine," she snapped, "I know what you mean." In the next instant she could have bitten her tongue. "That is," she croaked, "ah, what did you mean by 'total exclusivity'?"

"No other men," he growled. "I damned well don't intend to join any long line forming at your front door."

"It's blackmail!" Lacy cried, not wanting to give up. "It's unfair! I told you how much this job means to me. You've got a real meatball mentality, do you know that? I bet you're convinced the whole female population of the world is divided up into 'good women' and 'bad women,' with no in-between! It's exactly what I'd expect from a—a—Spanish half-Irishman!"

"Basque," he barked. "*Basque*, not Spanish. There are Basques living in France as well as Spain, for your information. Besides, I'm just as American as you are. I was born here."

"Then you ought to know better," Lacy retorted loftily.

He glared at her for a long moment. "Seven p.m.," he said. "My car will pick you up promptly at six-forty-five. That should give you time to change and freshen up. The new work guidelines for *Fad* magazine stipulate no more overtime on Fridays, so you shouldn't have any problems with that." He made some more notations with the pencil on the paper before him. "Also, no last minute requests to shift our date to some other evening, please. Other nights are out because of my heavy workload. And as I've told you, weekends I'm out of town."

"I'm not going to let you do this to me again," Lacy screeched. "You practically forced me to have sex with you in Tulsa. Yes, you did! I couldn't find my way out of that penthouse and you knew it when you brought me up there! All that ginger ale, and dancing and—and the rest of it!"

There was another sizzling moment's silence as their eyes locked.

"Clean out your desk, Miss Kingston," he said with menacing softness. "I'll call down and have *Fad*'s payroll department write you a check for your wages through the end of this week."

"I haven't got a desk! I'm sharing a corner table with four other junior fashion writers! That's the way it is around here."

"If you stay, I'll see one's assigned to you," he said indifferently. His hand was poised over the intercom button.

That's the way he does business, Lacy thought, keeping her eyes fixed on the finger that was ready to call the secretary in the outer office and give the command to fire her. Hard, ruthless, powerful—it was so different, she thought despairingly, from the way he made love.

"I can't do it, I live on the West Side," she protested. There was nothing even remotely fair about this; at the end of the three months' employee-re-evaluation period, he could fire her along with all the rest of the *Fad* staffers who were going to get the ax. It looked like the publishing business was going to be just as bad as fashion modeling, and for the same reason. She didn't believe a word about dinner and the theater; it was just the same old line all over again. "I don't even get home until six. How can I be across town by seven!"

After a moment's silence he said, "I take it that's a 'yes'?"

Lacy gritted her teeth. "How long is this supposed to last?" she demanded. "I mean this so-called 'Friday-night date.' Are we talking about the whole three-month job freeze? Or what?"

She'd seen his big frame stiffen. For the first time the arresting gray eyes looked at her with an expression that was not coldly furious or challenging, but knowing and slightly vulnerable. It made her own soft flesh quiver as though it had been pierced by quick, sensuous arrows.

"Why don't we," the black panther's voice said huskily, "see how it goes?" The dimple-indents flickered at the corners of his hard mouth and then disappeared. "I'll call down and have them find you a desk," he told her.

When Lacy took the elevator down to the floor of the *Fad* editorial department, she noticed that people seemed to glance at her, then hurry out of her way. Managing editor Gloria Farnham was waiting at the door of her office, oddly enough, just to greet her. A couple of assistant editors, including Jamie Hatworth, were lurking in the background; they seemed to be waiting to greet Lacy, too.

"Oh, Stacy, sweetie," the managing editor said, grabbing both of Lacy's hands in hers. "So sorry we seemed to have lost you in the absolute shambles of everything taking place this morning. But I did see your little accident in the auditorium. Are you all right? Do you need a cup of coffee? A Band-Aid? Would you like to go lie down in the lounge?"

Lacy shook her head. She saw that two building servicemen were carrying a file cabinet and a lamp out of a corner editorial office, and a third stood by to supervise.

"We're just getting things fixed up for you," the managing editor said, taking Lacy by the arm and steering her past the furniture movers. An associate editor was grabbing down some framed photographs of fashion models wearing surreal gowns by Kenzo and Tohji Yammamoto from the office wall, looking over her shoulder at Lacy apprehensively.

"How do you like it?" the managing editor said, waving her hand to indicate the corner office. "If you're not comfy here—the air conditioning is a beast, it does blow right down your neck sometimes— you will let me know, won't you?"

"It looks very nice," Lacy said diplomatically, watching the associate editor clean her things from the top of the desk and throw them hurriedly on top of the framed pictures she had just taken down.

"You'll love it," Gloria Farnham said with enthusiasm. "The only thing is, sweetie, I'm afraid we can't take you off the little Seventh Avenue Garment District assignments just yet." She pushed her hair back quickly and smiled her vague smile. "Personally, I wouldn't want to tie you down with beginner's stuff at all those obscure dress houses Jamie's got you going to—I think you've got too much talent. But the new management was very definite about it when they called down a little while ago. No change in assignments yet was what they said.

"But I guess you know that already," she finished meaningfully.

"That's OK," Lacy said, looking around. She was beginning to feel rather numb. But she was putting two and two together. And it added up to awful.

When the president and chairman of the board relayed a command to *Fad* magazine to find a desk for her, this was what happened. It was a wonder they didn't give her the whole editorial floor, including the restrooms. And they assumed, of course, what Michael Echevarria was getting for it. Who wouldn't?

"But a little basic run-through in the Garment District for a few weeks won't hurt a bit, love," the managing editor consoled her, giving Lacy's hand an affectionate little pat. "After all, you're still, ah, a beginner."

"You can say that again," Lacy muttered disconsolately.

10

As Lacy made her way late Friday afternoon through Fishman Brothers' loft on Thirty-second Street, where the sewing machines were still going rapidly and noisily to fill the orders for the now-famous Disco Queen line, she was feeling particularly beleaguered and out of sorts.

Nothing was going right in her chosen career of magazine fashion writing, especially since her meeting with the black panther of Echevarria Enterprises, Inc. A person would think that Harvard public-relations expert Harrison Salstonstall Potts IV and the literally explosive Fishman Brothers fashion showing would be enough for one person to cope with. She never thought there'd be more.

It had been a hectic week, scheduled with back-to-back lingerie and rainwear assignments. And this had been an especially bad Friday, trying to do interviews with the owners of an establishment called Tiny Lady Training Brassieres. Now it looked like her life was once again in danger of being reduced to absolute chaos, Lacy couldn't help thinking, thanks to the sudden appearance of the tycoon from that night in Tulsa. She needed a sympathetic shoulder to lean on. A shoulder belonging to someone kind. Someone with worldly experience who might know, perhaps, how this outrageous demand from the president and chairman of the board of *Fad*'s new owners could happen. She wasn't going to divulge all the details, because not even Irving Fishman would believe them, but the dress manufacturer seemed like the man to confide in. After all, she remembered, he had a daughter, too.

As Lacy made her way down the length of the Fishman Brothers workroom, with its rows of rattling machines and busy seamstresses at work on piles of mega-color purple and green satins, she could see that the door to Mr. Fishman's tiny glass office was closed and that he seemed to have someone with him. Too late it occurred to her that an afternoon at the end of the week was probably not the best time in the world to visit the successful fashion entrepreneur Mr. Fishman had just become. But before Lacy could turn back, he saw her and stood up at his desk to beckon her inside.

"My dear genius young lady," Mr. Fishman said, embracing her warmly and placing a large audible kiss on her cheek, "so how's it with you? I see you still have your job at the magazine, they should be so lucky to have you yet. Speaking of that, Mr. Potts the fourth called me to have a long, friendly conversation, and he tells me he's returning to Boston to open his own public-relations firm, now that he has a world-renowned promotional triumph like Fishmans' Disco Queen behind him. I wish him the best of luck.

"Why don't you join his firm, Lacy dear?" he asked. "I get the very great impression Potts the fourth would like to have you in Boston."

"Oh, no," Lacy murmured, genuinely appalled. "I really don't want to do P.R., Mr. Fishman. I—I have too many things I'm involved with as it is." She shot a cautious glance at Mr. Fishman's visitor, who had gotten politely to his feet, balancing a superb alpaca topcoat in one arm and a handcrafted Mark Cross saddle-leather briefcase in the other. "If you're busy, I can come back another time."

"Busy?" Mr. Fishman boomed genially. "Never too busy for you, my gorgeous young woman. Permit me to introduce Mr. Alexander van Renssalaer," he said, turning to the other man, "a lawyer for the insurance company which underwrote the former great but now destroyed Zebra establishment. He is just paying a friendly visit to clear up a few liability questions, which, I am happy to say, are no longer a problem, thanks to the fact that Mr. van Renssalaer also happens to be a friend of Mr. Potts the fourth, who went with him to Harvard.

"This," the dress manufacturer said introducing Lacy with a fond smile, "is Miss Lacy Kingston, the famous fashion model of a few years ago, now a writer for *Fad* magazine and also the marvelous young lady whose original idea was the late, lamented Zebra disco promotional dress showing."

Lacy winced. Mr. Fishman had obviously forgotten that her participation in the Zebra disco event was supposed to be a deep secret. The lawyer extended a firm, nicely manicured hand and seized Lacy's tentative one with a particularly interested smile.

"*Fad* magazine," he murmured. "You people have just been bought out by the Echevarria conglomerate, isn't that right? Good luck. Not many employees survive their takeovers."

The insurance-company lawyer was certainly very attractive, from the top of his close-cropped, rather reddish hair to his broad shoulders, clothed smoothly in finest heather-gray English worsted, and the thick, sturdy soles of his handmade Rawson Smith brogues. Everything about him spoke decisively of breeding. The name, van Renssalaer, was one of New York's oldest and finest. That penetrating look in his amber eyes had taken thorough stock of Lacy from the moment she'd stepped into Mr. Irving Fishman's office.

"A rough type, Echevarria," the lawyer said in guarded tones, "and ruthless. He's a very dangerous man to work for."

"Well," Lacy said, "I—why, do you know him? I mean, does he have the reputation for being dangerous, ah, generally?"

"There are all sorts of reputations," Alexander van Renssalaer smiled at her, "and Echevarria's got several. Which one are you referring to? Financial? Personal? His way with women?" He shook his reddish head. "Tsk, tsk, tsk," he said by way of description.

Lacy had just remembered with a guilty pang that this perceptive New York corporate lawyer was, after all, talking to Michael Echevarria's regular, exclusive Friday-night date. "Just asking, actually," she said quickly. "It's not all that impor—"

"It's a subject, if you'll allow me to say so," the lawyer said, with a flash of predatory white teeth, "that needs a whole luncheon to do it justice. Anyone, my dear, who works for Echevarria should really know what he or she is getting into. It would be my pleasure, Miss Kingston, to tell you all about it—say at the Yale Club, noon tomorrow? I love eating at the Yale Club even though I went to Harvard. I'm also an expert on how Echevarria operates. I've certainly taken him to court enough times."

Lacy stared at the broad-shouldered man, who looked at her with undisguised interest. Tell her how Michael Echevarria did business? After her interview with him in the *Fad* publisher's office, she already knew! "Some other time," she breathed, inching toward the door of Mr. Fishman's little office. "It's nice of you to offer, but I really have to go now."

"May I call you at *Fad*?" the urbane voice persisted. He followed her to the door and held it open. "You're a writer, is that what I heard Irving say?"

"I'll give you her number," Mr. Fishman offered approvingly. "She works so hard—what this beautiful girl needs is a nice lunch every once in a while in a cultivated atmosphere like the Yale Club. I don't know it personally, but I hear the food is excellent."

Drat Irving Fishman, Lacy thought, beating a hasty retreat through the Fishman Brothers' busy workrooms. He was kind, he was sweet, but after all, she thought uncharitably, if it hadn't been for him, she'd never have seen the Zebra Lounge go up in smoke and flames in what had definitely been one of the most terrifying experiences of her life. Now he was trying to be a one-man dating service.

Lacy pulled the collar of her denim jacket up

around her ears as the wind on west Thirty-second Street tore down the gritty canyons of the Garment District. As she did so, she saw out of the corner of her eye that the burly man in the doorway across the street snapped to attention.

The sight of that broad figure trying to be furtive was the last straw. Impulsively, Lacy decided to take a cab. She was running late as it was. And, she remembered, she was out of her *Fad*-magazine bus tokens. Even more impulsively, Lacy nodded to the man in the doorway, lifting her hand and crooking an imperious finger. *Come here*, her gesture said in no uncertain terms.

He started across the street toward her. Lacy couldn't help thinking he looked rather tired and cold. "Couldn't you even grab a cup of coffee while you were hanging around out here?" she wanted to know. "There's a deli on the corner of Seventh and Thirty-second."

"I hadda wait," he told her gruffly.

His name was Joe. She'd gotten that much out of him when he'd nearly fallen on top of her trying not to lose her on the crowded stairs of the IRT Thirty-fourth Street subway station. But he wouldn't admit that he was following her or watching her. Or who had hired him to do it. It wasn't hard to guess. Joe had picked her up in the lobby of the Fad Publishing Company at 5:00 p.m. last Monday, and he'd been tailing her ever since. She didn't have to be Sherlock Holmes to deduce that Joe was a walking, watching guarantee of the "exclusive" part of her Friday-night date.

At first she'd been so furious to find what was obviously a private detective following her that Lacy had slammed around her apartment to express her outrage that Michael Echevarria could have done this. To have put a tail on her, just to see if she was going out with other men! Dishes had rattled on their shelves as she stamped through the kitchen. She could almost hear the black panther saying coldly that he was only protecting his Friday-night "exclusive" arrangement.

"Come on," Lacy said, now taking the detective by his burly arm and pulling him toward a taxi that had just stopped in the middle of Thirty-second Street. "Make it easy for yourself—we'll travel together." She practically had to push the heavyset man into the cab ahead of her. "I've got to go to Daitch Shopwell and get some groceries before I go home. You wouldn't," she said suddenly, feeling an impish devil prodding her, "want to eat spaghetti with me for dinner tonight, would you?"

"Miss Kingston, please." His rough-hewn features wrinkled up in anguish. "You wouldn't wanna get me in big trouble, would you?"

Lacy smiled at him. He looked about fifty, probably a former detective with the NYPD, that's what they usually were on television. From what she could tell, he was practically on 24-hour duty. Joe had been downstairs in front of her apartment building no matter how early she'd left for work that week, and he came back with her at night when she returned from *Fad*, no matter how late.

"Are you following me, Joe?" Lacy asked. "You would tell me if you'd been tailing me all week, wouldn't you?"

He twisted his eyes at her, dumbly.

Why was she letting Michael Echevarria do this to

her? she asked herself. The answer was *She needed her job*.

That's no answer, she argued. Why didn't she tell herself the truth? *You're putting up with all this because you're falling in love*, her inner voice admonished her.

No, I'm not! she protested. Don't be ridiculous, I've never been in love in my life!

And what makes you think there isn't a time and place for everything? the first voice jeered. Even you, Lacy Kingston?

No—but not like this! she complained. Michael Echevarria is hard, ruthless, a chauvinist exploiter of women! You know what he thinks of me! Never, *never*! Not with *him*!

Why not? the inner voice countered. Have you been able to forget him since the first night you met him? Does he haunt your dreams, make you miserable, do you long to be in his arms, feel his kisses again?

The truth was devastating.

"I'm falling in love," Lacy murmured, staring wide-eyed at Joe's beefy form next to her.

"Please, Miss Kingston," the detective almost screamed, "don't say things like that! I'll lose this job! I gotta wife and two grown kids in Mamaroneck!"

As the taxi sped up the West Side Highway, Lacy felt a sudden rush of compassion for the man beside her. She was, after all, a tenderhearted girl; she couldn't help it if Michael Echevarria brought out the worst in her. She slipped her hand under Joe's big arm consolingly, even as he gave a muffled shriek. "Have you ever met Mr. Echevarria personally?" Lacy wanted to know.

Silence.

"Oh, come on, Joe," Lacy persisted, "it's been pretty dull for you this past week, hasn't it? I'll bet your whole report sheet, or whatever it is, is blank."

"I logged you every place you went, Miss Kingston," he said stiffly, looking at her out of the corner of his eye. "Even when you had lunch with the tall blond guy."

"Mr. Paul, from the Thornton Modeling Agency," Lacy said gently.

"Yeah."

"He's gay," Lacy said even more gently.

"I'll put it down on the report," he said, "and check it out."

"But somebody," Lacy murmured, "is already checking it out, aren't they, Joe?"

"Please, Miss Kingston," he said, rolling his eyes to look at her without moving his head. "Don't ask me that."

The taxicab stopped on Broadway at Seventy-ninth Street in front of the Shopwell supermarket, and Lacy let him go.

"OK, Joe," she told him determinedly, "I'm going to see that you and I get something out of this. No more subways, OK? No more crowded Seventh Avenue buses, right? From now on, we're on Mr. Echevarria's expense account." As Joe stared at her, she pointed to the taxi meter. "That means," she told him sweetly, "you pay."

11

At seven-thirty sharp that evening a Rolls Royce limousine with dark-tinted windows picked Lacy up at her apartment house on west Eightieth Street and whisked her through Central Park to the East Side, where it delivered her to a very select, and impossibly expensive, condominium tower on Sutton Place. The Rolls Royce's good-looking, very polite and silent young chauffeur in gray livery saw Lacy into the arms of the condominium doorman. He in turn escorted her inside to a private elevator with all the care of a Brink's armored-car driver depositing several million dollars' worth of cargo in canvas sacks at Fort Knox.

Going up in the mahogany and gold-mirrored elevator, Lacy stared at her reflection with a mix of emotions. At the last moment she had decided to dress for her so-called date with the president and chairman of the board of Echevarria Enterprises, Inc., in an old lavender cashmere sweater that went well with the smoky blond of her long, curly hair and a purple and gray tweed skirt. She'd thrown an old beige belted London Fog over her shoulders, thinking that whatever Friday night's activities consisted of, she'd save wear and tear on her really good clothes. She really didn't care, she told herself, whether he liked it or not.

Still, her heart jumped into her throat when the elevator doors opened and she saw the black panther waiting for her in his condo foyer in another magnificent black tuxedo.

She had to admit that he looked absolutely fantastic. He held a drink of Scotch in his hand, his long, tanned fingers grasping the glass tightly as he took in her sweater, skirt and London Fog and the old white plastic boots she wore. His chiseled features flickered with some expression she didn't recognize.

Wow, she thought, staring back at him. Before, he had only to touch her hand and all the *zap! bam! powie!* zeroed in. Now all he had to do was *look* at her!

"Hi," Lacy whispered feelingly. It seemed like the right thing to say.

But actually the black panther was so heart-stoppingly beautiful in his marvelously tailored tuxedo, his dark curls tamed, his imported cologne so warm and musky in her nostrils, that Lacy half closed her eyes and actually swayed.

She caught herself just in time. No matter what she was there for, he had a name now, Michael Echevarria. He was owner of the conglomerate that had just acquired *Fad* magazine. He was the boss over all her bosses. He was also the cold, furious executive in the publisher's office who'd told her that her job was in jeopardy unless she dated him exclusively. In a word, he was despicable.

"Come in," the black panther said in his low voice. His hard, handsome face was just as impassive as it had been Monday morning when he'd stood on the stage of *Fad*'s large auditorium zapping all the poor magazine staffers with his ruthless directives. "I have something I want you to do."

I'll just bet, Lacy told herself.

She flinched when he took her by the arm and steered her from the foyer into the living room of the apartment, which was decorated, Lacy saw somewhat apprehensively, in a style that was pretty ruthless and commanding, too. The décor was Sutton Place Expensive Contemporary, with leather, chrome, spare Finnish design work, hand-woven Greek fabrics and dark, waxed woods. It all had the unmistakable mark of an exclusive East Side, perhaps even international, interior decorator. A curious note was a bank of *étagères*, brass-trimmed glass showcases for a collection of eighteenth-century miniatures painted on ivory and set in diamond-and-gold frames, lovely enameled snuffboxes, raw hunks of semiprecious stones and antique gold and silver jewelry. He had said he loved beautiful things, she remembered; it certainly looked as though he didn't mind having them around. The *étagères* and their contents looked like a collectibles show someone had staged for the Metropolitan Museum of Art.

He didn't pause to let Lacy stop and look. "The bedroom," he said, his hand on her arm.

Lacy gritted her teeth. He was certainly getting right down to business. Talk about overbearing and crude! Besides, she had no intention of cooperating!

Still, the prospect of having the black panther make love to her returned now, with all the sneaky force it had had when she'd stepped out of the condominium elevator. Just the thought of it brought a hot, rushing sensation, like an invisible Jacuzzi roaring through her.

He was obviously too determined to get what he wanted to realize that given half a chance, the magic that had happened in Tulsa could easily overwhelm her. That she would probably be in his arms, willingly, eagerly, if he so much as kissed her. She had to fight the crazy, uncontrollable effect he had on her every moment she was with him. Stop thinking about such things! she told herself.

Lacy stumbled a little nervously on the inches-deep softness of a fabulous rug in orange and black geometrics. Three sides of the sternly masculine bedroom in silver, charcoal and beige were smoke-tinted beveled mirrors. They reflected back an image of a delectably slender young woman in a London Fog raincoat looking as though she were ready for anything.

"Good night, what's the rush?" Lacy cried. "It isn't even eight o'clock yet!" Obviously there would be no candlelight dining. Obviously there wouldn't even be romantic waltzing to music from *Dr. Zhivago*. He thought he had it made with her job on the line.

She came to a sudden stop. The bed that dominated the room was emperor size, truly regal in its proportions, covered with a charcoal and beige silk bedspread. Laid out on the spread was, incredibly enough, a dark-green silk chiffon evening gown with a *V* neck, long transparent sleeves made of the same filmy fabric, matching dark-green strappy sandals in silk and a scandalously brief pair of lacy bikini panties.

"Get dressed," the black panther told her. "We're going out to dinner."

Dinner? She could only stare at the green gown on the bed. Did that mean they were going to have a date after all? Her next thought was that she was the only person in the world who knew that this particular subtle shade of dark green set off her dark-blond hair and creamy-gold skin to perfection.

She gathered he had bought a long, green formal gown for her to wear to dinner. It was a lovely dress, her very own shade of green.

Well, Lacy thought, dinner it is. She wasn't in the mood to complain. As she lifted the green silk chiffon, she ran her fingers along the neck seams, looking for a label. Her guess would have been Galanos or a Givenchy. But there was no label, and all the long seams were exquisite handwork, no machine stitching at all. The dress was a gorgeous piece of couture, she realized with something of a shock, with its simple lines, lavish yards of incredibly fragile silk fabric and thousands and thousands of tiny little hand stitches.

She guessed he'd called some New York designer to whip up this dress for their first Friday evening. It had only taken a fortune to do it.

"It will fit," the low voice said from the doorway. "It was made from your measurements, supplied by your modeling agency."

Good lord, the private eyes had been at it again! Naturally the president and chairman of the board of the Echevarria Enterprises conglomerate could afford unlimited time and expense hiring people to look up details like that. Even her 35-22-36 vital statistics!

Lacy stared down at the beautiful green dress. "I'll be out in a minute," she said, turning her back.

It only took a few seconds to strip off her lavender sweater, the tweed skirt and her mauve silk panties and bra and put them on the bed beside her. She perched on the edge of the coverlet to pull on the green silk bikini and matching panty hose. Only after a few seconds it dawned on her—she was not exactly alone. She looked up to see him still standing there in the doorway.

In total silence her stunned, emerald gaze locked with that totally impassive stare.

"I've seen you naked before," he reminded her before she could speak. His interested gaze watched a crimson glow beat in her temples and up to her hairline as he took a sip from the drink in his hand. "I didn't know women blushed anymore. It must be a lost art."

"I practice a lot," Lacy gritted.

He wants me, she was thinking with a slight ringing in her ears. I've been thinking all this time of how he affects *me*, and I've forgotten the way he looks. Hot and smoky. In his eyes, in his voice.

"Get dressed," she heard him say. "We have reservations at the restaurant for eight-thirty."

She was blushing so, she could feel the blood beating in her face like a bad case of sunburn. She slipped the cool, slithery green chiffon silk over her head and put her feet into the delicate dark-green silk sandals. He came around behind her to pull the zipper of the gown up the back.

"I need more lipstick," she managed. She shied away from the brush of his hands against her bare skin. "I should put on a brighter red to go with—"

"Be still a minute." He was standing so close behind her she could feel his breath on her hair.

Seconds later she heard the click of a box snapping open. He evidently tossed it on the bed behind him, for in the next moment both his hands put a cold, heavy object around her throat, taking some time with the catch.

In one of the beveled mirrors on the wall opposite the bed, Lacy saw herself standing in a stunning dark-green chiffon gown that fell in flowing straight lines from the fabric's firm clasp on her breasts to froth like foam around her feet. It had been a long time since she'd worn fabulous *haute couture*, but even the famous unused Virginia Slims ad couldn't compare with this. Around her throat, Lacy saw, her mouth dropping slightly open, was a magnificent show-stopping necklace of emeralds and diamonds that, if they were real, would have been worth several years of her salary as junior fashion writer for *Fad*. With Gloria Farnham's annual wages thrown in, too.

"Nice," she murmured, staring. "I've never seen better fakes." Even imitations of this quality, she knew, cost a small fortune.

Somehow, though, as she watched the green fire and brilliant sparks clasping her throat, she had the uneasy feeling that what looked like white gold or platinum and replicas of marquise diamonds and large square-cut emeralds were real. The diamonds sent a shaft of sparks in the soft lights of the bedroom when she breathed, and the deep green depths of the emeralds exactly matched the shade of her eyes.

"They *are* fakes, aren't they?" she asked.

His big, powerful hands rested lightly on her chiffon-clad shoulders as he stood behind her. In the mirror, Lacy saw his dark head bend slowly and descend to the back of her neck, and she felt the inexpressibly shivery brush of his lips there.

"What do you think?" he muttered, his teeth taking a little sensuous nibble of her smooth skin.

The old, familiar instant paralysis was back. The feel of his mouth was as overwhelming as the imperial ransom of emeralds and diamonds that rested so heavily against her throat.

"God, you're beautiful," he whispered as he lifted the weight of her hair to run warm, firm lips under the curve of her ear. When Lacy shuddered, he said huskily, "You're the most beautiful thing I've ever seen. You're just as I pictured you, wearing this."

Lacy closed her eyes. Mr. Rushmore was back, she thought, with an irrepressible shiver of joy. Just the memory of all those fantastic kisses, the earthquakes of passion, sent answering rivers of fire running through her. Who could forget that once-in-a-lifetime experience, that night in Tulsa, the magic that had lasted—and that had given her anguished hours of insomnia just trying to get it out of her head? She knew at that moment, trembling, hating herself, she would have given him anything he wanted.

"Let's go eat," he murmured against the cloudy curls of her hair.

Unfortunately, Lacy knew almost at once that dinner was a bust. The president and chairman of the board of Echevarria Enterprises, Inc., had chosen the great New York restaurant Lutece, renowned for its superb

French cuisine and elegant atmosphere. But they had rushed through the main dining room as though the New York Fire Department was close behind them, leaving Manhattan's most prestigious and fashionable patrons gaping at Lacy's stunning couture gown, her jewels and crowd-stopping beauty, to a table in the back that was almost a semiprivate dining alcove.

"I want to see the people here," Lacy wailed. "Do you call this dining out? If we get any farther back, they're going to collect us with the garbage in the morning!"

"The food is excellent," the black panther said stonily, bending his dark head to the menu. "Please keep your voice down."

"Then why are you ordering steak and potatoes?" Lacy demanded, settling herself in her chair and craning to see into Lutece's main dining room.

"It's not steak and potatoes," he said between clenched teeth. "It's *chateaubriand avec des frites*."

"Blah—it's steak and French fries!"

She knew perfectly well why she'd been rushed to the back of Lutece. The chairman of the board of the Echevarria conglomerate didn't want to be seen with a notorious moonlighting ex-runway model from wholesalers fashion shows in the Midwest, even if she was done up breathtakingly in a fabulous couture gown and diamonds and emeralds. He just wanted the world to get a tantalizing glimpse of her, Lacy fumed, probably to fuel the rumors about his ways with women. His ambivalence was sickening, she decided.

"I won't contaminate the rest of the people in here," Lacy muttered. "You really didn't have to put me in quarantine on Lutece's back porch!"

"You look exquisite," he said grimly from behind the menu. "Stop complaining. We're seated out here because I want to have you all to myself."

Well, that much was true, Lacy thought, staring at the thick parchment Lutece menu he held up before him. Their waiter would practically have to have roller skates to get their food to them while it was still hot.

She saw him put down the menu with a decisive gesture, but managing to convey that he really wanted to reach over the table and grab her with his big, tanned hands and drag her to him and kiss her until she was breathless.

"Drat," Lacy said, shaken, as she dug into the crisp French rolls and salt sticks the waiter had brought with the flowerets of sweet, unsalted butter.

Their dinner was a monumental experience, a procession of tiny succulent shrimp steeped in white wine and tarragon, a delicate *potage cressoniere*, its verdant texture both crisp and ethereal, followed by a melting *turbot Normande*. Lacy was still devouring the last of the sauce, scraping it up with the tines of her fork, when the chateaubriand arrived.

"Do you always," her dinner partner asked sourly, "eat like this?"

"Always," she said, deliberately innocent. "I make starvation wages at *Fad*." And starved as a model as a matter of routine, she could have added.

When they were discussing politics, Lacy found he was a Republican. "How can you be a Republican?" she cried, incredulous.

"How can you be a Democrat?" he said icily.

They glared at each other while he lit up a long,

black Havana cigar. At least, Lacy glared; he puffed away imperturbably, safe behind a concealing smoke screen. Lacy coughed and choked ostentatiously, without much success.

"Those cigars are made by Cuban Communists," she protested, trying to wave away the smoke with her hand. Air pollution did devastating things to the skin. "You should be buying American mades. It's unpatriotic!"

"I know," he said around the cigar clenched between his teeth. He was studying her intently. "The emeralds match your eyes, Lacy." He cleared his throat. "I'm still trying to match the name up with the person."

She was having the same trouble herself. She looked away uneasily, remembering how impossible this whole arrangement was. Friday-night dates. Dinner at Lutece in crazy jewels worth a fortune and a custom-made gown. He was some weirdo, after all, she tried to convince herself. In spite of all the wonderful things that had happened in Tulsa.

"Do I get to take the necklace and the dress home with me?" Lacy asked him carefully.

"No."

"That's what I thought," she muttered under her breath as the waiter bent to pour her another glass of Dom Perignon '79 with her dessert, *souffle au chartreuse jaune.*

Surprisingly she found he had liberated ideas about women. At least in some areas. He was for women's rights, he said.

"That's ridiculous." Lacy finished her glass of champagne and held it out for more. "It doesn't go with your image, does it?'' She stared pointedly at the perfect Armani tuxedo, all his carefully stated power base, and the Communist cigar.

"I was raised poor, dirt poor," he said imperturbably. "St. Vincent's Orphanage was in a poor neighbourhood, even the hand-me-down clothes we got were worn out. When I was growing up, I saw poor women go out to work to support their families. It wasn't a matter of choice. I also saw they didn't get paid enough for what they do. They still don't."

Well, that was a revelation, Lacy thought, looking at him over the rim of the crystal tulip champagne glass. "Are you going to raise the pay scale then," she asked sweetly, "for women employees at *Fad* magazine?"

His eyes were enigmatic through the cloud of cigar smoke. "I might, if you can show me how to make it profitable."

"Ha! Spoken like a true Republican. Never let a profit interfere with sentiment." Lacy finished off her third glass of wine. "And you," she accused, "were raised in an orphanage!"

"And foster homes," he said, watching her pink tongue as it caught a drop of champagne at the corner of her mouth. "While we're at it, you don't put butter on salt sticks. It isn't done."

"The French do it," she said loftily, "and they invented them."

He put down his cigar to stare at her skeptically. "You've been to France, I take it?"

"Sure," Lacy said, lifting her chin. She was suddenly aware of how tired she was. She'd been on her feet all day in the Garment District, doing interviews and trying to have a confidential talk with Mr. Fishman, and in spite of the lovely green silk backless sandals she wore, her feet hurt. The wine was going to her head, she knew dizzily. She could feel it.

"The first time I went to Paris was when my school sent the sophomore French class over for six weeks. It was crazy. Can you imagine," she giggled, "two dozen teenage girls in Paris? We drove our teachers wild. We didn't learn any French, but we faked it like mad to meet French boys. That was our club project —meeting boys and psyching out our teachers. It was the trip of a lifetime."

The president and chairman of the board, Lacy could see, wasn't bowled over by the kooky charm of her story about the class trip to France. He probably didn't believe her. One dark eyebrow was up rather disapprovingly. "You've had three glasses of champagne," he observed.

"Have I?" Lacy asked, smiling happily. In spite of his apparent lack of interest in her story, she went right on making amusing dinner conversation about her high-school French class and the big white clapboard colonial house in East Hampton, Long Island, she'd grown up in, the pony her father had bought for her and her two older sisters and the reputation the Kingston girls had for being spoiled tomboys and the neighborhood brats, even though they were all later elected homecoming queens and successive winners in the Miss Long Island Beauty Pageant. People, Lacy told herself, had enjoyed her stories before; she had a certain reputation, actually, as something of a comedienne. She even launched into her best bit, about the boa constrictor her oldest sister, Felice, had ordered from a direct-mail pet catalog and what her mother had said when it arrived by UPS.

He puffed for a long moment on his cigar, eyes narrowed, before he said, "How did your mother get rid of it? The boa constrictor, I mean."

"Oh, she didn't," she replied, propping her elbow carefully to one side of the remains of the *souffle au chartreuse jaune* and resting her chin in her hand. "I had very liberal parents. They believed in pets, and, you know—children not growing up with negative attitudes towards repulsive forms of wildlife. They read Dr. Spock all the time. Daddy built a cage for it in the garage. The boa wasn't too bad at first—it ate mice, but then it graduated to eating white rats.

"Then it sort of developed this thing for our next-door neighbor's miniature poodle. It was like it was in love with it. Gastronomically," Lacy added, not able to resist doing her truly comical imitation, which she hadn't done in years, of Felice's boa constrictor weaving from side to side behind the wire mesh of its cage, eyeing a small white poodle with gourmet lust. But the wine got the best of her, and she had to grab the table suddenly with both hands. "We had to give it to the zoo," she gulped.

"Then you must have had," he said, taking the cigar out of his mouth to stare at her strangely, "a very . . . untypical childhood."

"Well, I suppose you could say my family is sort of . . . nutty," Lacy said, wishing the room would stop reeling. "My mother and father were wonderful to us —my mother has a degree in psychology—even if we were, you know, sort of impossible. All of us—my sisters and I—were, well, it's embarrassing to say this, but people said sort of, uh, unusually pretty," Lacy said, blushing. "But my parents always encouraged us to do what we wanted to do, even when they knew it would be hard. Like when I started modeling. That was tougher than anybody expected. Especially when you're just a teenager. I can't describe what a shock it is to have your face and body treated like a commodity. And what a drag it is when you go from assignment to assignment with your feet hurting because you're carrying all your makeup and clothes around with you. And fighting off people making passes at you. I was only seventeen," Lacy said morosely, "when I slugged Peter Dorsey. I laid him right on his back, the louse. He finished me off with what he did to me, though. I'll never forget it." How could she? she thought; she'd never had a big contract after that.

She saw his face go suddenly rigid as he stared at her. "Who," he said with sudden deadliness, "is Peter Dorsey?"

"Peter Dorsey is the source of all my troubles," Lacy explained, discreetly smothering a hiccup. "He is New York's most lecherous photographer, and he ruins plenty of girls. I'm not going to bore you with what he did to me, but it was plenty. On the other hand," she said, giving him an unfocused smile, "if it hadn't been for him, I wouldn't be where I am today."

The chairman of the board, she saw, vaguely puzzled, looked as though he had gone back to chewing pieces of scrap metal. "Peter Dorsey," he said, chomping out each word, "is a photographer in New York?"

"Yes," Lacy said. Violently he pushed back his chair and got to his feet. "What did I do now? Aren't we going to have more champagne? What about coffee?" she cried, disappointed. "Don't you want a brandy and another cigar?"

"I'm going to take you home," he said through clenched teeth. "After—after we've gotten you out of that dress."

They went back to the condominium tower on Sutton Place in the softly purring Rolls Royce limousine with the dark-tinted windows, and Lacy, exhausted after a hard day in the Garment District and two dinners, one of spaghetti she'd had at home and the other at Lutece, plus several glasses of *chenin blanc*, Château Rothschild *superieur* '78, and a half bottle of Dom Perignon, fell asleep on the black panther's shoulder. She didn't even wake up when he lifted her carefully from the Rolls and carried her in his arms through the condominium's underground garage to the elevator and her first regularly scheduled Friday-night date as per their arrangement.

12

Lacy was having the most marvelous dream. She had a tremendous headache—which wasn't the marvelous part—and she had to hold her throbbing brow with both hands, moaning softly, needing somebody to do something about it.

Then there was this beautiful, sleek black panther, naked with soft, subdued light on his satiny skin, making his body gleam like the gold in the *étagère* cases in his Sutton Place apartment, who padded across the thick carpeting to the bathroom to bring her a glass of water and two aspirins.

"I feel sort of sick," Lacy told him plaintively. She put the aspirins in her mouth and took a big gulp of cold water without opening her aching eyes.

"Do you need to throw up?" the black panther said, purring all around her protectively in a soft, velvety voice. He held her close against his lithe, muscular body comfortingly.

"No," Lacy said, sighing, "I just want this headache to go away."

"You had too much wine," he murmured. He pressed her face against his big chest with its fine mat of wiry black hairs and tenderly supported the back of her head with one big hand. "And you worked too hard this week, much too hard."

They lay down together in the lush vegetation of some beautiful Serengeti plain with the dark stars above them and the warm breath of the jungle caressing their perfectly bare, intertwined bodies. In this drowsy, languid state of her dream, Lacy felt the heat of a large, firm hand on the curve of her hip and turned into it, sighing again, pressing the hard points of her nipples against his slightly furry chest.

"It was all that spaghetti," she whispered, reminding him of the dinner she'd eaten at home before they ever went to Lutece. Not believing him, of course, when he said they really had a dinner date.

But all these problems were solved now, she knew, because she was back where she belonged, in the silky paws of that powerful body that stroked her hips and the length of her thigh so carefully and buried its softly breathing lips into the warm recesses of her throat. She felt the panther's grip on her tighten abruptly when she moved her bare knee to slip it between the sprawl of his long, muscular legs.

Lacy clung very tightly to him in the lovely dream, sliding her arms around his neck to close her fingers in his thick, slightly damp hair, which smelled like pine smoke and Ralph Lauren's Polo. He was big and hard, Lacy found dreamily, the rod of his flesh wanting her so fiercely that it seemed it moved slightly, searching her out.

"Darling," the black panther growled into her throat, "you're making it tough for me to hold you like this and not do anything. Can't you—"

The tall grass where they lay shifted under them, the warm winds of Africa blowing hot and voluptuously as he tried to pull Lacy's hips away from his groin just a fraction. But Lacy clung to him even more tenaciously, her legs and hips seeking him until she was half lying across the sprawl of his big body, absorbing the motion of his slow, labored breathing as his chest rose and fell.

"Sweet darling," he murmured raggedly, resigned to the demanding weight of her pressing body, "you're everything I've always wanted. You're so warm, so wonderfully responsive, and so exquisitely lovely—ah, Lacy, I've been looking for you all my life. God, how I want you right now!"

"I want you, too," Lacy told him drowsily, her lips softly kissing the hard, clenched line of his jaw. "I adore you actually," she whispered, her mind sliding off into the warm, slumberous darkness. "I've never forgotten you." She yawned. "You're the most fantastic lover I've ever had."

Under her, he went very still. "Lacy, don't tell me that," he growled. "I don't want to hear about your other men."

But as the dream folded its shimmering gray wings about her and bore her off to sleep, Lacy was trying to explain to him about prom night and Bobby Sullivan in the front seat of his Buick. Who probably had, she realized years later, no more experience with sex than she'd had. All that it had amounted to that night was hurried fumbling and quick pain, and then it was all over. Leaving Lacy to wonder why it had happened in the first place. She had vowed it would never happen again. At least not until she met the man who was perfect, and she fell in love with him, and then it would be wonderful. Just as it was now. Whereas poor Bobby Sullivan was married now and had a perfectly lovely wife and a little daughter, even though he still couldn't look her in the eye when they met on the street in East Hampton.

Lacy couldn't be sure she was actually explaining all this. The story of how it had all happened was perhaps still in her head. Unspoken.

"Lacy," he said, his eyes staring up into the darkness as he held her against him, "what I wanted to tell you that morning in Tulsa was—*unh!*" He shuddered as her groping hand seized the hot, silky center of his power, her fingers wrapping around the throbbing flesh to close on him, grasping him tightly. "Oh, God," he grated after a long moment, "you haven't gone to sleep like this, have you?"

But she had.

As the first light of dawn crept over the towers of Manhattan's East Side and made its way into the windows of the exclusive condominiums of Sutton Place, Lacy awoke with a start.

She was in bed, she realized, opening her eyes wide. Naked. And the president and chairman of the board of Echevarria Enterprises, Inc., was in the bed with her. Actually, she saw, trying to focus her eyes, he was propped on one elbow watching her, looking rather haggard.

Lacy blinked. It was definitely *déjà vu* to be waking up with him like this. "You haven't slept," she muttered, seeing his red-rimmed eyes.

He looked down at her tenderly. "I couldn't have," he murmured, "even if I'd wanted to. You have your hand around a slightly overstimulated part of my anatomy."

"Good grief," Lacy cried, releasing him at once and sitting bolt upright in the bed. It was all coming together. What was she doing here? *The Friday-night date!* "Oh, no," she wailed. "I fell asleep! I just blew everything!"

"Take it easy," he said, watching the graceful arch of her body, the thrust of her breasts as she lifted her arms to clutch her head in despair. He checked the heavy gold Rolex on his wrist. "I don't leave for my Connecticut house until eight o'clock. We've got plenty of time."

"Time?" Lacy leaped out of bed. "My clothes! Who took off my clothes? I don't remember getting in bed with you!"

"You insisted on getting out of the dinner gown," he said calmly, lying back with his arms behind his head to watch her. "You said you wanted to hold up your end of the bargain and give it back. In fact, you threw it at me."

"Never! Oh, how do I manage to get into these things?" Lacy raked her hands through tangled hair. "It's too much, this whole thing—I must be going crazy! Designing that dress and having it made, and diamonds and emeralds, and feeding me dinner at Lutece! Not to mention putting a detective on my trail to see that I didn't cheat on you." She was searching frantically through the bedclothes to see if she could find her skirt and sweater. The green evening dress was on the floor. "It's weird—it's paranoid! You're not normal! I've got to get out of here!"

"Are you always this way in the morning?" he said, a slight frown between his eyes.

"Yes! No!" she cried. Actually she was a very good morning person. It just unnerved her to think she had fallen into bed with him when she'd promised herself that was the last thing she'd ever do.

"Don't worry about the detective," he told her. "You won't be seeing him anymore."

She looked around the room, modestly holding one hand over her breasts to see if she could locate any of her clothes. "Joe didn't make a pass at me," she flung at him, "if that's what you're worried about."

"I didn't say that." Now he was studying her legs appreciatively as she charged around the room, picking up his clothes from the floor and looking under them for her underwear. "He asked to be relieved of his job."

Where were her sweater and skirt and boots? Lacy wondered frantically. Had he done something with them to make sure she wouldn't sneak out on him again the way she had in Tulsa?

"He was too involved with the case." There was a warm, interested look in his gray eyes as he watched her. "He liked you too much. It's all in his report."

"You're crazy!" If she could only find her London Fog she could wear that. It was good enough to catch a cab. "He was old enough to be my father, for heaven's sake!"

"Everybody likes you too much," he observed, sitting up in the bed. His hand snaked out and caught her knee as she passed and pulled her down beside him. "I like you too much, too," he murmured. He put his lips to the side of her face. "I'm only protecting my interests." His mouth reached for hers.

"Let me go," Lacy cried, struggling. "It's not an interest, it's blackmail. Just because I let you make love to me once—"

"I want you," he said, his lips devouring the silky, tender skin of her shoulders. "Damn it, Lacy, I *ache* for you, don't you know that? I stayed awake all night," he muttered against her chin, "watching you sleep. I'm aching for you now, Lacy." His lips moved over the side of her face and the tip of her nose, seeking her mouth. "I can't believe that I want you so damned much. It's incredible."

No, no, she tried to tell herself, struggling in his grasp halfheartedly. This always happened, the feeling that she was drowning in his blazing desire. The sense that she had no control over herself when he held her was frightening. Her body, with streamers of blazing delight flowing into it, was already beginning to melt. Mount Rushmore was back, but so was the president and chairman of the board of the company that owned *Fad* magazine, someone called Michael Echevarria.

The thought sobered her.

"Michael?" Lacy said, pushing him away to look up at him with questioning eyes.

"Yes, darling." He was caressing the silky weight of her breasts now with his big hands, his eyes glowing. "Tell me what you want. I'll do anything to please you."

"I think we ought to talk," she said, trying to keep her voice from shaking as he bent his head. She felt his mouth and then his tongue kissing and circling her nipples. She gave a muffled whimper as the tight buds drew and contracted under the hot, tugging pressure. "The whole thing's a big misunderstanding." Without consciously wanting it, her body slid under him eagerly to glory in all that sleek, marvelous strength. His hand trailed softly down her legs, fingers spread to stroke the smoothness of her belly, and she melted as first one probing touch of his fingers and then another sought the suddenly aching folds of her flesh. She could only moan.

"What do you want, darling?" he murmured, looking down at her with smoky eyes. "Tell me."

She couldn't stand it any longer. "Kiss me—I love it when you kiss me!" Her body was going crazy, and there was still all that *zap! bam! powie!* yet to go! "Please, Michael!"

But he resisted the tug of her hands. "You like the way I kiss, do you?" The Antarctic-gray glare was softened now by a warm, gleaming light. "First tell me that you want me as much as I want you. And no fooling around this time, Lacy." His opened lips brushed hers tenderly. "Tell me you want to be here, in bed and in my arms, like this. Making love. Without giving me a hard time about it."

Her softness flowered around his fingers' erotic stroking. "Talk later," she gasped. She felt a shudder course through his big body as she drew her knees up to clasp his thighs.

Quickly, his control slipping, his hard body moved over hers, positioning itself urgently between her legs. "Oh, Lacy, damn." His hard mouth rocked against hers. "What you're doing to me—it's got to be—"

His hands slid under her hips to lift her to him. "Take me," he rasped. "Darling—just take me!"

It all happened at once. The fiery blaze of his kiss covered her mouth as he arched and exploded into her. There was no thought of slow, sensual lovemaking; the firestorm broke in a burst of searing, unthinking fury. They spun out of time and consciousness, driving even more wildly together. Then it was over almost too quickly, with Lacy's shivering cry and his hoarse, ecstatic shout in her ear. It seemed a long time before they came to rest more calmly in each other's arms.

After a while she felt his body jolt with laughter against her.

"That's what comes of waiting too long," he grinned, pulling her close. "All night is definitely my limit." He lifted his head and the flash of his incredibly white teeth showed in his hard, tanned face. "I didn't hurt you, did I, sweetheart?"

Zounds, Lacy thought, raising a wobbly hand to her streaming forehead. She'd thought the night in Tulsa had been a once-in-a-lifetime experience! She found herself staring up at him. Was it he? Was it she? Or was it both of them together? Would another time be just as fantastical? Even the electricity of his fabulous kisses had gotten lost somewhere in the volcano exploding like that!

"I thought you were terrific, Michael Echevarria," Lacy said with some difficulty. Her mind felt numb. It wasn't just Mount Rushmore anymore or the black panther or any of her wild imaginings. It was *he*, she realized sadly. The president and chairman of the board. The man she was in love with.

She raised her hand to stroke his lips, which were still damp with her kisses. She put her finger against the tip of that straight, chiseled nose and dropped it to the shallow groove in his upper lip, exploring the reality of him—his mouth, his even white teeth. Oh, why couldn't he be different? she groaned. Why had she picked this ruthless Wall Street raider to fall in love with?

He was staring at her just as intently. "I would never want to be rough," he whispered. "I want to cherish you, Lacy. It means a great deal to me."

"Mmmmh," she breathed. How could one person put so much into his eyes? They were eloquent. His eyes said things he never said. Most of the time when they talked, they argued.

"Although having you go berserk like that," he murmured against her fingers, "has its attractions."

Her eyes widened. "Berserk? You must be kidding Mich—"

He cut off her words with ardent lips. His tongue caressed the stiffness until her mouth gave in to him, claiming her sweetness with a slow, confident thrusting. His body pressed her down, responding with its own returning arousal. "Let's keep it our little secret, shall we?" he said softly. "But you do go berserk, Lacy. You love making love to me, don't you? You just can't help yourself, right?"

There it was again, she thought. He was gorgeous and wonderful, but basically he was insufferable. He really thought she was his—his—

"I wish you had waited in Tulsa without running out on me," he murmured into her neck. "I had something I wanted to say to you."

"Wait," she began, knowing what was coming. If

he was going to bring up the terrible fifteen hundred dollars, he had to give her time to explain.

"I wanted to ask you," he said, kissing her eyelids and then the tip of her nose, "if you felt good enough about . . . what had happened, good enough about me, about everything, to be mine on a long-term basis.

"Lacy," he said quickly, "I want to be with you. I've never felt this way in my—"

"What long-term basis?" This couldn't be happening, Lacy was telling herself. "You're not talking about marriage," she said, her eyes narrowing suspiciously, "are you?"

His arms tightened around her. "Will you listen a moment?" he growled. "Don't start yelling, Lac—"

"You mean live with you? Be your mistress?" she cried incredulously. "Is that what you mean?"

"I want you with me, Lacy. That's quite a commitment for me, but what we have between us—I've never—you have to realize this situation needs stabilizing," he said firmly. "I want you in a nice setting, one that does you justice, a good address here on the East Side.

"Now wait a minute," he said, his arms restraining her. "Just wait a damned minute, will you? You can have everything you want, a decent automobile, the right kind of wardrobe, a bank account, no limits, you just have to name it. And I want you to quit that damned job at *Fad*."

"You *what*?" She felt as though she were going to explode even though he was holding her down.

"It's going to take austerity measures to keep *Fad* magazine from going under," he said grimly, "and that junior writer's job will run you into the ground. I don't want you worn out, exhausted, the way you were last night. I want you to stay just like you are—sexy, adorable, beautiful.'' His hand lifted a curl of her smoky-blond hair and twined it softly around his finger. ''For me, just for me. I can't get enough of you, Lacy.''

''You're going to terminate me at *Fad*?'' Lacy said disbelievingly, ''so I can be your mistress full time? Is that what you said?''

''I said I wanted you to quit the job,'' he told her, scowling. ''I didn't say anything about terminating you.''

''Good grief, is there a difference?'' Her whole body stiffened in his arms. ''Do you know what you're saying to me, Michael?''

''I wanted to make you this offer in Tulsa,'' he said, his jaw clenching, ''before you ran out on me that morning. Before I ever knew you had a job on that damned magazine.''

''Make me an *offer*?'' Lacy put her hands against him and tried to pry him away. ''Are we back to that? Do you think you're buying a business?

''Don't answer that!'' she yelled as she rammed him in the chest and sat up.

''Lacy, be calm.'' He raised himself on one elbow, his large biceps bulging. ''Stop it. There's nothing to get excited about.''

''You're disgusting, Michael Echevarria,'' Lacy cried. She'd never been so crushed, so humiliated in her life. She didn't know what she'd expected, but being a sex object in some apartment he paid for was—monumentally insulting!

She bolted from the bed and began flinging open closet doors. ''Oh, I can't cope with this! It's too much!'' She found her skirt and sweater where he'd hung them up very neatly. Her boots were on the floor of the closet. ''I should have expected it, that you'd kick me out of my job, anyway. How could anyone expect you'd keep your word?'' She threw her London Fog onto the bed. ''You must be crazy—do you think I'd lie around all day in the buff, painting my toenails and eating chocolates and watching the soaps while I wait for you to come for me after work—''

''That's enough,'' he growled, sitting up.

''—and use my body?'' Lacy was so wounded by his betrayal that she picked up the thing closest to hand, the green silk sandal she'd worn to dinner at Lutece, and flung it at him. It hit him square in the middle of his forehead, she saw, horrified. He didn't even flinch.

''Control yourself,'' he growled. He jerked up in the bed, the muscles in his chest knotted, eyes like hot, furious lazers.

''You're a decadent, rotten rat,'' Lacy yelled. ''*You're* the one who propositioned me, remember? Wanting me to go to bed with you for money— *yeccchh*!'' She stepped into her lavender and gray tweed skirt and yanked it up around her waist. ''I hope you're satisfied with everything you got here this morning! You only had to pay for my dinner!''

''You haven't got your underwear on,'' he said in a steely voice.

''I'm not going to wear any,'' she flared at him. ''I'm a tramp, remember? You even had to put a detective on my trail, to watch me! Yah, yah, yah,'' Lacy taunted, lifting her skirt and flapping it at him. and flapping it at him.

"My God!" He was out of bed in a shot. He looked around for her bikini panties and found the green silk ones lying on the floor. "Put something on under that," he said hoarsely. "Or so help me, I'll throttle you!"

"Don't you touch me," Lacy shrieked, backing away.

She squared her shoulders defiantly. "You want underwear, you'll have to pay me for it," she burst out. She flipped her hand over, palm up. "Pay me, Michael Echevarria—I'm speaking to you in terms you understand. Right here!" Beside herself with fury, Lacy jabbed the palm of her hand with her index finger. "Fifty bucks for the panties, seventy-five for the bra. One hundred and twenty-five smackarooties, no sales tax becau—" Her voice trailed off.

For a moment, Lacy realized, somewhat dazed, that she'd probably pushed Michael Echevarria as far as anyone ever had and still stayed in one piece.

But he surprised her. He managed to pull himself up to his naked six feet four inches and take a deep, steadying breath. "Anything you want, Lacy," he said in a strained voice. "As soon as you put on your underwear."

Lacy took the green silk bikini panties out of his hand warily. He watched her as she stepped into them and hiked them up under her skirt. He stared at her for a long moment before he said, "Right, I'll get my wallet."

From the look on his set, stony face, Lacy knew she had gone far enough. Why did things get so wildly out of hand when they were together? He made her do the craziest, most inexplicable things, and taunting Michael Echevarria was so easy, just like waving a red flag in front of a bull. Of course, Lacy told herself, it wasn't her fault that he was absolutely rigid, exploitative and humorless.

She watched him stride across the room to pick up his tuxedo jacket from a chair. He took out his wallet and yanked out a handful of bills.

"You misunderstood the whole thing in Tulsa," Lacy began, feeling defensive. "Will you listen to me? I was only trying to get rid of that little pest in the bar and you overheard what I said and grabbed me, and I was terrified someone would think it was all for real, and I panicked."

He laid his jacket back in the chair. "It's not important, Lacy," he said grimly.

"But it *is*! Listen, Michael, what I said in the bar was a joke." Lacy was beginning to feel a little less apologetic as he stood there, scowling at her. "And now you think I'm so great, you want me to be your mistress? In a fancy East Side apartment? I don't know, Michael, I don't think you'll ever understand, I swear I don't," she fumed. "You're so into money and power games—"

"I don't want to hear this," he growled. "I told you, it's not important."

When he started back toward her, Lacy bit her lip. She had every right to lash out at him—he had just tried to trick her out of her job on *Fad* magazine, and the offer to be his mistress was degrading, insulting. What she'd said he was—a decadent, rotten rat—was true. But when he came across the room to her, from the neck up Michael Echevarria was in a towering rage. The rest of him was towering, too, ready and eager, saying that if she'd just stop arguing and be reasonable—

Lacy clapped her hand over her mouth just in time.

"What the hell?" He stopped short, the money in his fist. "Are you," he said in a hard, grating voice, "going to be funny again?"

Lacy wanted to shift her eyes, but she couldn't. He was so wonderful, even when he tried not to be.

"You're such a jerk," Lacy gurgled, her shoulders beginning to heave. She couldn't stand it when he put his hands on his hips, naked body braced, glowering at her. "Anybody else would have known right away that I wasn't—that a fifteen-hundred-dollar-a-night h-h-hoo-hoo-hook—hahahaa!" She couldn't help it—she collapsed on the edge of the bed, hilarious tears oozing helplessly. "I have to go home," she wheezed. She didn't even have taxi fare with her. "Oh, I can't stand it! It—you—oh, you should see your—ah—f-face!"

He stared at her. "Damn! Are you a complete flake? I swear to God, Lacy, sometimes I think you're—you're emotionally unbalanced!"

Lacy whimpered, her hand clutching her stomach, as he turned on his heel and walked away. Poor Michael Echevarria. No wonder he wanted her so much! He was absolutely, grimly, totally without any sense of humor at all.

"Right," he said with his back to her. "I'll call down for the Rolls."

13

On Monday, Lacy's rewritten story on Fishman Brothers' new dress line, which Mr. Fishman had rechristened Disco Flame Queen after its sensational debut at the now-destroyed Zebra Lounge, was given the title "Tacky-Max Triumph" and scheduled for the January issue of *Fad*, bumping a lead article on a major sportswear house's new baggy jeans.

When she got over the first shock of finding her story rushed into print, Lacy couldn't get to managing editor Gloria Farnham's office fast enough.

It was obvious that Gloria didn't know that Lacy's days at *Fad* magazine were numbered. It was probably, Lacy told herself, just a matter of the executive order to fire her being stuck in the personnel office's paper work again.

"Panty Pants Jeans will hate it, Stacy dear," managing editor Gloria Farnham said, not listening to what Lacy was trying to tell her. "Panty's one of our biggest advertisers, too—they'll probably cancel their ads for six months and spend the money at *Mademoiselle*. But I can't help it, sweetie, the Fishman story is delicious. And besides, Panty's not going to launch Dutchman's britches in denim for a spring line, it's a bomb. No, babycakes, 'Tacky-Max' goes in, I just can't help myself. Besides, it's got more luscious details on the fire than the dailies carried. It's a scoop."

"It's only my first article," Lacy moaned, trying to approach the subject of being fired cautiously. "The Disco Flame Queen story is so late—it will come out almost two months after it happened. The back pages will be fine, really. I mean, none of the other junior—"

"Silly Stacy!" the managing editor cried. "Nobody ever came in here *not* wanting to go Big Time, really! In the front of the book, and a lead position, too! You're just too modest. I love you for it, honestly I do."

"People come and go around here," Lacy persisted. "I mean, you never know who's going to be next, do you? I might not even get past the three-month re-evaluation. Think about that."

"I *love* 'Tacky-Max'," the managing editor said with untypical firmness. "Everybody else does, too. Now, sweetie, Jamie Hatworth's just dying to see that marvelous rough draft on the Tiny Lady Training Brassiere fantastic exclusive. Why don't you go in your office and whip it up and rush it on over to her?"

How could she explain, Lacy fretted, to somebody like Gloria that for reasons best left unmentioned, the president and chairman of the board of *Fad*'s conglomerate was going to get rid of her once and for all? Probably by the end of the week?

There really wasn't anybody else Lacy could confide in. Because everyone knew, or thought they knew, how she'd gotten the corner office while the rest of the junior writers were still sharing a utility table in an elbow of the art department. That hadn't exactly made her Miss Popularity.

Lacy was still feeling it was her duty to prepare somebody for the blow when she wandered into the assistant editor's office.

" 'Tacky-Max' is a good job of writing," a harried Jamie Hatworth assured her. She put her baby sitter on hold with a quick "I'll get back to you, Lotus—I've got somebody here I want to talk to" and gave Lacy a weary smile. "You were there at the Fishman Brothers' fire, you got a big story, *Fad* is giving it a big play. So what's the problem?"

"They, uh, bumped the Panty Pants article and lost a lot of money," Lacy gulped, not wanting to meet the assistant editor's eyes. "We'll lose the Panty Pants ads eventually. That's what Gloria said."

"We lose ads all the time, don't worry, it's *Fad*'s publishing disease. 'Tacky-Max' is a good lead, kid. You write with a light, zany touch, you're different. It would have," the small woman said kindly, "gone in, anyway. Is that what you want to know?"

Lacy stared over Jamie's head at a large four-color blowup of the current front cover of *Fad*, featuring Brooke Shields wearing Che Guevarra-type combat fatigues in red sequins. She was realizing that her attempts to let people know that she was going to be the first and probably only person axed during the job freeze because she was a flop as the conglomerate president's girlfriend were definitely hopeless.

"The corner office has lots of space, actually," Lacy muttered unhappily. "I mean, there's room for all three junior fashion writers in there if one of us converts the modular executive bar into a desk."

"I wouldn't touch that one," Jamie Hatworth said, sighing, "with a ten-foot pole. Just keep turning out the light, funny stuff, gorgeous. You're out ahead by a mile.

"In more ways than one," the assistant editor added under her breath, picking up the telephone receiver again.

When Lacy carried a copy of the proof of the new lead story on the Disco Flame Queen promotion at the Zebra to Mr. Fishman, he was ecstatic.

"It's as good as what *People* magazine did, if not better," the dress manufacturer encouraged her. "You write so well, dear young lady, with the flair of your own unique personality. You should be very proud of yourself that this old establishment of *Fad*, which, you should pardon the expression, hasn't kept abreast of the times so much lately, recognizes your superior talents. So what if the story is a little late? Consider it a profile piece, like in *The New Yorker*, which is always months behind in getting around to the subject.

"Let me give you," Irving said, lunging for his dress racks, "a token of my appreciation, which is past overdue. As a favor to me, you should have your complete pick of our new, improved model of Disco Flame Queens."

"I think they're a little young for me," Lacy said, politely refusing an orange satin mini with the face of Wayne Newton in neon-colored bugle beads on the front that Mr. Fishman held up for her.

"Young?" he cried, replacing the disco dress on its hanger. "What is young at your age? You are maybe an old lady of twenty-one, twenty-two?"

"I'm twenty-three," Lacy said, full of sadness. "Almost twenty-four, actually."

"So now one of the most beautiful women I've ever seen in this business, and believe me, I have seen some beauties, is retired from the fashion business and is working as a very talented writer, an intellectual! What a gift, to have such loveliness and brains, too.

"And now I see," Mr. Fishman said with a note of triumph in his voice, "there is a man, also, a wonderful man. Not that your life hasn't been full of men following you undoubtedly, threatening to jump off tall buildings because you don't even look at them, but this is a special person, yes? Who has your heart now?"

Lacy sighed heavily. She was hoping the gossip at *Fad* about the president and chairman of the board of Echevarria Enterprises, Inc., and one of the magazine's newer junior fashion writers hadn't penetrated the Seventh Avenue dress houses. It just made things that much more difficult.

"Why do you ask if I've got a man, Mr. Fishman?" Lacy asked cautiously.

Irving Fishman took his cigar out of his mouth to regard her with a calm, fatherly air. "Because you have the look, my dear gorgeously beautiful lady, of a woman in love. Believe me, I know the look of love when I see it. Here, let me give you the Neil Diamond number in blue. It's a gift, blue goes better with your hair."

Lacy had a terrible sinking feeling. So it was true. Even Mr. Fishman could see it. She was in love.

"It's over, Mr. Fishman," she confessed, not able to keep the pain from her voice. "Something happened I can't talk about. Besides, he's not in love with me. He was just using me."

"My poor darling," the dress manufacturer said, quickly patting her on the head. "Such distress, it's tearing me apart! I can't conceive of such a schlemiel. Take my advice and forget this Cossack, whoever he is. Obviously he is not only crazy, he doesn't deserve you. Go to lunch with this very cultivated handsome lawyer, Mr. Alexander van Renssalaer, who can't get you out of his mind. He told me as much when he called me recently. Also, he left his card in case I should persuade you to go to the Harvard Club with him."

"I don't need to go to the Harvard Club for lunch," Lacy said, dabbing at her tears with her finger tips. "Honestly, Mr. Fishman, Mr. van Renssalaer is nice, but I don't need to be in love with anybody else right now, not even a lawyer. I can't help it—every man I meet only wants one thing. It's so degrading. One of my biggest troubles as a model was trying to keep from being hassled, you know? And believe me, I don't mind being retired from modeling, not at all. I could tell you about lecherous photographers, for instance—"

"So you've heard," Mr. Fishman said, sticking his cigar back in his mouth, "about Peter Dorsey.

What a disaster! Peter Dorsey, one of the biggest fashion photographers in the business, strictly *Vogue, Harper's Bazaar, Fad, Gentleman's Quarterly*, but a lech, a real lech, you should thank God you didn't have any trouble with him like some of the girls tell me. He went out of business Tuesday morning.''

"What?" Lacy said, staring.

"He was a young man," Mr. Fishman said, gesturing eloquently with his cigar. "But he was practically an institution in the trade. The Cecil Beaton Award, the New York Dress Institute Award, he was making good money, fantastic money. But who knows what goes wrong? Maybe he was a poor manager. All of a sudden Tuesday morning he comes to open up his studio and there is a crowd of process servers, bailiffs with trucks to seize his equipment and carry all of it away, you name it. My brother-in-law in Brooklyn who is connected with a moving business tells me he heard they wiped him out. Also, they took away Peter Dorsey's lease. The models who were waiting to shoot pictures for Macy's summer catalog, they had to take everything back to the store."

"Oh, no!" Lacy cried, feeling as though a bolt of lightning had struck. She suddenly had a good idea of what had happened to Peter Dorsey, and why. "Where is Peter Dorsey now?" she asked in a trembling voice. "They didn't take him to jail, did they?"

Mr. Fishman shrugged. "I heard it was nothing sexual, but maybe they should put a lech like that in jail, who knows? Actually, I was told in the Thirty-first Street Deli this morning when I went in for bagels and coffee that Peter Dorsey, the photographer, was having his mail forwarded to a Trappist monastery in Vermont. Although this I frankly refuse to believe, because I happen to know personally that Peter Dorsey is not a Catholic.''

"I can't believe it!" Lacy cried, horror struck.

But actually, she could.

As soon as she could leave Fishman Brothers' loft, Lacy went straight to a telephone booth on Thirty-first Street and Seventh Avenue to call the *Fad* editorial offices.

It was all true, Jamie Hatworth confirmed. Peter Dorsey Photographics, Inc., had folded overnight, leaving a backlog of photographic assignments for some of New York's biggest fashion magazines and advertising agencies just hanging. Including a batch for *Fad* magazine. *Fad*'s art department was hysterical. And, yes, the rumor was that Peter Dorsey had called one of his friends on *Vanity Fair* just before he left town to tell them he was voluntarily joining a Trappist monastery. It had always been one of his lifelong ambitions.

"It can't be," Lacy groaned, hanging up the receiver. She remembered now, too late, what she'd said at dinner with Michael, about Peter Dorsey being responsible for all the troubles in her life. But anybody who knew her wouldn't take her seriously, would they? She'd had several glasses of wine and she was practically out on her feet with exhaustion! *What else had she said*? She remembered saying something about his expensive cigars and Fidel Castro's Communist Cuba. She supposed Cuba was safe enough.

What had happened seemed perfectly clear. People didn't go out of business overnight and join Trappist monasteries when they weren't even Catholic. What had descended on Peter Dorsey, even though he richly deserved it, was all her fault. She had to take full responsibility for it naturally.

And if she didn't know already the way Michael Echevarria's mind worked, and the power he could wield, her new private eye stood in a doorway on the east side of Thirty-first Street, his hands shoved into the pockets of his trench coat. So much for Michael's promise he wouldn't have her followed. As long as she worked at *Fad*—and it wasn't going to be long now, Lacy knew, his detective was going to track her movements, down to every last hour of what he thought was their bargain.

Lacy sagged against the telephone booth. She'd just had a horrible memory of something that had occurred that night in the Sutton Place apartment. It wasn't very clear, but it seemed that she'd had this weird semiconscious dream and headache and had just rambled on and on about what had happened in the front seat of the Buick with Bobby Sullivan that fateful senior-prom night six long years before. There was no telling what she'd set in motion with that one! Had she said all that out loud, or hadn't she? She tried to think. It was no good—her mind was a blank!

With shaking hands, Lacy dialed directory assistance and got the number for the East Hampton firm of Harrison, Sullivan and Weems, Certified Public Accountants. It took her several long moments to get Bobby Sullivan to the telephone. Lacy realized she hadn't exchanged more than a dozen words with Bobby since high school, and there was, after all, a terrible burden of guilt that lay between them. She wasn't surprised to find that his voice, when he came on the line, was extremely wary.

"Lacy, is it really you? Listen, where are you calling from?" he asked very cautiously.

"I'm calling from New York City," Lacy said, putting her hand over one ear to shut out the noise of midtown Manhattan traffic. "From a telephone booth. Oh, Bobby, are you all right?" she cried. "I mean, is Harrison, Sullivan and Weems still in business? Nothing's happened this morning, has it? I mean, the office was still there when you came in, wasn't it? There hasn't been any trouble?"

There was definitely a note of alarm in Bobby Sullivan's voice as he said, "You're calling me from a telephone booth? What do you mean, is the office still here? Lacy—what in the hell, have you heard of a bomb threat or something?"

"A bomb?" Lacy said faintly. She really didn't think Michael Echevarria would go that far. "I'm calling to—" She found herself strangling on the words. "Oh, good grief, Bobby, I don't want anything to happen to you!"

But there was no guarantee, was there? The whole experience that night with Bobby in the front seat of the Buick had left a scar on her life, there was no arguing with that.

She could no longer ignore the screams and noises very clearly in the background at Harrison, Sullivan and Weems.

"We're starting an evacuation," the voice of Bobby Sullivan said over the racket desperately. "Lacy, don't hang up—oh, my God, I knew we shouldn't have done those tax forms for that crowd in Queens! Lacy, your contacts in New York, did they tell you what we should look for?

"I mean," Bobby Sullivan shouted over the noises of crashes and hysterical shrieks, "is it smaller than a breadbox, or is it large, black and shiny? Tell me what they—"

But Lacy did hang up. There was nothing more she could do, she told herself, leaning weakly against the side of the telephone booth and closing her eyes. Either there was a bomb in Bobby Sullivan's office out there in East Hampton, or there wasn't. She supposed you could hire anybody if you had enough money. And the president of Echevarria Enterprises had plenty of that.

There was only one way to find out for sure.

"I'd like to speak to Mr. Michael Echevarria," Lacy managed to say when the company operator answered. The next voice she heard was that of Michael's secretary. Lacy bit her lip, suddenly uncertain.

"May I ask who's calling, please?" a cool, crisp woman's voice asked her.

She never thought she'd have to do anything like this. Like calling him at work. It was possible they wouldn't let her through to him. After all, he was one of the richest and most powerful men in the country. Corporate secretaries filtered calls for executives just so they wouldn't be bothered with people they didn't want to talk to. There was no reason he should want to talk to her now. Not after Saturday morning in the Sutton Place condominium.

"He's in a meeting right now," the voice continued. "If you leave your name and number, I'll see if he can get back to you."

"It's Lacy Kingston," she said, without hope.

Astonishingly there was only the barest second's wait and then Michael Echevarria's cool, authoritative voice came on the line. "Lacy," he said quickly, "what's the matter?"

Lacy clutched the telephone receiver with both hands, not able to speak in a sudden rush of emotion. He was there! He was going to speak to her! He couldn't still be furious with her, or he wouldn't have answered the telephone as though he had practically leaped on it when his secretary told him who it was! Now his low, quiet voice was so near and shatteringly familiar she wasn't prepared for the tidal wave of happiness that swept over her.

"Oh, Michael," Lacy cried. It was so nice to know that this powerful president and chairman of the board of a great conglomerate would talk to you, even though you'd hit him in the head with a shoe the last time you'd seen him. Most men would never have forgiven that.

"I'm in an important conference, Lacy." His tone wasn't impatient—in fact, it held a note of concern. "What is it? Are you all right?"

"Yes. No!" She wasn't sure how she should put this. She wanted to be discreet. "Where is Peter Dorsey?" she blurted. "Something terrible's happened to him, hasn't it?"

"Ah, I see." His voice changed, became rather cool. "Your former friend had severe financial troubles, I suppose you've heard." Then with an abrupt edge: "He hasn't threatened you or anything like that, has he?"

"Threatened me?" Visions of a commando raid on a quiet Trappist monastery in the hills of Vermont swept through her head. "Oh, no! Please let him be a monk and be happy! He *has* gone to a monastery, hasn't he? He was so young!"

"Is this," the voice on the other end of the line said grimly, "what you're calling about? That you're worried about this . . . photographer? I'm informed that he has an estranged wife and a daughter in California. They've agreed to take him in temporarily."

"Oh, rats," Lacy moaned, slumping against the door of the telephone booth and ignoring the several people outside who were banging on it and pointing at their wristwatches. Michael Echevarria's voice sounded definitely chilly and unfriendly. "Bailiffs came and took all Peter's equipment, sent his models away, locked up his studio. It must have been terrible."

"I frankly don't understand your interest," he growled, "considering what this man did to you."

Lacy moaned again. So he *had* managed to misunderstand what she'd said at dinner. Michael Echevarria thought it was Peter Dorsey who had—that is, not Bobby Sullivan—but *Peter Dorsey*.

She didn't know if this made things better or worse. "I'm really not all that worried about Peter Dorsey," Lacy tried to explain. "He deserves everything he gets, as long as he isn't dead, or anything like that. I just—" She breathed a small, audible sigh. *Forget Peter Dorsey*, her inner voice told her. The important thing now is that Michael is on the line, he's still speaking to you. He's talking about all this very calmly and rationally. "I really don't," Lacy said humbly, "know why you bothered. About anything. Not after last weekend."

There was silence on the other end. Then the president and chairman of the board said rather huskily,

"Lacy, I don't want anybody to hurt you, do you understand? I don't like it even if it happened in the past. Make that especially in the past, when you were too young to take care of yourself. I don't understand what in the hell your parents were thinking of, to turn you loose in New York City in the damned modeling business, alone."

Lacy took a quick, in-drawn breath. He could shake her to her shoes when he spoke to her so caringly, so tenderly in his low, vibrant voice like that. "Michael—" she began. There were so many things she had to tell him. Perhaps they weren't finished after all, she thought with a surge of joy that surprised her.

"I'm sorry, I am in an urgent meeting," he went on. "I haven't got time to discuss all this now. The Rolls will pick you up Friday, regular time. You don't have a problem with that, do you?"

"Oh, no, not at all," Lacy cried eagerly. "Yes, I really want to talk to you, I want to explain—"

"Friday," he said tersely. And hung up.

Lacy gathered up her purse and coins and got ready to turn the telephone booth over to the restless crowd that had gathered outside. It seemed she hadn't told Michael about Bobby Sullivan after all. Or there surely would have been some massive devastation on the eastern end of Long Island by now.

On Friday morning, early, Lacy was called into managing editor Gloria Farnham's office, where a large group of *Fad* staffers, mostly editors, were standing around drinking champagne, even though it was barely ten.

It must be somebody's birthday, Lacy thought, glad to be a part of the crowd for a change.

"Congratulations, sweetie, you've just been promoted! Darlings," Gloria Farnham cried, seizing Lacy's hand and holding it up in the manner of a fight referee announcing a new Golden Gloves champion, "meet our new assistant editor, Stacy Kingsley!"

Everyone lifted champagne glasses in Lacy's direction, and there were a few weak cheers.

"Who?" Lacy said, trying to get out of the managing editor's grip. She searched through the crowd and found Jamie Hatworth standing by the window with Mike. The layout artist's arm was around the editor's shoulder, but she looked rather pale.

"You'll work in tandem with Jamie, love," Gloria went on, "she's dying to show you everything she knows. But you'll keep your convenient little office out here, lambie pie—there's a man coming in to fix the air conditioning today."

"I can't be an assistant editor," Lacy burst out, dismayed. "I've only been here six weeks!"

"Oh, yes you can, dear," the managing editor said. "They loved your 'Tacky-Max' article upstairs. It just blew them away—didn't it, gang? So here we are, and here *you* are—our new assistant editor!"

There were a few louder cheers at that.

"But that was only one article," Lacy protested. "And I haven't even finished Tiny Lady Training Bras. Not to mention Princess Di Maternity Sportswear and Hanes body stockings."

"Don't say that, sweetie," the managing editor said loudly. "They've been tracking all your stuff upstairs, management's read every word you've written. The big brass loves your enormous talent!"

"Yeah," someone in the back said, sourly. "You're loaded."

"Oh, no," Lacy whispered, the awful truth finally dawning. She was feeling as though she could drop through the floor of Fad Publishing Group's Madison Avenue office building, right down into the lobby, and not even feel it. Her work had been read upstairs? Every word of it? First what had happened to Peter Dorsey. Now this!

"Well, anyway," one of the associate editors in a striped Ship 'n Shore shirt said rather grudgingly, "you *can* write, if that's any consolation."

"I'm not going to take it," Lacy protested. No one appeared to be listening. "For the very good reason," she said, raising her voice, "that I'm still in training as a junior fashion writer, remember?" She could see Jamie Hatworth coming to her through the crowd. "I don't know the first thing about being an assistant editor!"

"Shhhh," Jamie Hatworth soothed, "that's show biz, honey. We'll work it out—you're assigned to me, remember?"

"I'm humiliated, that's what I am," Lacy groaned. "What happened to 'senior fashion writer,' anyway? Did I just jump over that? What happened to 'editorial assistant'—or have they abolished that, too? Oh, this is really mortifying."

The close-packed members of *Fad*'s editorial staff all appeared to be pleasantly ignoring her. The associate editor in the Ship 'n Shore shirtwaist got the plastic stopper out of another bottle of Andre champagne.

"You've got plenty of talent, kid," the layout artist said, his arm still around Jamie Hatworth's shoulders. "It just came on pretty fast, that's all."

"Shut up, Mike," Jamie told him. "I'm assigned to show you the ropes, Lacy. You'll make out all right."

"I refuse to be an assistant editor," Lacy told her in a trembling voice. "That's your job. I'm not going to take it! I'll only fall flat on my face!"

"You heard what Gloria said," Jamie told her. "We both have the same job. For a while."

That was the whole point. "I'll refuse to accept it," Lacy cried. "I'll only be making a fool of myself, don't you see?"

"They're not only going to fix the air conditioning in your office," the layout artist said, passing Lacy a plastic glass of Andre Very Dry, "but some Sutton Place decorator is coming in to give it the works. They were bringing in some black and chrome Finnish stuff this morning. It was on the freight elevator. And I hear you're getting brown hand-woven drapes and a smoked-glass partition to block out the view of the air shaft."

Lacy froze. Why had she been so stupid as to think that everything was going to be all right? It took a little time, but when you examined the complicated scheme involved, it was truly masterful.

"Excuse me," Lacy said, suddenly subdued. "I have something I have to do."

Two minutes later she was in her office. When Irving Fishman picked up the other end of the line, Lacy took a moment so that she could try to speak in a fairly normal voice. She didn't want to yell at Mr. Fishman. He was an innocent bystander.

"Darling girl," Mr. Fishman boomed cordially. "How are you this morning? Your friend Mr. Alexander van Renssalaer called yesterday to ask if perhaps you would consider the Knickerbocker Club for his invitation to lunch, and I told him, 'Why not?' I understand the Knickerbocker is even a more cultivated place than the Yale Club and has better food, although personally I don't know it.''

"Mr. Fishman, *please*," Lacy told him, trying not to yell. "I have a very important favor to ask you. Do you still have that Disco Flame Queen number with Michael Jackson in bugle beads on the front? In poison blue and in a size eight?"

14

When the elevator doors rolled back at 8:00 p.m. that evening at Michael Echevarria's apartment on Sutton Place, Lacy was wearing Fishman Brothers' fabulous Disco Flame Queen best seller in acrylic mega-blue satin. The effect, Lacy could see instantly in the black panther's eyes, was totally paralyzing.

Lacy's tall, five-foot nine-inch figure was once again a perfect foil for the outrageous blue satin disco dress with the pensive head of Michael Jackson emblazoned across the chest in glittering multicolored glass beads. Although labeled a size 8, the dress actually looked a full size smaller because of its skimpy cut. The hem ended an inch above Lacy's knees, and the side slits were slashed to midthigh. Puffy cantaloupe sleeves in blue satin reached to Lacy's elbows and would have given a top-heavy look except for the exposed expanse of Lacy's truly glorious legs—legs with strappy Roman sandals laced to above the calf and with four-inch heels, all in black patent leather. A little disco hat, covered with midnight sequins, was cocked over Lacy's right eye. Her long blond hair had been teased into a thousand ringlets that stood out from her face in a six-inch-deep cloud. Lacy's delicately carved eyelids glittered with iridescent purple eye shadow. Her wide mouth was a sensuously pouting deep-red gash. Overall, Lacy Kingston was a triumph of tacky-max raised to high art. In contrast, the president and chairman of the board was magnificent in white tie and tails.

They stared at each other.

"Good grief," Lacy murmured.

"My God," he exclaimed.

In that instant it appeared they had checkmated each other.

Lacy knew she'd gotten under his skin this time with the gaudy Disco Flame Queen extravaganza. It took *her* a minute to recover from his absolute perfection in white tie and tails.

"Where are you going?" Lacy cried, aghast.

"Where have you been," he snarled, "dressed like that?"

Lacy gave a smothered yelp as he dragged her from the elevator and into his apartment foyer.

"Have you been sitting in bars again?" he grated, propelling her through the Sutton Place contemporary living room with its black leather and chrome and the lighted *étagères* that held his collectibles. "I'll strangle you if you go back to doing that!"

"What's the matter with you?" Lacy cried, trying to drag her hand out of his grip. "You sound like I've got some sort of hang-up. You're the one with the bar-sitting fetish, not me!''

"Lacy," he said, breathing hard.

"It's Fishman Brothers' Tacky-Max," she yelled, still struggling. "You ought to recognize it—you've been reading all my stuff, checking up on my work so you'd have an excuse to fire me, right? Oh, don't deny, Michael Echevarria, that you've been reading everything I've written at *Fad* magazine, that you've had it sent to your office so you could catch me in something!''

"I've read your work, yes," he admitted stonily.

"Of course you have! Don't bother to deny, either, that you tried to get me promoted so I could fall on my face!'' In a frenzy of hurt and frustration, Lacy grabbed the little disco hat from its bobby-pin moorings in her cloud of curls and tore it loose and flung it on the floor. "Assistant editor—oh, really! You're really into rotten power games when you want something. And you want *me*, right?''

"I don't deny that," he said.

"You're playing dirty again," she accused. "Promoting me to a job I know absolutely nothing about is a great way to have me blow everything, isn't it? Then, when I mess up, you can fire me and set me up as your mistress! I'm just another corporate maneuver, admit it! I'm just another profitable acquisition!''

Lacy kicked at the little disco hat lying on the floor, then decided to stamp on it viciously. He took a step back, eyes narrowed.

"You got promoted because you have talent. Which is more than I can say for most of the *Fad* editorial staff.''

"I'm not listening to you," Lacy cried, putting her hands over her ears. "I always get into trouble that way!"

"It's my impression," he said evenly, "that you could catch onto the assistant editor's job fast enough if you wanted to. If you worked as hard at it as you've been working since you started at *Fad*."

She stared at him wildly. "It's a trick," she panted.

"No trick." His expression was icy. "The magazine's full of dead wood; that's why every staff member is currently being evaluated. You were at the employees' meeting—you heard what I said."

Lacy stared at him, confused.

"The 'Tacky-Max' story was fresh and original. If you can write like that, the magazine needs you.

"And if," he continued, his eyes deliberately raking her from the soles of her Roman-sandaled feet to the top of her puffed hair, "you can demonstrate you're serious by giving up your compulsion to be—humorous."

"You don't mean that," Lacy said shakily. "You don't really think I ought to be an assistant editor."

He shrugged his broad shoulders. "Suit yourself. But you're not going out tonight dressed in that—dressed in that damned thing. Go get changed."

"No, don't cut me off like that," she protested. "I want to discuss this with you."

"Later," he said, taking her by the arm to steer her toward the bedroom. "I want to get you into something more presentable."

"No," Lacy said, trying to hang back. "Listen—I can choose my own clothes! I'm wearing what I *want* to wear!

"In spite of your nasty mind, I haven't been sitting in a bar somewhere," she cried rebelliously.

"You're not going to the opera with—Michael Jackson all over your chest," he said with clenched teeth.

"The opera?" She tried to resist as he pushed her through the bedroom door and toward the bed. "You mean we're doing the opera scene now? Like, last week dinner on the back porch at Lutece, tonight the *opera*? Where are you going to hide me this time—in the ladies' room? Throw a blanket over me and prop me against the wall?"

He held her firmly by the shoulder with one strong, tanned hand. "I'm not going to hide you anywhere, you're being ridiculous. Although, believe me, Lacy," he growled, "considering your lack of . . . restraint in these matters, it's a temptation." His other hand worked to find the zipper on the back of the blue satin Disco Flame Queen number.

"Restraint?" she shot back, wriggling in his grasp. "Lack of restraint? Just because I won't let you bully me—treat me like a—a—*thing*?"

"I'm taking you to the Metropolitan," he said calmly as he unzipped the satin disco dress and slid it from her shoulders. "We're going to see *La Bohème* by Puccini, with Placido Domingo. The tickets cost me a fortune, getting them at the last minute like this."

Lacy stared at him in disbelief. "What, out there in New York City with all those people?" she said, grabbing her suddenly bared bra with both her hands. The Fishman Brothers' Michael Jackson special slid down around her knees and fell in a crumpled pile at her feet. "You mean you trust me not to jump in the orchestra and start molesting the violin section? You mean you think I can control myself?"

"I never accused you of anything like that," he said somewhat distractedly as his eyes followed the dress.

"Not directly, no," she cried, "but it's all you've been saying since we first met!"

He seemed not to be listening. He was staring at her suddenly revealed willowy body in a scrap of lace brassiere and midnight-blue bikini panties.

"You're going to be Professor Higgins to my Eliza Doolittle, that's what you have in mind, isn't it?" Lacy cried. "We're going to play your version of *My Fair Lady* with good restaurants, fine wines, couturier clothes and now grand opera? Tell me, is this for the assistant editor's job at Fad? Or is it your idea of a training program on how to be your high-class mistress? That is, after you fire me!"

"Lacy." He was clenching and unclenching his jaw so that a small muscle contracted spasmodically. "You're wearing a black garter belt again," he said in an unsteady voice.

"The garter belt goes with the disco look," Lacy snapped. "Look, there's one thing we need to get strai—"

He abruptly pulled her to him, the Antarctic ice breaking up under a warm, rushing spring flood. "Lacy," he murmured with a strained reluctance, "you drive me crazy." Both his hands were on her hips, pulling her against the hard, muscled length of his legs and his hips. "No other woman—" He lowered his dark head to her. "No other woman has ever had this effect on me," he growled as his lips touched hers.

By now, Lacy knew, shutting her eyes, kissing Michael Echevarria should be reasonably predictable. All the *zap! bam! powie!* should be a foregone conclusion. But actually she never knew what was going to happen. It was different every time. There was certainly nothing predictable in this new, stunning electricity that was more intense than anything that had ever happened before, as it leaped from his mouth and shot through her body into her very bones.

"Oh, Michael," Lacy murmured breathlessly.

She felt his teeth nibbling at her lower lip, then his tongue seeking the warm, sweet recesses of her mouth. Passionate waves of excitement shook her. He was shaking, too, as his strong body clasped her to him so possessively it left her gasping. His hands explored her, stroking and caressing the small of her back, then sliding up her bare shoulder blades, moving quickly under her arms to seize the heavy curve of her lace-covered breasts. She shuddered, throwing herself into those big, warm hands. A long hard finger hooked into the top of her garter belt and circled it, strong and firm against her fevered skin.

Garter belts turned him on, she thought dizzily. Everything seemed to turn him on. No other woman had ever done this to him, that's what he'd said. She'd reduced the president and chairman of the board to a hot, surging thrust of molten lava.

"Lacy—beautiful Lacy," he growled against her mouth. "This is madness."

Lacy could have melted for pure joy in his arms

right then. The room reeled about them as she tried to burrow closer to that big, magnificent body. She heard the answering rasp of desire deep in his throat.

Suddenly he stiffened. "We can't do this." She felt him trying to pry himself away. He pulled her clutching hands down. "You have to get dressed."

Lacy closed her eyes, drunk on the moment. "Forget it," she murmured, reaching for him again. "Let's just put an opera record on the stereo, and let's say we went."

He bent and picked up a long dark-red length of evening gown from the bed. Before Lacy knew what was happening, ruby-colored velvet folds descended over her head.

"Hey!" she protested. Then, as her head emerged, "Listen, I hate Puccini. I don't want whatever it is you've got for me to wear this time. Are you listening? Can we do that kiss over again?"

He definitely wasn't listening. He had stepped back to view the effect.

"Oh, my," Lacy whispered as she saw her reflection in the mirrors on the far side of the room.

If this was another custom-made gown, it even surpassed what had been done last time. A reasonably sane, normal woman could be excused if she had a nervous breakdown wanting to wear it. The ruby-red velvet was cut to a deep, revealing décolletage held up by thin velvet-cord straps that dazzlingly displayed Lacy's creamy-gold shoulders and breasts. The deep-red folds of the gown clasped her body in a Renaissance bodice and then dropped away to fall in heavy, regal folds that swept the floor. It was almost a costume. The opera was going to have a bad time competing.

Lacy bit her gleaming red underlip. How could anyone turn down the opportunity to wear this in the more glittering places of New York City? The answer to that was, she couldn't.

"I have to do something with my hair," she muttered. The disco cloud of curls had to go. "It doesn't work with what I'm wearing."

She pulled out the rest of the bobby pins that had held the little disco hat in place, grabbed her hair in both hands and crammed it into a French twist at the back.

As Lacy squinted at the mirrors on the far side of the room, she knew it had worked. Her hair swept up gave the right imperial effect, enhanced by a border-line carelessness. As she put the bobby pins back into place to hold it, she felt something cold and heavy slide around her throat.

The necklace Michael Echevarria was putting on her was a shade of ruddy gold that indicated the true antique, probably not of the last century but of the one before that. Rococco swirls of gold flowers and vines worked in the ancient thick metal were studded with smooth cabochon stones, either rubies or garnets.

The gown was designed to match the priceless necklace, Lacy saw, a little dazed. All that antique gold. She couldn't help wondering if the Smithsonian or the Frick Museum had found anything missing lately.

"Since your ears are already pierced, I think you can manage these by yourself," he murmured at her ear. His hand offered a set of matching gold earrings over her shoulder, each with a precious red stone in its carved-flower center.

"We're going by armored car, of course," Lacy quipped. It was nothing to joke about; she'd never seen anything like the heavy gold necklace; even the great diamond and emerald suite paled by comparison. Did anybody have this much money, even Michael Echevarria?

In the mirrored reflection, his dark, chiseled features watched her with an intent expression that said how beautiful she was.

So much careful planning had gone into this. The ruby velvet gown. The antique necklace. He was looking at her, Lacy realized with a shock, like a work of art that he had in his possession at last. The concentration in those brooding gray eyes was astonishing.

"Michael?" Lacy said uncertainly. That stare made her uneasy. If she had to choose between being an art collectible and a rehabilitation project, she'd choose the latter.

"Michael," she murmured, surrendering, turning around and moving into his arms.

"You're so lovely I can't believe it." He cleared his throat. "Lacy, I think I want you more than I've ever wanted anything in my life. It's incredible."

Want? she thought, staring back. He was viewing her like a hungry man views a thick sirloin steak! Was that all she meant to him? She loved him! She was absolutely wild, crazy, freaked-out in love with him—couldn't he see it?

"Michael, darling," Lacy murmured experimentally. It was the first time she had called him that.

"My God, sweet Lacy," he muttered, his gray eyes dazed. "I think—"

The telephone in the bedroom began ringing. Two low, musical notes, but definitely a telephone.

"Boston," he murmured abstractedly.

"Lovely." Whatever Boston was, it would have to wait. One minute more and he'd know she loved him. His mouth was only inches away from hers, the tension unbearable.

"One of our banks is going under." His voice was low and husky. "The examiners have been working all weekend."

Lacy slid her hands under the formal coat, feeling his fine, hard body warm through her finger tips. "Let's not go to the opera," she whispered.

"If that's what I think it is," he muttered, "I'll be going to Boston. I'll know just as soon as I answer that call."

His words broke the spell. Before Lacy could tighten her hold on him, he pulled his hands away.

"Michael?" Lacy cried, her fingers clutching air. She watched him stride to the desk in the corner of the room to answer the phone.

He can't do this, she told herself. A few seconds more and she would have told him she loved him! She stared, dumbfounded, as he spoke a final word into the telephone, hung up and came back to her, a towering, splendid figure in formal evening clothes.

"It was Boston," he said with a slight frown. "The one call I had to take here tonight.

"You look very lovely in that dress," he added, moving past her and going to a long line of doors that covered one wall of the room.

She looked very lovely in the dress? His dismissal of her was totally absent-minded! Lacy watched as he slid back his wardrobe doors to reveal seemingly endless racks of suits.

"There's no time to call for the Lear jet," he was saying. "Damn, I'm going to have to take the shuttle out of La Guardia."

Lacy listened in disbelief. They'd been practically in the middle of a kiss! She could hardly believe this was happening. She watched as he pulled a Louis Vuitton suiter out of the closet and threw it on the bed. He began to toss socks and underwear into it from one of the wardrobe chests.

"Do you need all those socks?" He seemed to have forgotten her completely. "Or are you packing for a centipede?"

"I don't know," he said, tossing a couple of immaculately laundered Brooks Brothers shirts after them. "Why don't you pick some out for me?"

Still numb with the suddenness of it all, Lacy bent over the bed in her exquisite red velvet gown, the gold antique necklace swinging forward heavily, and chose six pairs of French-made elasticized men's socks. She rolled them up neatly to put in the Vuitton luggage. She gathered Michael Echevarria was taking the shuttle jet to Boston. That meant they weren't going to the opera.

She still couldn't believe it.

"Haven't you got a valet?" With all these clothes, he must have somebody to take care of them. She trailed behind him to pick up the pieces of his formal evening clothes he was discarding.

"He's on vacation," he said from the bathroom. She heard him swearing under his breath about a missing electric shaver. "See if you can find me a pair of black shoes in there," he called out to her. "There's a shoe rack in the closet."

Lacy found not one but several enormous shoe racks filled with handmade boots, both Western and military style, loafers, lounge slippers, evening pumps and glove-leather oxfords of all descriptions.

One moment, she told herself, holding up a pair of Gucci wingtips in black kid, she was all dressed up like the front cover of *Town and Country*, on her way to be publicly displayed at the Metropolitan Opera wearing a fortune in gowns and jewels, and the next minute the president and chairman of the board had forgotten she was there. So much for being a priceless work of art. "Michael," she said crossly from the depths of the closet, "have you ever been married?"

"No." He came to stand in the door of the bathroom barefooted and bare chested, clad only in black trousers. "See if you can find a shirt for me," he said, throwing the electric shaver onto the bed next to the overnight case.

"Am I going to Boston with you?"

"No. Not unless you're an accountant." He pulled off the evening trousers, showing a brief glimpse of symmetrically muscled legs and dazzling black-on-black houndstooth Cardin briefs before stepping into a pair of tailored gray pants and zipping them up. "You don't happen to be an accountant, do you?" he said seriously.

That was the last straw.

"I'm not an accountant—I'm a writer, remember?" Lacy folded up the white Brooks Brothers shirts and put them into the suitcase. "Who's going to take me to the opera? Or should I start getting out of these clothes?"

"The detective, Moretti." He picked up the shirt she'd laid out for him and shrugged his big shoulders into it. "Don't forget a couple of ties, will you?"

he said. "He's Italian. All Italians know opera, he can probably follow *La Bohème* with a score. You two should have a profitable evening."

"Well," Lacy said, glowering as she watched him select a Countess Mara from the tie rack and toss it around his neck, "I hate to bring this up, Michael, but here I am in a red velvet dress that looks like I'm going to play Lady Macbeth and some sort of antique gold necklace and earrings worth a fortune—"

"Venetian," he said, throwing his head back and lifting his chin to loop his tie in a knot. "Eighteenth century. I bought it through an agent at Sotheby's in London last week."

"—all this jewelry worth a fortune," Lacy repeated carefully, "and you're going to send me to the opera with an *Italian private eye* for an *escort*? Is that correct?"

He cocked a dark eyebrow at her. "Yes, but you'd better get Moretti to check that damned trench coat before he goes in." He threw open a series of doors at the top of the mammoth clothes closet. "I need a hat —where in the hell," he muttered to himself, "are my homburgs?"

"Michael, are you listening to me?" Lacy trailed him to the desk as he called down for his Rolls Royce. "You're making a mistake again," she warned. "I'm not some sort of parcel-post package you can send across town to hear Puccini. With a watchdog you've hired because you think I'm some sort of tramp you can't let out of your sight."

She was a *thing* to him, Lacy told herself. In spite of all the magic when he held her, in spite of all the gowns and jewels, she was really only a body, something to decorate, an exceptionally fine piece for his collections!

As he began to speak into the telephone, Lacy watched him with narrowed eyes. She said in a perfectly conversational tone, "I'm going to cut my hair and have my forehead tattooed with the words *U.S. Navy*." When he kept on talking, she gritted her teeth. "I'd like to have a Ferrari before I report here next Friday night. Say one that's sort of a smoky-blond color, to match my hair. And since I don't really care for mink, I'll settle for a full-length coat in Russian sable."

"What else do I need to do?" the chairman of the board muttered, hanging up the telephone. "Where's my briefcase?"

Very deliberately, Lacy took it from the floor where it was propped against the desk, and handed it to him. "And I'd also like to have a microwave oven and a new blender," she continued sweetly, "because my old blender is worn out. I'm flying to Bermuda on Thursday. I'd like to have one of those gorgeous Australian white cockatoos. They're expensive, but everybody who is anybody has one. And I'm going to buy a tape of Pavarotti singing *La Bohème* on my way home tonight at a Broadway all-night record store, and invite my private eye up to my apartment to have a drink and be cosy and listen to it with me. I even have some left-over spaghetti in the freezer."

He looked around the bedroom with a slight frown between his black brows. "Looks like that's it," he told himself. Then, still absently, "Have I forgotten anything?"

"I want to kiss you goodbye before I ransack your condominium and take the loot and leave the country with it," Lacy murmured as she helped him into his black Chesterfield overcoat.

"Yes," he said. "That."

He put down his briefcase swiftly, folded his Marks and Spencer black leather gloves carefully and stuck them in the overcoat pocket. He laid his homburg on a nearby chair. Then, very deliberately, he reached out for her.

"Urk!" Lacy breathed as the black panther swept her into his arms.

His warm mouth closed over hers and all the lightning flashes and rolling thunder hit her in spite of his being in a hurry. All the *zap! bam! powie!* with a few spirals and comets thrown in. His arms crushed her so that she couldn't move. He pressed against her, and if it hadn't been for the tailored bulk of the Chesterfield overcoat, she wouldn't have been surprised to find him aroused and ready for her, even as his tongue thrust hotly, deeply into her mouth.

Lacy was still clinging to him, her eyes half-closed in ecstasy, her fingers digging into the soft melton cloth, when he pulled back and looked down at her.

Something in Michael Echevarria's eyes glimmered like silver fire. "A Ferrari with a custom paint job to match your hair," he murmured softly. The ironical indentations at the corners of his lips that would have been dimples on anyone else flickered entrancingly as he spoke. "Full-length sable coat, cockatoo, microwave oven, Waring blender, yes." His head bent, and his mouth brushed the tip of her ear, then nibbled gently on the lobe. "No, you can't cut your hair, tattoo your forehead or go to Bermuda." He lowered his lips to her neck and nuzzled the smooth skin there, making her shudder and press against him with a little moan. "And no tapes of Pavarotti singing *La Bohème*, because Moretti's not allowed past the front door of your apartment house." His mouth returned to hers for the briefest of sizzling kisses. "I'll call you."

He released her, bent and picked up his briefcase and retrieved the homburg hat from the chair.

"Call me?" Lacy whispered, stunned. "You'll *call me*?"

"I have your home telephone number somewhere," he said, adjusting the homburg brim with a flick of his thumb.

She'd never given him her home telephone number. But that didn't mean he didn't have it. She was surrounded, spied on, investigated. It was outrageous!

"Michael," she cried as he strode past her, "I'm not going to be your mistress, do you hear? You can't treat me like this!"

"Probably from Boston tomorrow," the tall figure in the homburg and Chesterfield said, going through the bedroom door.

Then she heard the front door of the condominium slam.

15

Saturdays, Lacy thought as she pushed the vacuum
cleaner across the living-room rug of her west Eightieth Street apartment, were the pits. No matter what
unbelievable and sometimes fantastic things happened with Michael Echevarria on Friday nights,
there was no escaping the fact that Saturdays were a
return to earth. So much so that she was finding it
increasingly hard to cope. How could you be in love
with the president and chairman of the board of
Echevarria Enterprises, Inc., and know at the same
time that your personality was splitting right down
the middle?

Last night she, Lacy Kingston, had been standing
in a Sutton Place condominium wearing a couple of
hundred thousand dollars' worth of antique jewelry
and a couturier-made ruby velvet evening gown, on
her way to the Metropolitan Opera with her very own

private eye, who was wearing a brown suit, foam-rubber-soled shoes and a trench coat. Now, on Saturday afternoon, she was pushing a vacuum cleaner in her own modest apartment, dressed in the bottom half of a jogging suit, frayed basketball high tops that had once belonged to her older sister Felice, and her own ancient Junior Miss America sweat shirt. She was watching a very boring football game between Georgia and FSU on television while trying to get through her housework fast enough so that she could get to a Broadway Laundromat with her wash before it turned dark.

It wasn't just the unpredictable events of Friday nights that were tearing a big hole in her life, Lacy recognized, pausing to hold the vacuum cleaner in place with her foot while she adjusted the old Diane von Furstenberg scarf that covered her hair. It was the whole chain of events that had happened since that fateful evening in the penthouse in Tulsa.

How had she managed to live before Michael Echevarria made his appearance in her thoughts and dreams? She had asked herself this more than once in the past few weeks. The answer was simple. Happier. More peacefully. Almost never, ever feeling badgered, outmaneuvered and humiliated. Almost never being provoked to lose her temper and do wild, inexplicable things.

Now, for a whole list of reasons she didn't want to go into, Lacy found herself in love with a man who was the worst possible choice for any woman. Good heavens, just the way they had met, in a hotel bar in Tulsa, proved that!

Sure, he was gorgeous, sexy, powerful, successful, fabulously rich, and his lovemaking was fantastic. He was also miserably domineering, ruthlessly insensitive and dealt with people as though they were objects, not thinking and feeling human beings. He'd bought everything he ever wanted in life, just as he had bought—or thought he had bought—her, Lacy Kingston. He *wanted* her. He hadn't said a word about love, had he? She was the only one who had been ready to blurt out that terrible word last night in his Sutton Place condominium before the telephone rang.

When you came right down to it, Lacy told herself as she turned off the vacuum, pulled out the disposable bag and carried it to the kitchen and the garbage, it was plain that being in love, at least with the president and chairman of the board of Echevarria Enterprises, Inc., wasn't going to work out. Some more experienced, beautiful woman, who was worldly wise, stronger and more confident than she, would probably be able to handle it. Lacy Kingston, who looked so good from the outside, was a loser where it counted most.

If being in love was a time to live joyously, drown in heady sensations and fantastic experiences with a fabulous partner, then her track record was a mess. Her first Friday night meeting with Michael Echevarria, she'd drunk too much wine at Lutece, was exhausted after a hard day's work and had fallen asleep in his arms. The next morning, she admitted, had been a disaster. There had been tender, unforgettable moments that looked as though things might be really wonderful—very quickly followed by what she was beginning to see was their usual misunderstandings and arguments. She had to admit she'd made things worse by taunting him. What in the world had gotten into her to make her say what she did about underwear that morning? When he was always ready to believe the worst of her, anyway?

Last night, when she'd had her big opportunity to tell him she loved him, she'd let him fly off to Boston. Good grief, she'd even helped him pack!

I've been doing everything wrong, Lacy told herself, squirting large amounts of dish-washing detergent into a stack of breakfast dishes in the sink and turning on the hot water.

Last night she'd been carrying the fifteen hundred dollars in her purse, up to the full amount since she'd gotten her paycheck from *Fad*, intending to make her speech about what had really happened that night in the Tulsa hotel penthouse. She hadn't been able to do it. Her excuse had been that Michael Echevarria had flown off to Boston before the evening had even begun. But, Lacy admitted, biting her lower lip between her teeth unhappily, she'd had most of the money with her, too, that first Friday evening and hadn't given it to him then, either. Nor that Saturday morning when she'd left his apartment. What was the matter with her? Did she realize somehow in a murky, subconscious way that if she got things straightened out with Michael, it might change everything completely?

Like what? Lacy asked herself. Like he's going to ask you to marry him? Fat chance! He thought she was a toy, a work of art, a slightly over-the-hill but still beautiful twenty-three-year-old ex-model with a shady past who needed all sorts of supervision to keep her in line. She doubted very much that stubborn, hardheaded Michael Echevarria would change his mind about that.

"Yay! Yah!" a voice from the living room yelled. Lacy wiped her eyes with the back of her hand, flung the dishcloth into the sink and strode out of the kitchen into the living room.

Her very own private detective, Walter Moretti, was standing before the television set with a can of Comet cleanser in one hand and a plastic sponge pad in the other, dripping dirty water onto her newly vacuumed living-room rug. He wore a bath towel around his waist to keep his brown trousers from being spattered, and his coat jacket was off and his shirt sleeves rolled up above the elbows. He looked very different without his trench coat.

When he saw Lacy, he gulped. "The Seminoles scored," he said with an apologetic smile. "I got a bet on the game."

Lacy was not in a mood to be forgiving. "You get back into the bathroom, you worm," she told him, pointing her finger in that direction. "And don't you come out until everything sparkles. Then you can mop the kitchen floor."

The private eye retreated, holding the can of Comet cleanser in front of him like a protecting shield. "Miss Kingston," he cried, "you gotta let me out of your apartment. I'll lose my license—they'll put me outta business if I don't get out of here. I'm not supposed to go past the lobby downstairs. Mr. Echevarria's orders!"

"Don't tell me what you're not supposed to do," Lacy cried, snaking her pointed finger at him menacingly as she backed him up, step by step, toward the bathroom. She was tired of hearing about orders from Michael Echevarria. "You weren't supposed to try to feel me up during the second act of *La Bohème*, either, you turkey! You were the only person in the audience with a raincoat in your lap. It made the Metropolitan Opera look like a porno-movie theater!''

"It's not a raincoat," Moretti cried, running to the bathroom. He didn't close the door all the way; one eye peered at her. "It's not a raincoat, honest Miss Kingston, it's a trench coat. Like Colombo wore on TV. I always keep it with me."

"I'll just bet you do." She knew she was taking out her feelings on the private eye, but she told herself he deserved it. "And you fell on top of me in the taxi, you lech! You said it was an accident, but it was no accident when you started grabbing."

"I lost my head," the voice said humbly through the door. "I only sort of rested my hand on your knee at the opera, Miss Kingston. I thought it was my own."

"You mean you're a private detective and you can't even find your own knee?" Lacy scoffed. "I hope you don't specialize in missing-person cases!"

"Miss Kingston, a build like yours oughta be illegal," he said sulkily. "You obviously don't know what effect you have on a male's hormones. Believe me, it's very upsetting."

"It's not your hormones," Lacy said, pulling the bathroom door shut before he could remove his fingers. She listed to Moretti's yelp of pain unsympathetically. "You're unethical and untrustworthy and a masher. If you don't do a good job in there, I'm going to tell Mr. Echevarria you tried to attack me in the taxicab when you were supposed to be taking me home from the opera." Before she turned away she said, "Don't forget to clean the mirror on the back of the bathroom door."

"I haven't got any Windex," he sobbed.

"Under the wash basin in the cabinet," she told him heartlessly.

She had just finished scrubbing the last of the breakfast scrambled eggs out of the frying pan when Lacy heard a hammering on her front door loud enough to carry over the sounds of another Seminole touchdown on television. With a sigh she put down the dishcloth and went to see who it was.

When she opened the door, the tall, beautiful redheaded figure of Candy O'Neill with Sicky-Poo on a leash greeted her.

"Oh, Lacy, honey," Candy began at once, "I've got a shoot at the military academy at West Point modeling bikinis, the army finally cleared us to pose with the cadets, but only today, just after the game, and the ad-agency crew is going to pick me up in an hour."

"Not outdoors," Lacy murmured, eyeing Sicky-Poo, who was staring down thoughtfully at her living-room carpet. "Candy, it's November—you'll freeze to death in swim wear."

"Yes, I know," Candy groaned, "but it's for the May issue of *Bazaar*, and they don't care if it snows. Lacy, I've got to do it—I only got the job because Christie Brinkley's too sunburned from shooting evening gowns on the beach in St. Croix last week. Oh, honey, I need the money! Can you baby-sit Sicky-Poo until tomorrow night?"

"Oh, no," Lacy cried. She wanted to help Candy, who still hadn't gotten over finding Harrison

Salstonstall Potts IV with another redhead at the Zebra Lounge disco promotion and fire. But Sicky-Poo was a major undertaking.

"Who's that?" Candy said interestedly as Moretti emerged from the bathroom and stood staring with obvious appreciation at the redheaded model.

"He does bathrooms," Lacy said. She didn't have time to explain. "Gee, Candy, I don't know. I want to go do my laundry, and you know coin washers make Sicky-Poo nauseous. He *will* sit in front of them and watch the clothes go around."

The words were hardly out of Lacy's mouth when the Doberman discovered Moretti. It was hate at first sight. With a ferocious, gnashing snarl, the attack dog lunged into the living room, dragging Candy by his leash. As the private eye whirled, making a dash for the bathroom, Sicky-Poo hunched, coughed, and threw up against the door just as it slammed shut.

"He's all heart," Candy gasped, reeling the Doberman back on his chain, "but it affects his stomach. I'll clean it up, honey, don't worry.

"Could I," she said politely to the closed bathroom door, "borrow your sponge for a moment?"

"For you, beautiful, anything," a cautious voice said on the other side. The door opened a crack to let a large hand holding a wet sponge pass through.

At that moment, Lacy's telephone began ringing. "Oh, what now?" Lacy cried. To Candy she said, "Yes, go ahead and clean it up. I'll have to baby-sit Sicky-Poo, I guess. I know how it is, Candy—you've helped me out plenty of times."

As she started for the living room, Lacy added, "Don't let that man out of the bathroom. He's not finished in there."

"Oh, do you have a problem, too?" she heard Candy say interestedly through the bathroom door. Lacy raced through the living room to catch the jangling phone.

She grabbed up the receiver. "Yes, what?" she managed breathlessly.

It was several seconds before the cool, definitely guarded voice of Michael Echevarria said, "Lacy? Lacy Kingston?"

"I can't talk to you," she cried. "I'm entertaining a Doberman pinscher and friends!"

She slammed the receiver back in its cradle. But she had only gotten as far as the kitchen when the telephone rang again. She turned and ran back into the living room and snatched it up.

This was too much, she seethed. He was the one who had made the rules about no weekends. Obviously *he* could invade her privacy, but she couldn't invade his! "How's the weather in Boston?" she said rudely.

"Lacy?" His voice held a note of cold command. "Who's there with you? There's a man with you, you just said his name."

"I'm having friends in," Lacy snapped. "One of them just threw up on the floor, that's all. Where are you calling from now—San Francisco, Des Moines? Some other penthouse, some other town? Some other night's date?"

There was a longer pause on the other end of the line. "I'll talk to you later. About the drunk you're having the party for." His voice was grim. "This is a violation of our agreement."

"The drunk's name is Sicky-Poo," she shouted over the sound of Candy's voice and the Doberman's barking. "I can't talk with all of this going on! You're going to have to wait until Friday night."

"No, I've had too much damned trouble placing this call," he growled. "I'm at my country place in Connecticut. My business in Boston"—there was just the slightest hesitation—"closed out early. There was no way to save the bank, so I left.

"I want you," he said firmly, "to come up here. I want you to spend tonight and tomorrow with me. I'm sending the Rolls down for you."

Here it comes, Lacy told herself, staring past the living room into the kitchen, where the famous Virginia Slims poster was prominently displayed in front of the refrigerator. Now we go to weekends in Connecticut taking dinners and breakfasts together, sleeping in the same bed, making love. Next week the lease on the East Side fancy apartment!

"I'm all tied up," Lacy said coldly. "Sorry."

"We'll return to New York tomorrow night," he said as though he hadn't heard her. "Bring some clothes for horseback riding."

"What?" Lacy held her right hand to her ear to shut out Sicky-Poo's anguished yelps. Moretti was helping Candy clean up the hallway outside the bathroom. The racket of the Bulldogs finally scoring against FSU added to the mayhem. "I can't hear you!"

"What the hell is going on down there?" Michael Echevarria's voice demanded. "Are you in the habit of giving wild parties in the middle of Saturday afternoon? Get that crowd—get those Germans out of there! The Rolls will pick you up at three o'clock. Be there!"

Lacy gritted her teeth. She had just received a command from the president and chairman of the board. Report to Connecticut, Lacy Kingston, or you'll get yourself fired.

"I can't go to Connecticut," she yelled over the noise. "You can't call me up on my days off—you get Friday nights only! You're the one who said no last-minute substitutions!"

"Lacy," the voice on the telephone said warningly, "I want you here."

"No! I have to do my laundry. I have my own life to lead—did you ever stop to think of that? No, you didn't! Well, I have dirty clothes just like anybody else!"

"Lacy, I want you here. Now, in Connecticut. I regret," he said huskily, "that I had to leave last night, but I had no choice."

Lacy gripped the receiver with both hands, trying to hold onto her resistance. When he talked to her like that, in his low, purring black panther voice, her willpower melted.

"I have to baby-sit a neighbor's dog," Lacy said weakly. "It's an emergency." She was thinking that during the visit to Connecticut, perhaps she could finally get around to telling him that she loved him. "I really do have to take my wash to the Laundromat, too."

"That's no problem." Was that eagerness in his voice? "There are plenty of washers and dryers up here at the house, bring your laundry with you. Hell, bring the dog. Just make sure," he said quickly, "he rides up in front with Edward. I don't want dog hairs all over the back seat of the Rolls."

"Oh, Michael," Lacy sighed. There was always a possibility, of course, that once she got the fifteen hundred dollars straightened out and convinced him that she absolutely would not be an assistant editor on *Fad* magazine and told him that she loved him—that he would say that he couldn't care less. Total disaster. What was she going to do then? "Michael," she couldn't resist asking softly, "did you miss me?"

There was a silence so deep she could almost hear it whistling over the long distance wires.

"Yes, I missed you," he said in a firm, businesslike voice. "Wear some sort of clothes for riding, boots and jeans if you have them. Be in front of your apartment promptly when the Rolls calls for you at three o'clock."

With that, he hung up.

16

The long, low Rolls Royce limousine hummed its way up the West Side of Manhattan, through the Cross-Bronx Expressway and then onto the New England Throughway. It was a gray, windy autumn afternoon. Lacy, in Ralph Lauren jeans, Joan and David Western-style boots and a creamy Irish hand-knit sweater was in the front seat, holding the Doberman, with Edward, the chauffeur. Walter Moretti in his trench coat sat in the back seat with a large bundle of dirty laundry. Sicky-Poo had tried to bite the Italian private eye only once since getting in the Rolls and had thrown up on Edward, whom he seemed to like, only twice, and that was apparently due to car sickness. So the seating arrangement with Lacy holding the dog up front had proved to be the wisest way to travel.

In all, it was a tiresome hour and a half ride from New York City, with the detective complaining that he should have tailed them in his own car and worrying that Mr. Echevarria wouldn't like them all riding together this way.

North of Wilton the Rolls turned off the highway into the Connecticut countryside dotted with the low-stonewall-surrounded fields that marked the boundaries of the estates of millionaires. After some miles the Rolls took a winding private road overhung with centuries-old oak trees to a massive iron gate manned by a security guard. The guard promptly telephoned their arrival to the main switchboard of the country home of the president and chairman of the board of Echevarria Enterprises, Inc. He was waiting for them when they finally came in sight of the massive stone English manor house.

Michael's tall figure, Lacy saw as they pulled up in front of the steps and right behind a bright-red Ferrari parked in the driveway, was attired in a superb Harris-tweed hacking jacket that snugly followed the width of his shoulders and chest and narrow hips. He had on a black cashmere turtleneck sweater, fawn riding pants and highly polished English riding boots. The gray autumn afternoon light struck his hair, which the wind had ruffled into a few dark, untidy curls, and the planes of his set, carved features. He looked so beautiful standing there in his meticulous riding clothes that Lacy felt a sudden surge of emotion in spite of herself. No wonder her life was in such a mess! No wonder she'd acted like she'd lost her mind ever since she'd met him and done things even she couldn't explain! What woman, seeing the president and chairman of the board standing there like that, even with that wary look on his face, wouldn't do the same?

There was a scowl between his eyes when he saw Walter Moretti sitting in the back seat of the Rolls Royce clutching the bag of laundry.

"Well, we're here," Lacy announced, feeling somewhat nervous. The fifteen hundred dollars, she'd promised herself, and the explanations were definitely going to come up this time. She yanked open the door on the passenger's side of the limousine.

Too late, Lacy remembered Sicky-Poo, who promptly jumped his chain as soon as the door opened and propelled himself through midair, snapping and snarling at the tall figure in English riding clothes. The Doberman came down on all fours with a thud and then, overcome with the hostile emotions that his psychiatrist said traumatized his nervous system, hunched, coughed and vomited across the insteps of the impeccably polished leather boots.

"My God," Michael Echevarria said, staring at his feet.

"Don't move!" Lacy cried, rushing up the steps. "He won't bite—he just throws up on you!" She immediately tripped over Sicky-Poo and landed in his outstretched arms.

"Mr. Echevarria," Walter Moretti shouted, coming up the steps with the bag of laundry gripped to his chest, "I can explain all this. It's Miss Kingston's fault. I only did what she told me to do."

"Michael," Lacy murmured breathlessly, looking up into his widened, storm-gray eyes, "I'll clean off your boots with some of the laundry in the bag, honestly. Just don't worry about it."

He was holding her now, both hands tightly gripping her upper arms, looking down into her face. "It doesn't matter," he said with an obvious effort. Edward, the chauffeur, came up to drag Sicky-Poo away by his chain. "You look lovely." He lifted his hand to touch the shining blond sheath of hair that drifted around her delicately modeled features. "What did you do to your hair?"

"It's the way I used to wear it," Lacy said, shaking her head from side to side so that the long, silvery-gold mass slithered like silk. "My hair's almost straight, not curly. I changed it when I went into runway modeling."

She could tell he liked it. So close to him in his arms, Lacy's nostrils were filled with the aura of his cologne, some Swedish import, she guessed, sniffing appreciatively. Somewhere inside his chest the black panther's heart was going, *thud, thud*, she realized with a little shiver of anticipation.

"I like it," he said, still staring. "It makes you look different. More beautiful, if that's possible."

Before Lacy could open her mouth to tell him how much she appreciated that, a handsome medium-sized man in a black three-piece business suit and Yale tie who looked like a movie actor stepped forward. In a swift movement he snapped a color-sample book up to the side of Lacy's head.

"Unfortunately your hair's going to be hard to match, Miss Kingston," he announced, giving Lacy and the color card a comparative squint. "That blond color's not Basra Pearl, and it's not exactly North Sea Champagne, either." As Michael released her and stepped back, the handsome actor type took Lacy's hand to shake it. "I'm George Swithins, Miss

Kingston, special executive sales from Import Motors, Limited, Greenwich, Connecticut."

"What's he doing?" Lacy asked, wide-eyed.

"He's trying to get the color of your hair," Michael Echevarria said impassively, "for the custom-paint job on your Ferrari Testarossa."

"You're kidding!" It wasn't possible he had believed every word she'd said to him last night in his Sutton Place condo just to get his attention when he was telephoning and getting ready to leave for Boston. "Good grief—do you know how much Ferraris cost?"

He folded his arms across his big chest and regarded her imperturbably. "Around eighty-seven thousand, before sales tax. I never buy anything, Lacy, without pricing it first. You know that."

Lacy made a small strangling sound. Before her vocal cords could recover from their paralysis, the salesman from Greenwich said, indicating the Italian sports car parked in the driveway, "Would you like to take a look? It's red right now—Kuwait Scarlet, actually, is the shade, but the Testarossa's ready for a test drive if you want to see how she handles."

"Mr. Echevarria," Walter Moretti said desperately over the vicious snarls of Sicky-Poo, who was lunging on his chain at the Ferrari salesman, "where do you want me to put this laundry?"

"Oh, I can't believe this," Lacy moaned. "This is very funny, isn't it? Well, where's the white cockatoo? What about"—there was not the remotest possibility of this—"what about the Russian sable full-length coat?"

"Start with these," Michael Echevarria said, taking Lacy by the arm and steering her past the sports-car salesman and the private eye. Lacy stumbled slightly on Sicky-Poo's chain and then over a line of boxes stacked on the floor of the entrance hall to the English manor house.

The stacked cardboard boxes had names like Sunbeam, Waring and Proctor-Silex printed on their sides. Some of the containers had been opened to show a variety of assorted blenders in several colors and their attachments. Beyond the boxes of blenders there were larger shipping crates pried apart to display the chrome and glass shapes of a variety of microwave ovens. Somewhere in the shadows of the hall behind the microwave ovens, a faintly inhuman voice said, "Awrk? Awrk?" plaintively.

"I don't believe it!" she cried.

"It seems there are more kinds of blenders on the market," Michael observed thoughtfully, "than one would think. Also microwave ovens. Bloomingdale's sent these on approval." He indicated the boxes with a gesture of one big, powerful hand. "Take your choice."

"You can't do this to me!" Lacy burst out.

"Morton's Birds, in Westport, sent a very nice sulphur-crested cockatoo," he continued judiciously. "It's their most popular type."

"No!" Lacy knew what he was trying to do in front of Edward, the private eye and now the sports-car salesman from Greenwich. She wasn't that stupid. "Oh, how *low*. How dirty! You knew it was just a joke!"

She held an avocado-colored blender over her head as Walter Moretti and the Ferrari salesman backed hurriedly out the front door.

"Lacy, don't throw the blender," Michael said calmly. "Put it down."

"Dirty bird," the hollow voice said from the back of the entrance hall.

"The whole idea is to humiliate me, isn't it?" The blender wobbled over her head. "To show them you're paying off your floozy! Well, I'm not a tramp, even though you're trying to make me look like one! It was bad enough with gowns and jewels—but now! Blenders and microwave ovens?"

"I thought you said you needed a blender, and every kitchen should have a microwave oven," he decided firmly. "I want to give you everything you desire, Lacy. I told you, you just have to name it."

"I won't take your rotten Ferrari," she shouted, glaring at him. "I won't take your microwave ovens or blenders or anything, do you hear me, Michael? You can take your cockatoo and—"

"Lacy," he said, scowling, "if you don't want these things, just tell me what you *do* want, and we'll get it."

"You're not going to trick me!" She threw the blender at him, but he ducked, and it hit the wall with a crash. Lacy stood trembling before him, her breasts heaving indignantly under the Irish hand-knit sweater. "Why don't you go back to the hotel you own in Tulsa," she burst out recklessly, forgetting all her good resolutions, "and buy some other woman? That's what you usually do, isn't it? Come on, let your buddies know what you *really* do—you pick up hookers in bars! You are," she taunted him, "a closet degenerate, Michael Echevarria!"

She saw the fury in his eyes that meant winter had

come again to the Antarctic. "You don't know what you're talking about." She saw him make an effort to keep his voice down so that the others couldn't hear. "I don't pick up hookers. I don't care whether you believe it or not, but I never bought sex before in my life!"

"That isn't what you said to *me*!" He was right—she wasn't going to believe it. "You grabbed me so I couldn't get away and hustled me into a hotel elevator before I could scream for help. You kidnapped me! You said, 'I'm buying,' that's what you said! You said—"

"I know what I said," he growled, grabbing her arm. "Frankly, I don't need to explain this to you, but it so happens I came into the bar that night checking out the volume of business. It's something I always do when I'm in town. When I came in, there you were—selling yourself."

"Oh, really," Lacy cried, "don't try to wriggle out of this! You said, 'I'm buying.' Just like you try to buy everything else you want!"

A small vein throbbed in his temple. His mouth was grim, furious. "Look at me, Lacy. Do I look as though I need to pay a woman to go to bed with me?" He gave her arm a slight shake. "Answer me."

Lacy took a deep breath. Good grief, he was right! You just had to look at a big hunk like Michael Echevarria to know what he was saying was true.

"Why," she whispered, "did you do it? Why did you offer to pay fifteen hundred dollars when you could have had somebody else"—she gulped—"for free! You must have been out of your mind."

His hands on her arms tightened. "I was out of my mind," he growled, "you were right. I plead temporary insanity from the moment I walked into that damned bar and saw you dressed like a hooker and still looking like an angel.''

"It was a joke! I couldn't help it about the dress—I was modeling it for the Western Sta—"

"You were beautiful," he said, harshly. "When something is as beautiful as you, price is no object."

Her mouth dropped open in dismay. They were back to that again. "Look, I'm not just a great big collectible," she said, yanking her arm in his hard grip. "I brought the money with me. You've got a surprise coming, Michael Echevarria! When I give you your fifteen hundred dollars back, what are you going to do?"

She saw a flicker of some unfathomable expression in that hard face. Then his expression smoothed. "I'm going to take you horseback riding."

"I'm not going horseback riding; you're changing the subject. You think I'm lying, don't you?" she demanded. "Well, I'm tired of having you order me around. I won't be your mistress; you're not going to treat me like one. I'm not going to be forced out of my job at *Fad*. I won't do anything you tell me to do!" she yelled. "That's it!"

Michael Echevarria bent his dark head to her, sliding his arms around her softly. "Yes, you will, Lacy," he said softly, "you're going riding. The horses are all saddled."

His mouth closed over hers and smothered her protests, his tongue caressing her adamant lips, persuading them to softly open to him. Lacy closed her eyes. When she moved to him, his kiss deepened and grew hungrier. Lacy clung to him, shaken by the sudden sensuous heat that poured between them and the heady sweetness of the *zap*! and the *powie*! as if played by a whole symphony orchestra of singing violins.

"Aren't you, Lacy?" he murmured huskily against her partly opened lips.

"Where do you ride," she breathed, "around here?"

Forty-five minutes later, as Michael worked to disentangle her blond silky hair from a tree branch she'd ridden under, he said, "Somehow I have the feeling, Lacy, that when I'm with you, chaos enters my life."

"Well, you said you liked my hair down loose and wavy," Lacy grumbled. She hadn't seen the overhanging tree branch until she was right under it, and the horse she was riding was a tall, powerful hunter, not the easiest mount to control. He *did* insist on doing these things, anyway—Lutece, the opera, horseback riding. The first night she'd met him, Michael Echevarria had whirled her around the penthouse in a waltz to "Lara's Theme," from *Dr. Zhivago*. Would she ever forget that evening? she wondered, looking at the incredibly thick brush of his eyelashes against the hard planes of his cheeks as he carefully pulled another strand of her hair from the oak tree. "I don't ride English saddles very well," she murmured. "Daddy always let us use Western saddles at home."

"On Long Island?" he said, shooting her a look from under dark brows.

"My sisters and I wanted to be cowboys. Outlaws, actually. We were terrible tomboys," Lacy told him as she reined in her horse for about the twelfth time to keep from getting scalped. "All the other little girls in

East Hampton took riding lessons and had nifty little English riding boots and those little black jockey hats and Lord and Taylor riding jackets. But my father had lost his money right about then, so my sisters and I wore old jeans and cowboy hats and sort of slouched around, trying to look like Clint Eastwood. Daddy bought us the Western saddle. Then the next year my oldest sister, Felice, got into junior homecoming queen and the year after that Miss Universe tryouts, and looking like Clint Eastwood sort of got''—she shrugged—''harder to do.''

"But you ride very well''—the corners of his mouth quirked—''when you're not hung up in trees. How did your father lose his money? I thought he was a lawyer," he said as he freed the last of her hair from the oak twigs.

"When he stopped being a partner in a big law firm in Manhattan." Her horse jostled his hunter and brought them face to face. "He made some bad investments, so Daddy moved back to East Hampton and opened a small law practice there. We were supposed to be well off, with the big house and everything, but we weren't. We really needed all the money and clothes we won from beauty pageants, although''—she shrugged—''we weren't supposed to tell people that.''

Michael Echevarria rode beautifully, better than anyone Lacy had ever seen. The article in *People* magazine had said he was an exercise boy at race tracks in his youth, a homeless teenager who'd slept in the stables. No wonder he rode so well, she thought, studying him. As for how the three beautiful Kingston girls had worked the beauty-queen circuits —she supposed she couldn't tell Michael much about needing money. "When I started modeling, Daddy made me put my money into a savings account for college." She finally got out from under the oak tree and kicked her horse into a canter. "I made good money the first few years.

"*Race*!" Lacy yelled suddenly over her shoulder.

His reactions were good, but Michael Echevarria was untypically startled, a few seconds late in responding. Then, as Lacy bent her head over her horse's neck, tucked in her elbows and crouched forward for a gallop down the wooded lane, she saw the answering slash of a grin break over white teeth. She knew he was coming after her with a vengeance.

The horses charged down the November-brown woods, their hooves loud in the fallen leaves. The Echevarria country estate was miles of old, walled fields and meadows and twisted byways, a tremendous place by any standards, especially here, just outside New York City, where every acre literally cost a fortune.

It was no small feat to guide the big hunter under trees and around sudden curves in the lane hemmed in by field-stone walls. Lacy could hear Michael coming up fast behind her. Her hunter stretched its legs, trying to get his head, and Lacy fought to keep him under control. At the last moment she heard Michael's hoarse shouted warning, saw the lane come to an abrupt end at a gate and leaned forward, digging her heels into the horse's ribs.

The hunter lifted his coiled body, sailed over the gate and stone wall with a gliding motion, his stride faltering only for seconds on the unexpected down slope of a pasture on the far side. Lacy pulled him up quickly and turned his head to circle him. Michael's big black came thundering up behind her.

"Damn!" If she didn't know better she would swear Michael Echevarria's face had gone slightly ashen. "Do you do these things deliberately?" he barked. "Are you a total crackbrain? You—you—didn't know what was on the other side of that wall!" He pulled the big black under control, fighting its tossing head. "You—you're a good rider," he said grimly. "Or you wouldn't have taken that gate like that."

"Oh, he really likes to jump, doesn't he," Lacy breathed, her eyes sparkling as she bent forward to pat her mount's neck. "I could get used to hunters. There must be something in riding English saddle, after all."

"Lacy." There was a peculiar expression on Michael's face, gray eyes glittering as he moved his horse closer to hers. "If I ever let you—"

"What, Michael?" she asked softly. It was strangely satisfying to see him like this. He was even breathing hard. "If you ever what?"

"I think," he said, staring at her, "that either you're crazy, or you have more guts than most men I've seen. You're not like . . . any woman I've ever known, believe me." He rested his forearms on the pommel and leaned to her. "I still can't understand why your parents let you grow up the way you did."

Lacy sighed. "Oh, Michael, what's that supposed to mean?"

"Modeling," he said abruptly, "is too damned tough for an innocent young girl in New York. Even someone as . . . independent as you are. Why didn't your parents do a better job of taking care of you, Lacy?

"You know the sort of wolves that go after beautiful women," he said, chomping down on each word. "And they went after you, didn't they?"

"Is that what's bothering you?" she cried. "Good grief, Michael, I could take care of myself. It wasn't as bad as you think."

As she brushed her hair back from her eyes, she realized it wasn't the moment to tell him the whole story about Peter Dorsey. Their horses were dancing restlessly, wanting to gallop again. Was there ever going to be a right time? she wondered, despairingly.

They ate dinner prepared for two in front of a roaring fire in the Tudor-style den, rather than in the formal dining room, and the sense of cosiness, of being shut away from the world, was enhanced by a cold autumn drizzle falling outside. They dressed for dinner, Michael in his Savile Row tuxedo, which brought back a flood of memories, Lacy in a pair of gold silk crêpe de Chine trousers, a matching gold satin shirt and a black velvet jacket from Altman's that managed to look ten times more expensive than they actually were. Sicky-Poo was allowed to come in during dinner, but while the butler was pouring the Aufstadler-Rhone '78 during the first course of duck-liver *pâté en croute*, the Doberman had an anxiety attack. It ate part of a *Time* magazine from the coffee table and then threw up on the sheepskin rug in front of the fireplace.

"I hate neurotics," the chairman of the board said, viewing the Doberman coldly. "I had plans for that rug in front of the fire later."

"A little cold water and dish-washing detergent," Lacy began helpfully, but he had already shoved his chair back from the table. "Don't use violence," she cried, "Sicky-Poo has a defective hostility mechanism! His shrink says he identifies with the unresolved conflicts of the oppressor."

The tall figure in the Savile Row tuxedo went to the door of the den, opened it and pointed forcefully to the hallway. Sicky-Poo slunk meekly out of the den.

"How did you do that?" Lacy exclaimed. "That's incredible—I've never seen Sicky-Poo behave, especially when anybody told him to!"

"Intimidation," he growled, returning to the vichysoisse the butler had served. "It's a successful corporate technique."

Unfortunately, during the beef Wellington, they had a large argument about Republican foreign policy. "What are we talking about?" Lacy cried finally, exasperated. "Republican foreign policy doesn't exist, it never has. Good grief, it's a nonsubject!"

He just stared at her. "Nobody," he said in an even voice, "argues with me like this except you, Lacy."

Lacy stared back at him. "I'm not afraid of your successful corporate techniques," she said.

But for once she didn't want to start an argument. Instead, she began a long story about the time her middle sister, Charity, set fire to the roof of their house with a homemade rocket after reading the life of Dr. Goddard. At that time, Lacy explained, no one knew that Charity was going to become an astrophysicist.

Halfway through, when Lacy was giving her

famous dramatic impression of the East Hampton fire department scaling the front porch through her mother's rose beds, he was still staring at her with a curious expression.

"Usually," he said, interrupting her, "I find most dinner conversations with women excruciating."

"I thought you liked hearing about my family," she sighed. "I was only telling this to make you feel better. All right, I'll bite—what's so excruciating about your dinner conversations with women?"

"Boring," he said flatly. "But at least they don't argue."

"Do you want to go back to discussing Republicans?" Lacy cried. "Do you or do you not want to hear about my sister Charity? She has her Ph.D. in astrophysics now, and she's probably going to be an astronaut. She'll be the only astronaut who was first runner-up in the 1980 Miss America contest."

His eyebrows went up. "You fascinate me, Lacy," he said after a long moment. "I never know when to take you seriously. I love hearing about your sister." He reached into his tuxedo and extracted a silver cigar case. "Go ahead."

"You don't," she said, looking down at her plate. "I don't know why you keep leading me on, Michael, if you hate it so much."

He lit the cigar and blew a long cloud of smoke, watching her. "I don't hate it," he said finally. "Actually, I'm panting with breathless anticipation waiting to learn about your sister, the first Miss America astronaut." When he saw her stiffen, he said quickly, "As long as you're sitting there telling it to me. Is that better?"

"Hmmmph," Lacy said. But yes, it was better.

After dinner, with brandy glasses in hand, Michael took her for a tour of his English-style Connecticut manor house. Lacy admired the formal dining room, the library and the kitchen downstairs, which had been left shining by the servants. The furnishings in the lovely old mansion were nondescript but rather homey, leftovers from the previous owners. Lacy couldn't help hoping Michael Echevarria wasn't going to decorate the house in the blacks, browns and chrome of Sutton Place expensive contemporary, but his next words dashed that hope. The same interior-decorator friend, he told her, was going to go to work on the Connecticut place shortly.

Somehow, Lacy got the strong impression the interior decorator friend was a woman. Time was running out, she told herself. She had to break her good news to Michael, that she loved him, and start planning from there.

Upstairs, in the bedrooms that overlooked the English-style gardens, there seemed to be an excess of faded chintz and colonial reproductions. But then he showed her a series of rooms at the back that were newly painted and quite bare.

"Oh, pretty," Lacy murmured as she stepped into a big yellow room with a huge Peter Max-type pastel rainbow painted across one entire wall. "What's this going to be?" The only thing she could think of was a game room.

"Nursery," he said, closing the door behind them.

In the hallway, Lacy stopped to look at him. Michael had taken off his tuxedo jacket downstairs in the den before the roaring fire. Now the sleeves of his perfect London-made dress shirt were unfastened and rolled up to his elbows, exposing corded, tanned forearms that testified to his days as a dock worker and construction foreman. He looked particularly handsome, Lacy thought dreamily, with his dark hair tightly curled, his gray eyes in his chiseled face.

"Children?" she whispered. It was such a lovely idea; it fit into what she was thinking about, too.

He shrugged. "Planning ahead," he said in his president and chairman of the board voice.

Marvelous, she noted. Now she was positive she loved Michael Echevarria more than she could love any other man, ever. She would make him happy, too, she thought with a rush of emotion that left her eyes shining like stars. This beautiful house. And now children. He didn't know it yet, but she could give him everything he'd always wanted.

He took her by the arm and gently steered her down the hall. The next room was a master bedroom with an enormous early-American four-poster bed that had a ruffled tester and a bright heirloom handmade quilt for a spread. The furniture, highboys and spool-backed chairs, were warm waxed pine and walnut, and there was a lovely blazing fire snapping in a small brick fireplace. The covers of the four-poster had been turned back for the night and showed hand-spun linen sheets in their natural color.

She didn't need to be told that Michael Echevarria had probably designed the master bedroom himself. That he could get away from chrome and black fabrics if given a chance. This room had the mark of someone who had spent too much of his youth without a home, she thought, and now wanted one, and a loving family.

"It's perfect, it's fantastic," Lacy breathed. It was even in good taste.

The room actually revealed a great deal about him, she thought. The bed was expansive, warm, sentimental—and big enough to accommodate a whole crowd of children if they crept into bed with Mommy and Daddy on a Sunday morning. The room, the bed, were made for love.

Why wait any longer? Lacy thought, turning into his waiting arms.

"Lacy," the black panther growled, gathering her to him, "come to bed."

17

Lacy loved Michael more in that moment than she'd thought it was possible to love anyone. Everything she'd found out about him in Connecticut only reinforced the wonderful feeling, and she told herself that somehow she was going to get everything straightened out and make him love her, too. Perhaps he was in love with her now and didn't know it!

As she lifted her eyes to his in the early-American bedroom, all she wanted to do was revel in the warm, tender, passionate emotion she was feeling. She wanted to make Michael happy as he'd never been before, as a struggling orphan and then as a self-made millionaire. To do generous, creative things for him, like decorate his Connecticut house and perhaps go back over his New York condominium and rearrange it and make it look better. Love him forever. Marry him, and have his children.

"Michael, darling," Lacy cried in a burst of passionate joy, "I'm going to make love to you if you'll let me!"

It was a bold step, but she'd been reading *Joy of Sex* over again, this time with less shock and more care than she'd done several years ago, and she was much more confident. It was the ultimate expression of her love. Besides, she was sure it would blow his mind.

"If I'll let you?" There was a definite note of caution in his voice.

"Yes, you know what I mean," Lacy said. She unfastened his black silk cummerbund and dropped it to the floor. "Just relax, darling, and enjoy it."

He looked wary as she took the bottom of his dress shirt and pulled it up. "Lacy," he began as she unfastened his tuxedo suspenders and let them fall over his shoulders, "we've had discussions before about your sense of—" His words were choked off as her fingers dropped to the zippered front of his fly. "Humor," he finished in a suddenly hoarse voice.

Lacy gave a small gurgle of laughter. She knew he was remembering that when she'd started this sort of thing once before, he'd ended up with his tuxedo trousers around his knees and his arms immobilized in his white cotton dress shirt.

"Is anything the matter, Michael?" she inquired in a throaty voice.

"It's all right," he rasped as the zipper of the fly opened and her light touch explored the silky, taut thrust of his Cardin briefs. "Just go on—*yunnhh*," he shuddered, grasping her wrists in an involuntary movement.

"Trust me, my darling," Lacy crooned. "I won't hurt you. You're safe with me."

"Oh, hell," he groaned. But his eyes were gleaming, and the corners of his lips quivered uncontrollably. He shuddered again as her hands rose to unbutton the dress shirt and help him out of it.

He had the most fantastic body, Lacy thought, staring at the heavily curving chest muscles. She felt him flinch as she put her moistened lips to the slight hollow of his breastbone between the dusky male nipples. She ran her tongue deliberately along his satiny skin, tasting the slight saltiness, her nostrils filled with his clean, masculine odor, and licked carefully up the base of his throat. She met his eyes, which regarded her with a strange, untypically distracted expression. "You taste so good," she had to tell him softly.

"Lacy," he croaked, "what am I supposed to be doing—while you're doing this?"

"Standing still," she told him as she sank her teeth lightly into the powerful curve of his tanned shoulder. "Do you like it?"

"I love it," he managed.

She gave a few lustful nibbles down his arms and then lifted the big, heavy palm of his hand to press her lips to it. Her wet tongue stroked its hollow as the muscles in his forearms and biceps jumped in response.

"But I don't think I'm going to survive it," he muttered.

"Is this—ah, anything special, or did you just happen to think of—aaahh," he breathed as her free hand slid around his waist, and her fingers scooped softly under the waistband of the Cardins to seize the rock-hard planes of his buttocks.

"Actually, just a minute ago," Lacy confessed. "But I've been thinking about it for a long time. Well, not a long time." She used both hands to pull down first the evening trousers and then the feather-soft fabric of his underwear. "Just the past few min—"

"Never mind," he said quickly. "It's all right. Oh, God."

"Oh, Michael, you really are beautiful all over," Lacy murmured. "Being raised with just three sisters and no brothers and never really seeing a male figure without his clothes except in art books and museums has its disadvantages, you know. I always thought men looked a little ludicrous with everything—hanging out in front," she explained delicately. She touched him with adoring fingers, careful of the giant spasms that rattled his big frame. "But I could worship you. You look so primeval."

"Aaagh," he retorted, trembling. "Ah, Lacy, love—great god!"

"Yes, and godlike, too," she agreed, getting him to step out of his trousers, his heavy hand pressing into her shoulder. "Actually, more like that statue of Adam by Epstein in *Great Art of America*. You don't have to help, darling. Just relax."

"I never know what in the hell you're going to do," he muttered. His face was dark and flushed as he bent his head to her, but he obediently kept his hands at his sides. "Just as long as you don't tie me up, right?"

"Shoes," Lacy murmured softly. "We have to get you out of your socks and shoes."

He allowed her to guide him to the four-poster bed, and she pushed him down on it. His gray eyes were fascinated as she bent over him, her long blond silky hair brushing his face.

"Oh, darling," Lacy cried feelingly as she stretched the whole length of her body against his. "This is marvelous. Even I didn't know it was going to be this great!''

She had pulled off her velvet jacket. Now she stroked the hard, bare expanse of his chest with one hand while her other unbuttoned the front of her gold satin shirt and pulled it open. She lowered herself so that she could feel the nakedness of his skin against her own breasts which were cupped in the tiniest of gold satin brassieres. When he moaned, she reached for his mouth with her moistly swollen lips, her long hair drifting over his throat and shoulders. She gnawed teasingly at his firm lower lip, then deepened her kiss into his mouth with slightly awkward but passionate thrusts. His body contracted in a powerful convulsion, and then his big hand went up to grab the back of her head and hold her to him.

"Lacy," he rasped into her opened lips. "My own angel. My beautiful witch. Sweetheart!''

She kissed him thoroughly, exploring his lips, his teeth, the depths of his mouth with all the *zap! bam! powie!* that he'd used so well to set her afire, which was hers, now, as much as his, astonishingly. The furnace of heat she was generating rippled through his powerful body and stiffened against her pressing thighs.

Lying on top of him like that, Lacy marveled, was like resting on top of a volcano about to erupt. All the creative things she could think of to do with her hands, and her loving fingers, set him to gasping. He seemed to be barely controlling himself.

"I have to get your shoes and underwear off," she murmured, looking down into his clear gray eyes. "Michael?''

"Shoes," he said hoarsely. "Underwear. God, yes.''

"Well, you have to help," she reminded him, wriggling off the bed and tugging first at his shoes and then at his socks as he stuck his feet out cooperatively. She stood back a minute to peel off her gold satin shirt and her crêpe de Chine evening pants, kicking her backless sandals away but not taking her eyes off his big, sleek body as it lay darkly against the linen sheets.

"You're so gorgeous," Lacy murmured as she bent her head to touch her lips to the faint line of hairs that ran downward from his navel to the top of the elastic. As her teeth and tongue enjoyed little bites of the hairy flesh of his upper thighs, his big hands seized her hair blindly and buried his fingers in it.

"Don't stop," he croaked.

Quite carefully, Lacy eased the silky, clinging Cardins down his legs, her warm breath close to his swollen flesh.

"You're so responsive," she cried, his tormented body bucking under her as her lips caressed his velvety skin. "Oh, darling!"

Actually, *responsive* was a very weak word for it. His big, virile body was going to explode at any moment. "Unnhh," he gasped as her fingers tightened around him.

Somehow his shaking hands managed to reach up to strip away her brassiere and then yank feverishly at the bows on each hip holding the silky string of her gold bikini briefs.

"Naked," he gasped.

"Michael, are you all right?" she asked him, holding his heavy strength cupped in her hand tenderly. He lay quite still, staring up at the ceiling. "Oh, Michael, am I pleasing you? Am I doing this right?"

"Don't stop," he said hoarsely. "Beautiful, beautiful Lacy." He raised his arms, biceps bulging, and reached up to pull her to straddle him. "Incomparable Lacy," he murmured, "you drive me nuts."

"Oh, oh," she breathed softly. "Michael, you're supposed to be letting me do everything!"

"I am," he groaned. His hands slid down to the curve of her waist and then to her hips, seizing them. "I am, precious. I'm just trying to help. Oh, beautiful, sweet Lacy—"

"Michael, do you want me?" Lacy cried passionately. "Say that you do, my darling," she urged him, showering his face with hot, eager kisses. "Say that you're mine!"

"Are you kidding?" His gray eyes were wild. "I—yaarrghh," he rasped as her body settled on him fiercely.

"Michael!" Lacy screamed. She tried to fight away his hands that were taking charge, possessing her with seismic surges of gigantic proportions. "You're supposed to be letting me make love to you!"

"You are," he ground out, rocking her body against him with growing turbulence. "I am—we are! I'm yours, angel! Take me!"

His hoarse demands pushed her over the lip of the roaring volcano into its flames. His hands clenched rhythmically, dragging her up to take him in an upreaching thrust that brought a small shriek of excitement to her lips. She was drowning in convulsions—she was enveloped in molten lava as he took her devouringly. The world collapsed around them in the grinding roar of continents moving, seas surging, the blazing fall of comets. The ruffled tester over them trembled, the four-poster rocked with cosmic upheavals, assailed by their perfect wildness.

"Yowrrrmmmh!" Michael roared in loud, luxurious release as he pulled her down against him, his hands tightly tangled in her long hair.

"It was crazy," Lacy sobbed joyously as she fell against his wet, heaving chest. "Oh, Michael, I did make love to you, didn't I? Oh, it was marvelous. *You're* marvelous!"

"Call a doctor," he muttered.

"Oh, goodnight," she cried, raising up on her elbows to look down at him. His face was drenched, eyes tightly closed. "Are you serious?"

"Can't tell." His voice was faint.

"Oh, drat—did I really do something?" she panicked. "Michael, oh, good heavens, say something! Tell me quick—was this too much for you?" She quickly dropped her ear to his wet chest to listen to his heart. It sounded like a series of explosions.

"Resting," he managed huskily.

"What?" she asked, her ear close to his mouth. "Oh, I can't believe this! Resting what?"

"You'll find out," he growled, suddenly snaking his powerful arms around her to hold her close. As she squealed, he told her, "My turn next, beautiful Lacy."

"You couldn't," she breathed, staring down into his eyes.

The gray gaze narrowed. "Are you telling me I can't?"

"No," she gasped, giggling.

The enormously powerful body moving under her was already proving it could.

Lacy's first thought as a beam of sunshine fell across her face was how wonderful it was to wake up in an early-American four-poster bed with Michael's arms and legs wound around her tightly and his big body half-resting on hers. How could it be anyone but Michael? she thought dreamily. He always slept like this, holding her possessively as though she might slip away in the night, crushing her to him so that she could hardly breathe. He smelled marvelous, warm and damply male, his lips burrowed into her throat, his hair carrying the faint aura of Swedish cologne.

Lacy hadn't had much sleep. One would think that would make for a really haggard look with dark circles under her eyes. But she was finding out she always came awake in the morning with Michael beside her sort of—glowing.

They had talked the night away when they weren't making love. In the dark it was Michael who talked. Very brilliantly, too, on what had made the Boston bank fail and what made conglomerates work and why buying into publishing houses was mainly an ego trip, since their profits were small and they were riddled with management problems. They discussed the desirability of investing in hotels, Sutton Place condominiums, Connecticut real estate and diamond and gold jewelry. She'd been surprised when he quizzed her almost endlessly about her ideas on how to improve *Fad*. And because Lacy had good, sound creative ideas, she'd told him at length and with growing authority.

He *was* brilliant, she thought fondly, looking down at his handsome, sleep-softened face resting in the hollow between her throat and her naked shoulder. Even if his mind did seem to run in the predictable tracks of Wall Street, corporate development and making money. She had a very strong feeling that the president and chairman of the board didn't open himself up to many people and especially not in bed. He also, she had found out, lifting a dark strand of hair from his eyebrow very carefully so as not to wake him, had decided opinions on raising children. That is, preferably in a stable environment with two loving, devoted parents and material things, such as swimming pools and horses, and with good educations —private schools if necessary. He felt the worst thing that could happen to a child was not to have a home or anyone you loved or who loved you. That is, to be an orphan.

He was so dear and sweet, once you got to know him, Lacy sighed. In a way, it was a good thing he was going to find out that she loved him. It might be a little difficult at first, but she had so much to offer him, and they agreed about the important things, even if they did argue a lot.

"I want you, Lacy," a rusty, early-morning voice said into her shoulder.

"That's impossible," she said, startled. He was undoubtedly the most potent lover a woman could find, too.

"You're irresistible," Michael said, biting the silky flesh of her upper arm softly. "You have an amazing effect on me. You're sexy and wild and the most beautiful damned woman in the world, even at this hour." He looked up at her, his gaze smoky. "Even looking like you've spent the night in the subway. Let's make love."

He looked so happy, she thought, looking down at him tenderly as his large brown hand held her breast, his thumb lazily stroking her nipple.

Now was the time, Lacy told herself.

"I have to talk to you," she said, gently prying herself away from him. She lifted his arms, and he let them fall back on her, watching her with a lazy smile. She moved his legs to one side with an effort.

"We talked last night—all night," he reminded her. "It's good to talk to you, sweetheart, you're a very interesting and intelligent woman, as well as fantastically beautiful."

"Thank you," Lacy said modestly. She managed to get his big body rolled to one side far enough to slip out from under him.

"Now is not the time for conversation, though," he said, making a grab for her leg. "Lacy, where are you going?"

She couldn't help feeling a twinge of apprehension as she scooted across the room to her black velvet jacket lying on the floor. There was so much to try to explain, like how to get his fifteen hundred dollars back to him, and this warm, intimate moment needed a light touch. Pass it off like the joke it was.

She pulled out the roll of bills held with a rubber band from the pocket.

The big man on the bed stretched his whole muscular length, putting his hands over his head. "Yummmmmh," he growled, looking at her with a smoldering expression. "Lacy, come to bed."

Lacy bounced back and knelt down beside him, her long legs tucked under her. She could tell from the way his eyes traveled down her slender body that she didn't have his full attention.

"Michael," Lacy said, "look at me. I'm going to give you something."

"Right," he said, reaching out to stroke her thigh caressingly. "I can't wait, honey."

"La-di-da!" Lacy cried. She struck the frivolous, provocative Lacy Kingston pose that had almost made her famous. She opened her hand and let a shower of bills drift down into his face. "Michael," she crowed, "what happened in Tulsa was all a stupid joke, really, because I love you too much to let this thing go on any further.

"You've got to believe me—Michael?" she said quickly. "Why are you looking at me like that?"

Michael Echevarria wasn't exactly being swept away by her provocative charm. The gray eyes that had been smiling at her seconds ago changed to hard granite stones.

"Stop it," the president and chairman of the board ordered.

"I didn't spend any of your money," Lucy blurted. "It's all there. You've known all along it was a dumb joke, haven't you?"

"What the hell are you doing?" he snarled. "Put on a robe. You're stark naked."

Robe? What was he talking about? Lacy thought, giving a confused look down at her perfectly lovely bare body. All he talked about was looking at her and how much it turned him on. "Michael, I've never been in love with anybody in my whole life," she wailed. "This is a totally new experience! Good grief, don't you have a sense of humor about *anything*?"

"I refuse to discuss this damned subject of your idea of what's a joke. I thought it was settled."

"You *must* love me," Lacy cried. "You couldn't make love to me the way you do if you didn't!"

"I don't want to go through this scene again," he said, sitting up in bed and reaching for his underwear, "with some . . . ex-model employee who thinks she's in love with me!"

"Employee?" Lacy exploded, jumping off the bed to stand in front of him. "You haven't said that one before!"

"I should never have brought you up here," he said with deadly calm. He kicked a few stray one-hundred-dollar bills out of his way. "I knew it was a damned big mistake. Give a woman an inch and she thinks she's in love with you!"

"Michael, will you look at me, please?" Lacy demanded, putting herself in his way every time he turned. "When did I get to be just an 'employee,' instead of a magazine wrecker with an insatiable body? Why are you so sorry you brought me up to your Connecticut house?"

"Put some clothes on," he said, firmly pushing her aside.

"Is it because I look like I belong here?" she yelled. "Is it because I fit in so well? Because you picked me up in a *bar*!" She dogged his steps as he strode to a walnut Chippendale highboy, yanked open a drawer and dragged out a clean shirt. "You're a prejudiced chauvinist rat, Michael Echevarria—you're afraid somebody will find out you mistook me for a hooker! And *you* picked *me* up!

"Boy," she hooted scornfully, "what a dumb thing that was!"

"I can't blame you for being ambitious," he said grimly, "it was a good try. You overplayed your hand with the protestations of love, however."

"Never mind, Michael, you blew it," Lacy taunted him, matching him step for step to the clothes closet.

"But you thought about me as your wife, didn't you? You haven't been able to get me out of your mind!"

"Get dressed," he grated, taking her by the arm and steering her toward the door. "We're going back to New York."

"You thought about what a good wife I'd make," Lacy yelled, struggling to keep him from pushing her out into the hall.

"It hit you hard when I said I loved you," she insisted as he picked her up bodily and deposited her outside the door.

"Wife—*wife*, Michael—I could do that even better than being your mistress in some nifty apartment on the East Side," she shouted triumphantly as he slammed the door and locked it. "Like some broad you couldn't take to Lutece or the opera or horseback riding, right?"

"We're going back to New York," his voice came from inside the bedroom, "in an hour."

18

It was probably the worst limousine ride of her life, Lacy thought dejectedly, as she sat up in the front seat of the Rolls Royce next to Edward, the chauffeur, holding Sicky-Poo partly in her lap to protect the dove-gray upholstery. The tall, darkly good-looking chairman of the board of Echevarria Enterprises, Inc., sat in back in stony silence with several boxes of assorted blenders and microwave ovens and the covered cage that held El Magnifico, the sulphur-crested cockatoo.

When they reached the West Side and Lacy's apartment on Eightieth Street an hour and a half later, Lacy accepted El Magnifico and his bird cage because there was, after all, no one to take care of him unless he was returned to Morton's Birds in Westport. But she told Michael Echevarria what he could do with all his Waring and Sunbeam blenders and the half dozen or so microwave ovens still in their crates, standing on the sidewalk and delivering her message through the closed window glass of the Roll's back seat while he smoked a large cigar and stared at her imperturbably. In the end, Edward carried everything up to her apartment, including her washed and dried laundry, and stacked it in a big pile in the middle of the living room.

"Miss Kingston, is this, ah, breakup for real?" the tall, blond, attractive chauffeur said, taking off his gray uniform cap and holding it in front of him politely. "Because if you're not going to see the boss anymore, I'd like to say that I have two tickets to championship wrestling at Madison Square Garden this Thursday night."

"Go away," Lacy cried, pushing him away. "I hate wrestling."

"You're the most beautiful woman Mr. Echevarria has ever, ah, taken out, Miss Kingston," the chauffeur said diplomatically, "and more fun, too. How about Chinese food Friday night?

"At least I could call you," he said as Lacy shoved him out and slammed the door.

Lacy flung herself into her prized bentwood rocker and stared at the neatly stacked mountain of appliances in the middle of her living room. On top of an unopened Tappan-microwave carton in a beautiful art deco brushed aluminum cage El Magnifico, the cockatoo, tilted an eye at her quizzically and cried, "Awrk?" in a plaintive voice. Squeezed under the table in the dining alcove where he was hiding, Sicky-Poo alternately moaned and slathered disconsolately. Lacy put her head in her hands and moaned, too.

This time you've done it, her inner voice chided her. Zany and irrepressible, OK, Lacy Kingston. But this time you went too far. You'll never learn when and when not to clown around. Just telling a man you're madly in love with him isn't enough. Dropping his money all over his head was not exactly the most enticing gambit, either. You just proved that.

She couldn't go on doing these stupid things; there was too much at stake. She'd messed up a weekend that should have turned out gloriously. As she reached for the telephone, Lacy took a deep breath. Somewhere there was a friend who knew more about these things than she did. Someone to confide in, someone who would give good advice.

But the voice that answered Jamie Hatworth's home telephone in Brooklyn Heights was not the assistant editor's. A man was shouting over the racket of Sunday-afternoon television and children's loud voices.

"Mike?" Lacy said, uncertainly. She wasn't having any luck at all. Of all times to pick. Jamie Hatworth had Mike, the layout artist at her house. "This is Lacy Kingston. What are you doing there?" she blurted before she could stop herself.

"Hey, Lacy, honey," the layout artist's voice greeted her, "how's the most beautiful blond in New York?"

And why not Mike? Lacy thought with a sinking feeling. Even Jamie, with all her problems, her unruly kids and her impossible job, had a love life. Everybody did. Except ex-models who were now Echevarria, Inc., employees in love with their president. Tall, willowy smoky-blonds with emerald eyes who picked the wrong time to be funny. Who had just won the prize for this year's total bomb in the romance department.

"Hi, angel," the brisk voice of the assistant editor came over the wire. "Good heavens, Lacy, what are all the waterworks about? Is that you I hear crying? Is anything wrong?"

"No," Lacy said, squaring her shoulders bravely. "I'm just watching a sad movie on TV." She was not about to ruin Jamie's Sunday afternoon with her lover, even if it was only Mike from the magazine art department. As Sicky-Poo began to howl broken-heartedly from his hide-out under the dinette table and El Magnifico added his sympathetic squawks, she wept, "Actually I was just calling to see if your kids would like to have a really fantastic sulphur-crested cockatoo I picked up in Connecticut this weekend."

But the worst was yet to come.

On Monday, Lacy drew nothing but bad assignments, including a tedious article on the proposed standardization of women's suit and dress sizes and spent most of the day in the library of the New York Dress Institute doing research. The only good thing about the standard-dress-size story was that it kept her away from her assistant-editor training sessions and the probing if sympathetic questions of Jamie Hatworth. But at six-thirty that evening the packages began arriving by United Parcel Service, which, Lacy found, ripping the first open, contained the coutu-rier-made gown in which she'd dined at Lutece, her matching underwear and the green silk shoes.

"This is a nice apartment you have here," the UPS delivery man said as Lacy signed for the box. He gave her last year's Liz Claiborne pant suit a particularly appreciative look. "You ever have a friend over for a drink now and then?"

"Go away," Lacy cried, kicking him out, too.

On Tuesday evening the red velvet Renaissance evening costume arrived, but the UPS delivery man prudently left the box resting outside her apartment door after getting the super to sign for it. On Wednesday, though, the Revillon Freres full-length sable coat in a size 8, with Lacy's name embroidered on its satin lining, arrived by the fur salon's special messenger, who apologized for the delay on the order placed last week, which was due to necessary alterations. Lacy burst into tears.

Michael Echevarria was dumping her, she realized, sitting down on her living-room couch with the sumptuous soft folds of the sable fur in her lap and wetting its beautifully crafted lapels with her tears. He was sending everything back to her except, apparently, the fabulous jewelry. He was closing out his account, dispersing the inventory, clearing the books! In spite of the fact that her misery was so deep that she could hardly face a day's work on *Fad* magazine anymore, Lacy knew there was only one way that she could respond and salvage her dignity and what was left of her pride.

On her way to work each day she mailed everything back to him from the post office: the delicate green chiffon gown with matching underwear and shoes, the dramatic red velvet costume and accessories, then the fabulous Revillon Freres sable still in its original gold-embossed box.

But so much weeping, both sorrowful and angry, had taken its toll. Thursday morning Lacy wore dark glasses to work to cover her noticeably red and swollen eyes, even though it made it difficult to see the computer terminal on her desk to try to write. She wasn't surprised to find managing editor Gloria Farnham standing at the door of her office just before lunch time, regarding her with an unusually thoughtful expression.

"There's an awful lot of space in here for just one person," the managing editor said, "don't you think, Stacy? And now that it's almost winter, the air conditioning doesn't get used much, does it?" She extracted a clipping from the slash pockets of the Dior jacket she was wearing and looked around vaguely before putting it on Lacy's desk. "Here, sweetie," she said, "I was just reading this morning's *WWD*, and I thought you'd like to have this."

Lacy waited until the managing editor had floated back out to the editorial room before she picked up the *Women's Wear Daily* clipping to read it. After she'd read it, she wished she hadn't.

"The on-again, off-again romance," the bible of the rag trade reported, "between Michael Echevarria, New York's most eligible millionaire and chairman of the board of venerable *Fad* magazine's conglomerate owners, and Dulcie Ford-Manning, socialite designer, is *on* again. Dulcie, whose firm, Ford-Manning Associates, did Michael's Sutton Place condominium for New York's Design Showcase in 1983, will once again put her talents to work with a new contract for the décor of his new home in North Wilton, Connecticut. The happy couple were seen tête-à-tête at Dulcie's cousin Trish Vanderbilt's Tavern on the Green fund-raiser Monday night for local Republican candidates."

Lacy crumpled the clipping and went into the employees' lounge to burst into tears again, not caring who saw her among the women staffers gathered there to eat their brown-bag lunches.

Now she knew, Lacy told herself, flushing the toilet loudly to drown out the sound of her furious sobbing, who was responsible for the Sutton Place-contemporary horror that made Michael Echevarria's condo the absolute pits. She wouldn't have believed it possible to feel the knifelike pain of betrayal over the *WWD*'s "off-again, on-again" description of his romance with the interior decorator. So there had been other women! Women before, during and after he'd met her, she was positive. It put their whole relationship on such a shabby, demeaning level Lacy could hardly stand it.

When she finally wept herself dry and came out of the editorial department's women's lounge, putting her dark glasses back on, she could barely make out the figure of managing editor Gloria Farnham waiting for her.

"Oh, there you are, Stacy Kingsley," the managing editor said, looking over Lacy's head to a spot far away in the publicity department. "Just take a quick lunch break, will you? We're moving your things out of the office until we can find you a spot over in graphics with the rest of the junior fashion writers."

Lacy couldn't speak, her tears surging up again. She didn't take a lunch break; instead, she took the elevator to the lobby of the Fad Publishing Group building and used a pay telephone there to call the New York executive offices of Echevarria Enterprises, Inc.

"May I ask who's calling, please?" the secretary in the office of the chairman of the board said.

"It's Lacy Kingston," she replied, trying to keep her tearful voice steady.

But the cool, crisp voice on the other end of the line said, "Mr. Echevarria is in a meeting right now. If you'll leave your name and telephone number, I'll see if he can get back to you."

There it was, Lacy thought. It had finally happened. He wasn't taking her calls. He—they—were through. Somehow, even though Michael had returned the fabulous gowns to her, even had the magnificent sable coat forwarded because it had already been altered, even though there was a deep, profound silence that indicated there'd be no more Friday night dates, she really didn't think he would reach into the levels of one of his newer acquisitions, *Fad* magazine, to take her desk away from her!

"How long will he be in the meeting?" Lacy persisted, resting her forehead against the cool marble wall of the lobby as she clasped the telephone receiver.

"Forever," the cool voice said crisply, and hung up.

Lacy stared at the telephone, which had just switched to a soothing humming tone in her grip. He wasn't taking her calls. He was seeing another woman. He'd gone from that disastrous scene in his bedroom in his country house in Connecticut Sunday morning to dating an old flame society decorator on Monday night in a fast switch that was unbelievable! His insensitive ruthlessness was incredible.

And you said you loved this monster? Lacy's inner voice jeered.

Not any more, she told herself, dashing away the last of her tears with the back of her hand. She lifted her head and stared across the lobby of the Fad Publishing Building, biting her lips. A firm, proud resolve was finally replacing the soggy despair of the past few days. Lacy picked up her purse from the ledge under the public telephone. This whole thing had gone beyond the bounds of anything personal. Now it was a matter of principle.

If her father had taught her anything, Lacy reminded herself, it was when to know you needed a lawyer. She opened her purse with a snap and rummaged around in it, looking for the business card Mr. Irving Fishman, of Fishman Brothers Frocks and Superior Sportswear had saved for her.

Less than a half an hour later Lacy was sitting at her corner of the utility table used by the junior fashion writers in the narrow elbow at the back of the art department, with all her things from her former office piled around her untidily, trying to finish her New York Dress Institute story on standardized sizes for women's dresses and suits but not able to see what she was writing very well through her dark glasses and her even more swollen and irritated eyelids, when she received a telephone call from the executive secretary in the *Fad* publisher's office asking her to report at once to the nineteenth floor. The president and chairman of the board of Echevarria Enterprises, Mr. Michael Echevarria was there, and he wished to talk to Miss Kingston.

"No," Lacy told the *Fad* publisher's secretary, and hung up.

She took her notes on U.S. Public Health Department statistics on average bust and hip measurements of women aged twenty-five to forty-five from her desk, crumpled them up and started gathering the paper shopping bags of her possessions together. The blow was going to fall, she thought stoically, but she was holding her pain and humiliation under control. She wasn't going up to the executive offices on the nineteenth floor to have the president and chairman of the board turn the knife in the wound one more time before he finally fired her. She had already planned to report back to the Leonard Thornton Model Agency in the morning, to see if the Western States Wholesalers had gotten their runway models lined up for their usual spring tour. She could take care of herself. She only asked one thing from life. That she never see Michael Echevarria again.

Lacy was just cramming her desk calendar with digital clock back into the paper bag Gloria Farnham had so thoughtfully provided, along with a half-eaten package of peanut-butter crackers that had been her lunch, when she heard the flurry among the desks nearest the elevators. Out of the corner of her eye, Lacy saw a tall figure in a gray worsted three-piece Cardin business suit striding toward her.

"No," Lacy cried, scrambling to get her purse, her tape recorder, the digital calendar and clock and the U.S. Health Department volume on physiological measurements by states into her arms. "Beat it!" she yelled as the lithe, powerful frame of Michael Echevarria loomed over her.

"Lacy," he said in a low, strained voice, "you called me, and my secretary just gave me the message about an hour ago. I want to talk to you. Why didn't you come upstairs?"

She tried not to look at Michael but found she couldn't help herself. He was still, she thought moodily, so devastatingly handsome, so outwardly marvelous, with his black curls tamed by an expensive barber, cool gray eyes and grimly sensuous mouth, that she had to brace herself to keep from responding. The broad shoulders in the conservative tailored business suit were lightly sprinkled with rain, as though he had left his office in a hurry without a topcoat and had taken a New York City taxicab, not the Rolls Royce. He always looked so young and appealingly handsome, she thought, dragging her eyes away, to be so ruthless and powerful and rich.

The entire floor of the *Fad* editorial department was trying to pretend that nothing was going on. That the president and chairman of the board of their conglomerate owners was not standing in the art department carrying on a conversation with Lacy Kingston, the new junior fashion writer—and verifying all the hot rumors that had been circulating for weeks. Ever since, in fact, Miss Kingston had fallen on her bottom in the employees' auditorium at her first sight of him. Managing editor Gloria Farnham was hovering at the door of her office, vainly trying to hear what was said.

"Go away," Lacy mumbled. She opened her purse and tried to pry the desk calendar and digital clock into it. "Drop dead. Don't come back. I'm not destroying *Fad* magazine with my body anymore— I'm leaving."

"I can't talk to you here," the chairman of the board said hurriedly, glancing around. "Hell, what are you doing back here in this trash heap? Why aren't you in your office?"

She stood at the utility table and drew herself up to her full five feet nine inches, which was almost tall enough to look him straight in his rigidly clenched jaw.

"You can't fire me," Lacy cried, sweeping off her dark glasses to face him proudly. "I quit! Got it right, Mr. Chairman? I quit! Quit!"

"My God," he groaned, seeing her face. He stepped toward her quickly.

"Lacy, what have you done? You've been crying," he said in a harsh voice. "You've been crying, haven't you?"

"Did you hear me?" she cried. "I quit! I quit!"

"Don't yell," he said quickly. "I have to talk to you, Lacy." He took her hand and tried to press something into it. "I want to give you this. The jewelry is in a safe-deposit box in your name."

"Yaaagh," Lacy cried, throwing the key to the safe-deposit box back at him. "Can't you give up? You know all these people are watching! It really turns you on, doesn't it, to make me look like—?"

"You can't keep the necklaces in your West Side place," he said, picking the key up from the floor, "because the insurance won't cov—"

"Money, that's all you think about!" Lacy swung her purse and hit him on the side of his head just as he straightened up. He winced as the digital clock fell out and grazed his shoulder. "Keep your junk, Michael Echevarria. I sent everything back to you in the mail! Can you get this through your head for once," Lacy yelled, "that everything I did was for *free*!"

There was a concerted gasp from the *Fad* editorial employees gathered at a distance around them. The back fringe was already scattering as managing editor Gloria Farnham ran to her office to pick up the telephone.

"Lacy," Michael said, catching her by the arm, "stop it. It isn't just the jewelry. That's not why I'm here. I want to—"

"Get your hands off me," Lacy shrilled. They were chest to chest, arm to arm, glaring at each other. "Let me go, you're—*harassing* me!"

Through the fabric of her lavender sweater and skirt, Lacy could feel the heat of his big, virile body, and she tried to stiffen against its familiar pull. He looked at her with a strangely vulnerable, tormented expression. Lacy's green eyes widened. Oh, no, it looked as though in another minute he would sweep her into those powerful arms and kiss her!

"Sexual harassment," Lacy breathed, remembering what Alex van Renssalaer had just told her during her lunch-time telephone call. "Sexual harassment on the job," she repeated, her voice gaining power. "Let go of me, you lecher!"

A squad of uniformed building security guards hurtled toward them out of the elevators, stumbling through the aisles of makeup and copy editing.

"Mr. Echevarria," the uniformed guard out in front shouted, "are you all right?"

"I'm being sexually harassed," Lacy was yelling, burning all her bridges behind her. "Help! Help! Call the feds! I'm being sexually harassed on the job!"

The last game plan of them all had just begun.

19

The late-autumn sunshine attractively illuminated the Palladian-style splendor of the dining room at the Yale Club, on Vanderbilt Avenue, and the large, prosperous crowd of New York alumni, mostly attired in charcoal worsted business suits and Bergdorf Goodman tweeds with only a token sprinkling of 1960s-style corduroys and plaid shirts. Alexander van Renssalaer had reserved a window table that offered a magnificent view of the sooty domes of Grand Central Station and the distant traffic on Forty-second Street. The Yale Club's headwaiter, Frank, pulled out Lacy's chair with an expression of approval as she smoothed the skirt of her subdued all-black velveteen suit, then gracefully lowered herself into her seat.

"I can't tell you how happy you've made me, my dear, coming to me with this problem you've had with

the head of a very suspect outfit like Echevarria
Enterprises, Incorporated,'' Alex van Renssalaer
said. He took advantage of the arrival of their white-
wine spritzers to cover Lacy's hand warmly with his
own. The New York lawyer's attractive, well-bred
features held an expression that would have been
vengeful smugness on anyone less patrician. "It's
about time somebody rang the bell on this parvenu
ape from Belmont race track and the Brooklyn docks.
Believe me, my dear Lacy, you're carrying the standard for right and justice, challenging him like this, not
to mention just plain old-fashioned good taste!''

Lacy tried to pull her fingers out from under his
firm clasp as tactfully as she could. Alex was being
terribly sympathetic and supportive; she supposed she
owed him a big debt of gratitude for pointing out that
Michael Echevarria had violated some very important
federal statutes by insisting she date him every Friday
night or else he'd fire her. As Lacy gazed at the
lawyer's rather long, aristocratic features, though,
she couldn't help being attacked by another miserable
wave of uncertainty.

She'd had two whole days to think over her moment of confrontation with the president and chairman of the board of *Fad* and second thoughts, Lacy
was finding out, were not always the happiest. She
was not the sort of person who wanted to cause
anyone serious trouble. That is, not the kind with a
possible jail sentence attached to it. Even if, for-
tunately, she was no longer in love with Michael
Echevarria.

To add to her unhappiness, she really missed being
at work. Did anybody at *Fad* miss *her*? Was anybody

writing her story on standardized women's and misses dress sizes? In the morning, when the staff gathered for coffee and Danish, did any of them even mention her name? And get it right—Lacy Kingston, not Stacy Kingsley—for a change?''

"You sweet girl," Alex van Renssalaer was murmuring, "when you get that expression on your lovely face, it breaks my heart." Under the table his feet pressed consolingly against Lacy's. "You've been through a lot, haven't you? You've conducted yourself with a great deal of courage and sensitivity in this sorry affair—ah, *matter*.

"A lot of women are going to thank you for your stand, Lacy," he assured her with a consoling smile. "This untutored clown Echevarria is utterly ruthless where the fair sex is concerned. Furthermore, his manners are abominable. Last year's debutante committee was in an uproar when that clod failed to respond to invitations from half of New York's finest families. He had to go inspect an oil field somewhere, that was his excuse. But we've got him this time, thanks to you." The handsome lawyer picked up a pumpernickel roll, divided it into precise small pieces and began buttering them rather vindictively. "I've been waiting for years to nail this arrogant horse boy, and now I'm going to do it."

"Good grief," Lacy cried, dismayed. It was worse than she thought. "Don't tell me Michael's had this trouble before—harassing women, I mean?"

The lawyer gave her an abstracted look. "Mmmh? Oh, yes, there have been plenty of women—you've only to look at the brute to know they throw themselves at him disgustingly. He lives up to his uncouth reputation with women the same way he does business —moves in like a pirate, trims up liquid assets, axes personnel with the zeal of an executioner.''

He reached for a baking-powder biscuit. "But then these people he's terminated have to report to the unemployment office for their dole at the taxpayer's expense. As a taxpayer and a Republican, I deplore federal handouts—they're a disgrace to our national work ethic." When Lacy moaned softly, he seemed not to hear. "Normally, my dear, we'd go to the Equal Opportunity Commission with your complaint and take this vulgarian straight to the wall, but we've got bigger fish to fry. We don't want a blundering federal bureaucracy to tie up a plum like this in the courts for months, years, with embarrassing investigations, depositions, countercharges and appeals.

"No," Alex van Renssalaer smiled at her, "we need swift justice now. That is to say, we're talking punitive damages."

"We are?" Lacy said, feeling more miserable by the moment.

The handsome lawyer hesitated. "I understand the cad even had you watched by a private detective," he said delicately.

Lacy stared down at the chicken salad Hawaiian the Yale Club waiter had just set before her. She'd almost forgotten about Walter Moretti. She hadn't seen him at all in the past week, and then only because she'd baby-sat Sicky-Poo so the detective could take Candy out to a Greenwich Village art theater rerun of *The Sound of Music*. She wondered if Walter was unemployed. From the way he was hanging around Candy, she got the impression the

Italian private eye had plenty of time on his hands these days. That, too, was her fault, she supposed.

"I have to tell you," Alex van Renssalaer was saying, "I've had several long telephone consultations with Jack McLanahan, the Echevarria corporate counsel. They're claiming, Lacy, dear, that there've been some, ah, expensive gifts which would put a different light on this alleged affair.

"Which is nonsense, of course," he said quickly. "The federal guidelines are clear. The crux of the matter is that he threatened to fire you if you didn't see him. Any claim of, er, remuneration doesn't enter into it."

Inwardly, Lacy shuddered. What she'd told Alex van Renssalaer had been simple enough: that the president and chairman of the board of *Fad*'s conglomerate had told her either she would have Friday night dates with him, or he'd fire her. And when she made the mistake of telling him that she thought she was in love with him, he'd dropped her and started going out with an interior decorator. Then her boss, the managing editor, took away her desk and moved her out of her office. Then she quit. Lacy decided she didn't need to add any further details.

"Well, as a matter of fact," she said, not able to meet the lawyer's eyes, "I did get ten blenders, eight microwave ovens, a full-length Russian sable coat from Revillon Freres, a sulphur-crested cockatoo—"

"A *what*?" he exclaimed. "Good lord, stuffed or alive?"

"Oh, alive," Lacy assured him sadly. "He was very sweet for a cockatoo, but I had to give him to my assistant editor's kids.

"My *former* assistant editor's kids," she added.

"You're not serious," Alex said, staring at her. "Surely you can't mean that you accepted gifts from this . . . hood!"

"Well, yes, but I gave everything back to him as fast as he could give it to me. He just wouldn't stop! You see," Lacy said with mounting desperation," "that was the whole point. I thought I loved him, and all he wanted to do was treat me like his sleazy—" She couldn't bring herself to say the word. "Well, anyway, it was very demeaning and exploitative!"

Now she tortured herself wondering if she wouldn't have been better off just loving Michael and leaving things the way they were. Was she ever going to be happy again, charging Michael Echevarria with what was, after all, a federal crime, as Alex had so helpfully pointed out? Shouldn't she have explored, just for a few weeks anyway, a life of humiliating decadence as his East Side mistress—if that was all he was ever going to offer?

Just the thought of how he made love, and how it was never going to happen again, brought tears to Lacy's eyes as she picked the pineapple chunks and macadamia nuts out of her chicken salad and laid them carefully on her bread and butter plate.

"My second cousin, Dulcie Ford-Manning," Alex van Renssalaer said rather stiffly, "has been pursuing Echevarria for two years, poor girl. All that tight-fisted orangutan ever gave her was a book on kitchen design from Hammacher Schlemmer last Christmas.

"Don't despair, dear heart," he added with grim relish, "this Wall Street stable hand has met his match. He'll find out what it's like to deal with a better class of people who know their rights."

"I don't know that we're a better class of people if we're going to do anything horrible to him," Lacy muttered, appalled to learn that the interior decorator who'd been dating Michael was related to Alex van Renssalaer. She lifted a lettuce leaf hungrily to see if there was any chicken under it or just more chunks of pineapple. "We certainly don't want to descend to Michael Echevarria's level and be horrible and ruthless ourselves, do we?"

"My sweet, beautiful plaintiff," Alex said with sudden, surprising emotion, "don't worry your beautiful head about it." He captured her hand, extracted her salad fork from it and dragged it across the lunch table so that he could kiss her fingers ardently. "The resources of my considerable law practice are at your disposal. Surely you know I have more than a professional interest in your case?"

"Please don't," Lacy told him. She looked around the dining room, embarrassed. Of all the things to have happen, Alexander van Renssalaer, one of New York's most outstanding young lawyers and scion of one of the city's oldest and most prestigious families, was kissing her hand for everyone to see.

"Echevarria has requested a meeting tomorrow in his office," the lawyer murmured, maintaining a tenuous grasp on Lacy's thumb. "I told their corporate counsel I'd have to consult with you.

"But darling," he said with barely suppressed eagerness, "Echevarria is going to make the only move he can under the circumstances. He's going to settle out of court. To put it in the vernacular, the bastard is going to pay through the nose."

As the waiter arrived with their hot apple pie à la mode, Lacy finally wrenched her hand away from the lawyer's fervent clutch. "But, Alex, we can't ask Michael Echevarria for money," she protested. "That's just playing right into his hands! Good grief, that's *his* way of settling everything! Now he'll think we're as ruthless and money crazy as he is."

"Lacy, dear," Alex van Renssalaer said as he wiped a smear of vanilla ice cream from his sleeve, "trust me in these matters, will you?"

"I don't know," Lacy moaned. "I'm having severe second thoughts. I never knew what you told me to say, that Michael was breaking the law with all those Friday-night dates, was going to lead to all this." She shuddered. "Settlements. Money. Meetings. Federal court. The penitentiary!"

"Lacy, I'm going to make you a *rich woman*, please try to understand." Alex showed his handsome white teeth in a happy smile. "Good God, you'll be eminently marriageable, don't you see? Didn't you say your father was a lawyer, too? Why, there isn't a fine old family in the country that wouldn't fall all over itself to have you, beautiful as you are, and with, say, four or five million in your bank account."

"Well, actually," Lacy murmured, "I haven't had all that many problems getting proposals, Alex. Last year—"

But he went on quickly. "Perhaps this isn't the moment to broach the subject, but surely you have some small conception now of the way I feel about you." He reached for her hand. "Darling Lacy," he said rather hoarsely, "I want you to meet my mother. The trip to our family estate at Rynderkill-on-the-Hudson is very pleasant, and I know you'll adore her. We could drive up just as soon as we know the ballpark figure Echevarria is going to settle for."

"I'm sorry, what did you say?" Lacy asked, because she hadn't been paying attention.

"I said, beautiful child," Alexander van Renssalaer smiled at her a trifle indulgently, "I want to take you home to the family estate at Rynderkill-on-the-Hudson to meet my mother. Don't you know what that means?"

"She likes company?" Lacy said blankly.

He sighed. "Of course she likes company. Dear heart, a trip to see Mommy means I'd like her to consider you as her future daughter-in-law. I'm sure you'll get her stamp of approval." His eyes kindled appreciatively. "You're so beautiful, my love—all the van Renssalaer men have married exceptionally tall, fine-boned blond women. It's rather a family tradition. Your unique, giddy charm will delight her."

Giddy charm? Lacy stared at him. Was that how he saw her?

Then she thought: One of New York City's most successful lawyers was proposing to her in the middle of the Yale Club.

Well, at least *somebody* wanted to marry her. And any woman in her right mind would be ecstatically happy to have a marriage proposal from Alexander van Renssalaer—would, in fact, jump at the chance to say yes. She would certainly like to see the look on Michael Echevarria's face when she showed up in his executive offices and casually let him know that she was engaged to his archrival, the prominent New York attorney who hated him almost as much as she did! For a moment it almost took her breath away. It was certainly neater, better than any threat to take Michael into federal court.

"You mean, marry you?" Lacy said breathlessly, wanting to be sure.

Alex van Renssalaer beamed at her. "Of course."

Going down in the Yale Club elevator, Lacy allowed the tall lawyer with his short-cropped reddish hair and intense, handsome features to draw her into his arms and place his mouth over hers. Unfortunately the kiss was a strange experience.

For the few moments that Alex van Renssalaer's lips were pressed against Lacy's, it was as though she had a total out-of-body experience. As though she floated, in fact, somewhere at the top of the Yale Club, above the swimming pool and gym, like a disembodied spirit, pleasantly viewing what was going on, but aloof from it all. When Alex van Renssalaer kissed her, there were no spirals, no stars, not the faintest echo of anything that remotely resembled an electrically charged *zap*! *bam*! or *powie*!

But that, she supposed, disconsolately, was a once-in-a-lifetime experience that was doomed not to repeat itself.

"Well, we could try it," Lacy said resignedly.

"Darling, we'll go to Tiffany's tomorrow and pick out a ring," he told her, giving her a hug. "After we find out, approximately, what Echevarria's going to fork over."

Later that evening Lacy received a telephone call from her father out in East Hampton, Long Island.

"Lacy," her father said in the stern tone of voice he used when addressing juries or his three headstrong, beautiful daughters, "what the hell's going on down there in New York?"

"Oh, Daddy," Lacy said, thinking fast, but filled with subliminal dread, "what do you mean, what's going on down here?" Lacy gulped, knowing her father had almost a sixth sense about trouble learned the hard way. "Everything's just fine, Daddy—I'm just between jobs again, that's all.

"Why," she said with false gaiety, "do you want to know?"

"I got a telephone call this afternoon," her father went on ominously, "from some corporate counsel who says he works for Echevarria Enterprises, Incorporated, your employers. And that you're bringing some pretty nasty federal charges against them."

"Urk," Lacy moaned, sliding down on the kitchen stool and bracing herself for what she knew was coming.

"What they're asking me to do," her father's stern lawyer voice continued, "is come into the city tomorrow for a meeting with the president and chairman of the board called—I have the name somewhere here on my desk—"

"Echevarria," Lacy moaned again. "It's a Basque name. But his mother was Irish."

"Yes, that's the one. They say you're charging somebody in their organization with sexual harassment on the job. Lacy, are you listening to me?" G. Frederick Kingston's voice boomed from the easternmost reaches of Long Island. "Do you remember how much money it cost both of us to get things straightened out with that damned photographer a few years ago?"

Lacy sank down on the kitchen stool and clutched the telephone receiver in a suddenly sweaty hand. She was being framed! Michael Echevarria was reaching out not only to her but to her *family* in a predictably ruthless maneuver! She might know he wouldn't stand still for what she was doing, getting a famous lawyer like Alex van Renssalaer, someone he hated, to represent her. Now he was striking her vulnerable areas, bringing her father into this. Michael knew that all he had to do was mention one word—*Tulsa*—and it would take years for Lacy to get it straightened out with her family.

Fight it, her inner voice told her. You're not a coward, Lacy Kingston. If Michael Echevarria wants to make this another lesson in humiliation because he can't force you to accept his sleazy proposition, all that's left to do is stand up and fight.

"First of all, Daddy," she began indignantly, "this is a setup. And I'm not going to let Michael Echevarria do this to me.

"And second of all," Lacy said, taking a deep breath, "I'm going to be an entirely different person from now on. I can't explain it right now, but I *am*. I'm probably never going back into modeling, and I certainly am giving up being a fashion writer. It didn't work out at all.

"Finally," she rushed on, "I'm engaged to a very wonderful man from one of New York's finest families. He's a lawyer by the name of Alexander van Renssalaer, and if you'll give me about fifteen minutes I can explain all this, believe me."

It wasn't fifteen minutes but an hour and a half later when Lacy finally hung up the telephone and ended her conversation with her father. She was still fuming as she dug into her closet looking for something to wear at the meeting with Michael Echevarria, his lawyer, Alexander van Renssalaer and her father, who was coming in from East Hampton at noon the following day.

She hadn't been kidding when she'd told her father she was going to change her life completely. A new Lacy Kingston, eventually to be Lacy van Rennssalaer, would appear at the executive offices of Echevarria Enterprises, Inc. As promised. When her doorbell rang, Lacy greeted Candy O'Neill with grim determination.

The tall, redheaded model was in old jeans and a Nautilus sweat shirt and wore her hair up in pink foam-rubber curlers, since she was meeting Walter Moretti for a date later that evening. But Candy's face was full of concern.

"Gee, Lacy," her friend told her, "are you sure you want to do this? I mean, practically *nobody* changes her image until she's over thirty. And has to go into something like fashion consulting because she can't get modeling jobs anymore. Don't you remember what hap—"

"Never mind," Lacy said, grabbing her friend by the wrist and dragging her inside. "I'm having a whole lifestyle crisis, and I need help."

"Are you sure you want to do this?" Candy said doubtfully. She handed her a Halston dress on a hanger that was of the softest French-silk gauze in taupe and gold tones, with a high neck, long tight sleeves that ended in demure roll-back cuffs and a full skirt of midcalf length. "Gosh, Lacy, I haven't worn this since I did the Tupperware Easter ad for *House and Garden* and they let me have it at cost because the account executive said it reminded him of Eleanor Roosevelt."

"It's perfect," Lacy assured her. "Just let me try it on and see how it looks."

"Oh, I don't know, honey," the model said, following her into the bedroom. "This might not be a good idea. You were always the queen of all that sexy pizazz and you know, glamourous, giddy—"

"Don't say 'giddy,'" Lacy cried. "Really, Candy."

"Well, zany, then," Candy said quickly, "and that great, mind-blowing sparkle. Like the Virginia Slims ad that never—"

"Don't remind me of my wasted life," Lacy groaned. "That's exactly what I'm talking about. I've got to change my image, grow more—severely mature."

She went on bravely: "Michael Echevarria has really taught me about ruthlessness and power moves. Tomorrow when I go to that meeting in his office, I'm aiming for something totally, fantastically regal, serious and unapproachable. Like dignity and conservative sockaroo. Like—like the front cover of the *Ladies' Home Journal*."

"Oh, wow," her friend said. She opened her makeup box. "What are we going for—the old Grace Kelly look? Meryl Streep? Linda Evans?"

Lacy opened her model's makeup box, too. "The best of all of them," she said glumly. "I'm going to win this time. I'm out to blow Michael Echevarria's mind."

20

When Lacy stepped into the glass-enclosed Manhattan tower offices of the president and chairman of the board of Echevarria Enterprises, Inc., shock waves swept through the room.

If an admiring pause in the conversation, Lacy knew from her years of runway modeling, meant that she was looking her loveliest, then this stunned silence certainly indicated that on a scale from 1 to 10, she'd probably scored about a 20. The Lacy Kingston New Image transformation she and Candy O'Neill had worked over for long hours the night before was an eye-popping success, to judge from the faces turned to her. Including, Lacy saw, her own father. For a moment, G. Frederick Kingston failed to recognize his beloved youngest daughter. Then, unaccountably, he smiled.

A glistening coronet of braided fake hair that perfectly matched her own smoky-silver tresses rode the crown of Lacy's elegant head, supporting an enchanting Princess of Wales cap of alternate twists of gold and brown faille, complete with a daring little nose veil, behind which her emerald eyes gleamed aloofly. Candy O'Neill's Halston dress in tones of taupe-brown and palest gold silk chiffon swathed Lacy's regally slender figure. An ever-drifting full skirt swirled around her long legs, and on her feet were a borrowed pair of Andrea Pfister classic pumps in the same taupe-brown shade of polished kid. Lacy's face wore an expression that was serenely imperial, as though she were listening to heralds announcing her arrival to examine the credentials of not terribly presentable foreign ambassadors.

The imperial serenity faltered a little when Lacy entered. She could see her gray-haired, distinguished lawyer father had apparently been having an absorbing, if not actually downright friendly conversation with the president and chairman of the board and a small man in the familiar wolfish black clothes of the conglomerate who was evidently the corporation lawyer.

"Daddy," Lacy cried, temporarily dropping her imperial detachment, "what are you doing in here? You were supposed to meet us outside!"

"Hello, puss," G. Frederick Kingston said, giving his daughter an affectionate peck on the cheek. "I thought I'd come early and look over, um, statements Michael's already made concerning the charges."

Michael? Lacy was unpleasantly surprised. What had they been talking about? Alex van Renssalaer shifted his briefcase to his left hand to shake hands with her father and the corporation's attorney. She had wanted her father and her fiancé by her side as sort of troops surrounding her. Not consorting with the enemy.

As for the enemy, Lacy could hardly ignore him.

Michael Echevarria, she saw with a very unmonarchial pounding of her heart, was on his feet behind an ebony desk the size of an Olympic hockey field, wrapped sleekly in an all-black business suit with pale-gray button-down shirt and dark-gray silk tie. His hard, good-looking face seemed more than usually taut; his silver eyes glittered. Were those fine lines of strain around his narrowed eyelids? The president and chairman of the board of one of the country's largest and most powerful conglomerates held a cigar clamped in his strong white teeth so tightly it angled ceilingward. It *was* strain, Lacy decided, with a shiver.

It had to come sometime—she had to meet that bone-chilling glare; she couldn't put it off, since they were both in the same room. But as Lacy steeled herself for the inevitable eye contact, she was considerably disappointed to find that Michael Echevarria's attention was fixed on Alex van Renssalaer.

"Get that society shyster out of here," Michael Echevarria barked, glowering at the New York lawyer. "He's not representing anybody here. Get him out!"

The forceful words jolted them all. Even the Echevarria corporate lawyer rather nervously began to rearrange stacks of Xeroxed papers he had laid out on a side table.

"Daddy, I need to tell you something," Lacy said urgently to her father. She had expected a calm, intense group around a conference table, with high-level negotations bouncing from one legal brain to another like a ball of lightning. Not Michael Echevarria snarling orders to throw out Alex van Renssalaer from behind a desk that looked like an anti-tank barrier. "Could you just stand here," Lacy hissed, "with Alex on my other side? For goodness' sake, can we look united and—*dignified*?"

"I am representing Miss Kingston jointly with her father," Alex van Renssalaer responded. "Sir," he said, turning to G. Frederick Kingston, "I'd like to suggest a conference with you before we go any further, regarding the vile and untoward events which have taken place as a result of this man's actions toward his employee, your daughter."

"Vile and untoward, hell," the chairman of the board snarled. He stubbed out his cheroot violently in a large silver ashtray. "This clown van Renssalaer isn't representing anybody except the outfit he takes money from, Ransom Tri-Star Technologies! I want him out of here!"

Why wouldn't he look at her? Lacy wondered. Her expression of queenly reserve was fading fast. The New Lacy Kingston was getting lost in the opening salvos of this *macho* blitz.

"Daddy," Lacy murmured, lifting the delicate little Princess of Wales nose veil between thumb and forefinger in order to see, "what's Tri-Star Technologies? Can we—?"

"You're going to get creamed, Echevarria," Alexander van Renssalaer was saying with a coldly aristocratic smile. "It's a federal rap this time. You've taken advantage of a sweet, lovely girl. What we're talking is an out-of-court settlement. Before you get in any deeper.''

"Regarding these allegations and others,'' the corporation's lawyer said quickly, holding the Xeroxed copies he'd gathered up from the table, "perhaps it would serve to clarify matters if the parties present referred to this statement by Mr. Echevarria as to what was actually involved in his relationship with Miss Kingston.''

"Christ, I'm going to have to do this myself,'' the chairman of the board exploded, coming around the edge of his mammoth desk.

"No, you don't,'' Lacy cried, stepping in front of Alex, who was skimming the Xerox copies the corporation's lawyer had just handed him. "He is representing me—you have nothing to do with it! Mr. van Renssalaer is a very prominent and successful lawyer from a fine old New York family.''

But the man behind her said, "We don't want to give the impression we won't listen to an offer, Echevarria. Isn't that right, Mr. Kingston?''

"I'll pass on that right now,'' Lacy's lawyer father murmured, "if you don't mind.''

"Let's get down to it,'' Alex van Renssalaer went on as he hastily scanned the Xeroxes. "You're hanging on the wall, Echevarria. What's the opening figure?''

"He's a damned gofer for Ches Ransom of Tri-Star, and he's after my ass, not settlements,'' Michael Echevarria growled, peeling off his suit jacket and displaying powerful shoulder muscles rippling under the gray Cardin shirt. "I want him out of here!''

"Honey,'' G. Frederick Kingston said pleasantly,

"I think you're in the line of fire. Why don't you step over here beside me?"

"What's this about a hotel in Tulsa?" Alex van Renssalaer was muttering as he held his bundle of pages up to the light.

"I think the idea of holding a fact-finding conference at this time," G. Frederick Kingston said, trying to move his daughter out of harm's way, "might not be a bad idea."

"Not under dispute," the corporation's lawyer was pointing out hurriedly to Alex van Renssalaer, "is the title to the Ferrari XKZ or the key to the safe-deposit box with the jewels which remain in the complainant's name and which are inventoried under 'Appendix A.' My client waives all rights—he very generously wants Miss Kingston to have them."

"I'm a changed person, Michael Echevarria," Lacy cried, giving the skirt of the clinging Halston an impatient twitch. "You're not going to make me lose my temper this time!"

"Get out of the damned way," he said, reaching for her. "I'm going to bash that smirking legal nit if it's the last thing I ever do."

"I can't believe this," the voice of her fiancé was saying behind her. "Fifteen hundred dollars?"

"Don't read that, Alex," Lacy cried. "I told you I gave everything back!"

"You conniving son of a bitch," the black panther rasped, reaching over Lacy's shoulder, "Ches Ransom put you up to this, didn't he?"

"What did I tell you?" Lacy neatly sidestepped Michael Echevarria as he tried to lunge past her. "You see what an unscrupulous rat he is, Daddy?

Just try to tell anybody like *that* you're in love with him!"

"Now, kitten," G. Frederick Kingston said mildly. "Listen to what he's saying. There's a corporate battle going, obviously, between Tri-Star and —"

"Don't you touch him," Lacy cried, drawing herself up proudly as Michael's menacing figure towered over her. "You come one step closer, and I'll kick you in the shins! Alex van Renssalaer is a wonderful man, and he respects me. We're engaged to be married!"

"Also enclosed," the corporation's lawyer was saying, holding another large bundle of Xeroxes under his elbow, "is the waiver of the three-day waiting period for blood tests required by New York State law. Or have I," he murmured, "lost my place?"

"You've lost your place," Michael said with deadly calm as he lifted Lacy's defiant form and pushed her into her father's arms. "He's not going to marry her. *I* am."

Alex van Renssalaer stuffed his Xeroxed copies into his briefcase and began backing away toward the office door.

"Actually," he said as the chairman of the board closed in on him, "I think my effectiveness in any ongoing negotiations here today is fairly well negated by now. I advise plaintiff's counsel to request a review of everything on record, like, tomorrow."

"Marry you?" Lacy whispered, staring at the black panther who was relentlessly tracking the New York lawyer to the door.

"I'll send over my associate, Norman Astor, Mr. Kingston," the New York lawyer said, picking up speed. "He'll cover your daughter's case in my absence."

"Alex, don't leave!" Lacy cried. It was some sort of nightmare! Michael Echevarria had just announced he was going to marry her, and no one seemed to be paying attention. The two people who should have come to her defense were doing nothing. Her father was smiling, and her fiancé was backing hastily toward the exit. "Come back," she yelled at Alex's retreating figure. "Don't listen to him! It's just another corporate maneuver to get me to drop my complaint!"

She saw the powerful figure of the chairman of the board lunge just as Alex yanked open the door.

"Restraining order, Echevarria!" the New York lawyer yelled as he shot out into the secretary's office. "You damned gorilla—I'll serve you with breach of peace if you touch me!"

"Now, honey," her father said consolingly. "Don't cry."

"I'm not crying," Lacy sobbed. She shoved the dainty toque with its nose veil to the back of her head and blew a loose strand of nylon hair out of her face. "He's always like this, Daddy. Michael Echevarria treats me like I'm just another takeover target!"

"You look lovely," the voice of the chairman of the board told her on his way back to his desk.

Lacy stared at him. It was the sort of vindictive maneuver Michael Echevarria would think of. Oh, he'd offered to marry her—but only because she'd forced him into it!

"Yes, here it is," the corporation counsel said, holding up a fresh batch of papers. "Mr. Echevarria offers to marry the plaintiff, contingent on early nuptuals scheduled in Judge Samuel Markowitz's chambers, room five-oh-one, New York City Supreme Court Building, Sixty Center Street, noon tomorrow. Attached you will find copies of the suggested premarital property agreement and the waiver of the three-day waiting period and blood tests.''

"Take some time, baby," her father was saying, "to think it over. Michael has made some counteroffers. You can—"

"Stop calling him Michael," Lacy wailed. "I can't stand it! For goodness' sake, isn't anybody on my side?"

All Lacy could think of was that Michael Echevarria had won again. Back to bashing her human dignity again. Back to exploitative maneuvers! What she really wanted to do, she thought, glaring at him through her tears, was pay Michael Echevarria back for the most humiliating fifteen minutes she'd ever spent in her life. He was inhumanly cruel, offering marriage under these circumstances. She didn't have a shred of self-respect left at all. She wanted to make the president and chairman of the board of Echevarria Enterprises, Inc., as excruciatingly miserable as she could. For as long as she could. She wanted her revenge.

"All right," Lacy said, drawing herself up with all the monarchial dignity she could muster, "deal closed, Daddy. I'll marry him!"

"Now, baby, stop crying," Lacy's father told her as he drove her up the West Side Highway to her apartment. "Nobody said you had to marry him—that was your own decision. And you signed the premarital property settlement—no one forced you to, remember? All I said was I thought you ought to wait and think things over, not rush into anything as precipitous as, well, a ceremony at noon tomorrow. Although frankly, knowing my sweet little girl, I can understand some of Michael's thinking about rush arrangements.''

G. Frederick Kingston smiled down at his daughter in a rather rumpled Halston gown, who was slumped beside him in the front seat, her little hat askew. ''It's not such a bad deal, puss. Considering the property terms Echevarria's offered, I'd marry him myself.''

''Oh, Daddy, please don't try to be funny,'' Lacy moaned, ''you really weren't any help to me, you know. When I walked in, I knew you were all up to something. You've stabbed your own daughter right in the back!''

''Now, Lacy, it wasn't that way at all,'' her father assured her. ''Actually, Michael talked to me for a few minutes before you arrived because he wanted me to know what he was offering. I'll have to confess it's rather flatteringly old-fashioned to be asked for one's daughter's hand in marriage. Not many fathers get that courtesy extended to them these days.''

''He's a rat,'' Lacy groaned. ''I'm betrayed—even my own father sides with him!''

''Now Lacy,'' G. Frederick Kingston said. ''Michael was considerate enough to have prepared personal references to show me as his, ah, prospective father-in-law. He had letters attesting to his good character from two U.S. senators, four foster parents, St. Vincent de Paul's Orphanage, the longshoremen's union of New York and the former director of Belmont race track. He went to a lot of trouble, dear. There are a lot of people out there who like him apparently.''

"Like him? Oh, Daddy, you just don't know Michael Echevarria the way I do," Lacy wept. "He's a snake, totally ruthless, and he's only marrying me to get me out of his hair! You heard what he said to his lawyer when we left, didn't you? About hoping to get a good night's sleep for a change? Oh, that was low, tasteless, dirty!"

"Now, Lacy," her father sighed. "I don't think he meant it in quite that way. Actually, I thought Michael looked a bit on edge. I don't think you realize," he said, sliding his car into a double-park in front of his daughter's apartment building, "you've dealt his company quite a blow. You seem to have put your trust in the wrong person, honey.

"Yes, I know," he said quickly, "this was probably van Renssalaer's idea from the start. But even I could see your, er, ex-fiancé had more than one iron in the fire when he showed up. I don't blame your, er, new fiancé for flying off the handle. These two young bucks have a lot going on between them. If you'll pardon my saying so," G. Frederick Kingston said firmly, "it was obvious to me that your lawyer friend didn't exactly come into the meeting today with clean hands."

Lacy slid down even farther in the seat of her father's Mercury Cougar. "I know I'm not going to convince you, Daddy, but did Michael Echevarria ever say anything about marrying me because he loved me? No! Not even once. I told you what he's been offering all along. It wasn't marriage!"

"Now, sweetheart, you signed a very generous prenuptial agreement that says you'll stay married for six months," her father reminded her. "It allows you to get a divorce after that if you're not satisfied, with the property settlement free and clear. Which includes the sports car, the fur coat and the assessed half-million dollars in jewels. That's very good-hearted of Michael, kitten.''

"He's just forcing all that junk on me," Lacy cried, "because he couldn't get me to take it otherwise. After all, what's he going to do with it? Who wants a forty-thousand-dollar Russian sable with *my* name embroidered on the lining, and a Ferrari with a weird custom-paint job to match *my* hair?

"No, you don't understand," she said, dabbing at her tears with the edge of the little nose veil. "If Alex van Renssalaer hadn't done a quick fade, I would at least have had *one* offer of marriage to fall back on. It's pretty humiliating, Daddy, to have a rat like Michael Echevarria say he'll marry you when a really eligible bachelor like Alex van Renssalaer just slinks out the door.

"But I've learned my lesson," Lacy vowed. "No matter what Michael Echevarria says, what he really wanted was to have me be his tacky mistress in a fancy East Side apartment! Daddy, you really don't know how much he *hates* to do this. It's just that his lawyers have told him it's the only way out!''

G. Frederick Kingston sighed. "All right, cherub, I'll take your word for it. I have a feeling, though, things are going to turn out better than you think. Perhaps," he suggested, "all this can be thrashed out on your honeymoon. Good lord," he said, quickly looking at his watch, "I've got to get home if we're going to be on time tomorrow in Judge Markowitz's office. How about if your mother and I come to town around ten o'clock to pick you up and help you get ready?''

It was Lacy's turn to sigh. "No, Daddy, really, I don't need any help. I've got a lot of things to do." Her emerald eyes were thoughtful as she reached for the door handle on her side of the car. "I'll just meet you there in the judge's chambers. I have a few things I want to do between now and then, so I'll just take a cab down in the morning." As Lacy got out of the car she did not raise her eyes. "I didn't mean what I said about your stabbing me in the back, I know you wouldn't do that. But, Daddy—"

"Yes, darling?" her father said fondly.

"About the honeymoon," his daughter said, slamming the door. "Just don't lay any bets on it, will you?"

An hour later, Lacy took the taupe-brown and gold dress down the hall to Candy O'Neill's apartment and a Proctor-Silex blender as a thank-you gift for the loan of the Halston.

"You can have a couple of microwave ovens, too," Lacy told her friend indifferently. "I'm getting married. I might as well give all this stuff away."

"I really want to meet Alexander van Renssalaer," Candy crowed. "He sounds fabulous! I'm so glad the Halston with the front cover of the *Ladies' Home Journal* image worked out. Listen, do you think we could do the same thing for me, like say something from the cover of *McCall's*?"

With a frown Lacy said quickly, "Look, Candy— do you mind if I invite, well, Pottsy to the wedding? You've gotten over that bad stuff that happened at the Zebra Lounge, haven't you? I mean, with Walter Moretti around, taking you out, things have certainly changed."

"Pottsy?" the redheaded model said. "Gee, I don't know, Lacy. I don't think Walter would like it."

"Leave Walter home," Lacy said shortly. "Look, come down in the morning around eight, will you? I've got a lot to explain. I'm getting married. Nothing big—in a judge's chambers at noon, that's all."

"Tomorrow?" her friend cried in astonishment. "Lacy, what happened? Is Alex van Renssalaer in some sort of trouble?"

"No," Lacy said over her shoulder as she walked away, "but actually he's about the only one I can think of who isn't. I'm marrying Michael Echevarria."

It was after seven-thirty before Lacy finally settled herself on her living-room couch with a bottle of Calvin Klein Crushed Berry and a box of Q-Tips to do her fingernails and watch the rest of *Entertainment Tonight* on TV. The Manhattan telephone directory still lay on the floor by the kitchen extension, where she'd dropped it after making the last of the telephone calls Harrison Saistonstall Potts had told her to.

That was it, Lacy told herself with deep resignation. After tomorrow's wedding ceremony she had the rest of her life before her. The dream—and that was all it had been—that had started in Tulsa was over. *Finito. Kaput.*

After tomorrow she was going to borrow her sister Felice's old Datsun and travel westward, perhaps to some spot in the desert in Arizona or New Mexico where she could stay for a long, long time and retreat from a world that had demonstrated it wasn't ready for an emerald-eyed smoky-blonde with a totally unacceptable sense of humor. At least that was the general complaint.

She knew she had a lot of rethinking to do now that her goal of being a fashion-magazine writer had gone the way of everything else. Sometime, somehow, she was going to forget Michael Echevarria and get rid, forever, of the nasty, unpleasant ache in her chest that was actually the result of too many weeks of suppressed rage and frustration. And not, she was sure, love.

When Lacy heard the buzzer for the apartment building's front door downstairs, she put down her bottle of nail polish reluctantly, not wanting to answer it. She'd taken her telephone off the hook. One frantic call from Alexander van Renssalaer wanting to explain everything and saying that he really loved her had been enough. When she pressed the intercom button in the kitchen, the line was full of static. All she heard was a crackle of a voice downstairs and perhaps the word *Edward*.

Edward? The only Edward she knew was Michael Echevarria's chauffeur. She certainly wasn't going to buzz to release the door lock downstairs and let *him* up!

"Please, Miss Kingston," the voice that was definitely Edward, the chauffeur's, pleaded through another burst of crackles. "I have some boxes to deliver to you. Boss's orders."

"No!" Lacy yelled and took her finger off the button, breaking the connection.

She had no idea why Edward had been sent over to

deliver something at that hour, but she didn't want to have to think about Michael, his chauffeur or her life's biggest disaster until tomorrow.

She'd just put a second coat of Crushed Berry on her left hand when the buzzer in the kitchen began its annoying whirring again. Lacy waited, trying to ignore it, but when it wouldn't stop, she put down the nail polish and charged into the kitchen.

"Go away, Edward," Lacy said into the intercom grille. "Go home to your employer and tell him whatever he's trying to deliver, he can stick it. I don't want it!"

"Miss Kingston," the chauffeur's anguished voice came back, "if I don't deliver these boxes, it's going to cost me my job. Please press the button and let me up."

Lacy slumped against the kitchen wall and closed her eyes. She wouldn't let him get fired; she wasn't that sort of person. And now that she wasn't in love with Michael anymore, what did it matter? Instantly the once-dormant devil inside Lacy whispered mischievously that there was really no reason why she should sit around her apartment that evening being miserable when there was someone downstairs who had once invited her out to championship wrestling and Chinese food. Lacy's stomach gave a tentative growl at the thought. She hadn't had dinner, and she was remembering the chauffeur's tall, slim physique, blond hair and admiring hazel eyes.

Gotcha! the little devil said, impulsively.

"Edward?" Lacy held down the SPEAK button on the intercom. "How would you feel about going out for sweet and sour pork?"

Actually, the devilish voice was saying reasonably,

Lacy needed to get out of her apartment, if only for an hour or two. She lowered her voice. "Edward?" the devil went on, "say just over to Broadway?"

There was a silence downstairs. Lacy bit her lips. Maybe Edward was too afraid of his employer to want to take her out.

"Edward?" Lacy repeated. There was nothing wrong with going out with the chauffeur, the inner voice assured her. There was nothing complicated about having Chinese food with a tall, handsome blond man like Edward; it was certainly better than eating alone.

"Yes," the chauffeur's suddenly choked voice came back through the intercom speaker. He coughed. "Yes, I'll take you out to a Chinese restaurant, Miss Kingston, just let me up."

Lacy had changed into a red cashmere pullover belted with a wide silver chain, faded Levi Strauss jeans and cowboy boots. She barely had time to run a comb through her hair by the time she heard the ancient elevator clank open in the apartment hallway outside.

"Hi!" she said, smiling gaily as she threw open the front door.

It was probably, Lacy realized a split second later, the most horrendous mistake she'd made in her whole life. Because it was not Edward standing there.

A terrifying apparition filled her doorway.

The most gigantic criminal she'd ever seen in real life or in the movies stood there. It was a horrible hulk in a black motorcycle jacket studded with steel buttons, with a hideously muscled T-shirted torso, narrow, threatening hips and powerful legs encased in black jeans and boots. Where his face should have been, there was only a black plastic cylinder that made him look like a clone of Darth Vader.

"Mugger!" Lacy croaked in instant recognition. Her brain was reeling in shock; she could hardly utter the words. "A mugger!"

"Jesus," the mugger growled with an inappropriate note of surprise.

"Help! Police!" Lacy squealed, trying to slam the door on one big black-booted foot. "Sicky-Poo!" she cried, trying that futile hope. "Candy! Mugger! Mugger!"

"Damn," she heard the monstrous figure say irritably. "Don't call that stupid dog—I just polished these boots."

The mugger scraped his black leather jacket open with his hand, and she could see the black T-shirt that strained over his massive chest bore the words HARLEY-DAVIDSON DOES IT HARDER AND LONGER.

"Never! Never!" Lacy cried, landing a kick on the black-booted shins. She followed that with a karate chop to the iron-hard midsection. "Mugger! Kill! Die!"

"Damn it," the mugger said again. He raised a huge leather jacketed arm to lift the plastic wind screen from his face and drag off the helmet.

Underneath the Darth Vader mask, Lacy saw quickly, was a hard-faced brute with tumbling black curls, a grim slash of a mouth and cold, steely-gray eyes.

"What the hell do you mean—Chinese food?" the mugger growled. "I'm going to give you all the Chinese food you'll ever need from now on. So lay off Edward."

21

"I told you I was going to marry you—you don't have to kidnap me!" Lacy cried as the leather-clad hunk in biker's clothes lifted her from the buddy seat of the Harley-Davidson motorcycle and set her carefully on her cramped, wobbly legs. "Where are we? I want to go back to New York!"

"This *is* New York," the menacing hulk said tersely. He raised Lacy's plastic visor and then pulled off her motorcycle helmet. As the glistening sheath of her pale hair tumbled down, he smoothed it back from her face. "This is Brooklyn."

She'd have to take his word for it, Lacy thought, looking around. The Harley was stopped on a narrow street in the midst of warehouses and docks, and the night air was filled with the strong, oily smell of New York Harbor. It could be Brooklyn, but if it was, what were they doing there?

As he released her to lock up the motorcycle, Lacy staggered around in a little circle dizzily. Her ears were still ringing from the spectacular ride over the Fifty-ninth Street bridge in heavy traffic and then their rocketing blast down the expressway south of the Gowanus Canal. She had the confused impression that if this was really Brooklyn, then they were only there because Michael Echevarria rode a motorcycle like a superbly skilled maniac. There had been a moment with a cross-town bus when she'd thought they weren't going to make it. During the whole ride, Lacy had clutched the big, hard body in front with her arms and legs in the four-pronged attitude of a terrorized koala bear clinging to the world's last eucalyptus tree.

What am I doing here? Lacy wondered. She'd been dragged out of her apartment and into the night and thrown on a gigantic Harley-Davidson motorcycle. Now she was in Brooklyn; that's what Michael had said. He parked the Harley across from the only lighted spot on the deserted street—an old brick building with a neon sign that announced, THE SEVEN SEAS BAR AND GRILL. "This is no way to treat a bride on her wedding eve," Lacy muttered under her breath. "It's ridiculous!"

The figure in the black leather jacket finished securing the motorcycle, pulled off his own helmet and tucked it under his arm. "I'm taking you to dinner," the familiar cool, authoritative voice of the president and chairman of the board said. "You told Edward you wanted something to eat, didn't you?"

Lacy stepped back a step. She didn't recognize this towering, sexy brute with his unruly black curls, narrowed eyes and bulging muscles in biker's leathers any more than she knew where they were. But it had to be Michael Echevarria, she thought, peering at him: the same hard, square-jawed face with its grimly sensuous mouth and flickering dimples, the glinting cool gray eyes. He looked like those tough boys in high school who'd wanted to date her. Only she'd always been too frightened to do more than hug her books to her chest and scuttle straight ahead, pretending she hadn't seen them or heard their growled invitations.

Good grief, Lacy realized with a shock, the way he looked now, Michael was a teenage girl's worst sex fantasies come true! The desire to have him ravish her with one of his hard, burning kisses was so great she had to clench her teeth to keep from blurting it out.

She gave a little startled squeak as the dark figure reached for her. But his big hands only straightened the front of her denim jacket and then buttoned it modestly over the provocative swell of her fire-engine-red pullover.

"Take me home," Lacy pleaded. "Please, don't do whatever it is you're going to do, Michael. This is no time for revenge. I still have to shampoo and set my hair.

"Don't you," she asked plaintively, "want me to look nice for tomorrow?"

"You always look beautiful," his expressionless voice said. "Just keep your jacket buttoned." He put a big arm around her waist and half carried, half shoved her ahead of him. "I have something I want to show you."

They crossed the dark, empty street to the Seven Seas Bar and Grill, Lacy struggling to free herself from his grip all the way. He pushed open the door.

"I need to go home," Lacy cried, bracing her hand on the doorjamb to keep from entering. "I need to pick out my clothes for the wedding! I'm not hungry anymore! Honestly, I was only kidding around with Edward!"

"So I gathered."

The arm around her waist propelled Lacy forward. Her protests were swallowed up by a blast of smoke, darkness, warmth and the noise of the bar's television set somewhere in the murk, tuned to the fights in Queens Coliseum. She quickly stopped struggling as she saw the clientele of the Seven Seas Bar and Grill in construction hard hats and windbreakers turn to them interestedly.

"Hey, look who's here," the bartender cried. "It's Mickey Evans. Long time no see, kid!"

Aware of the impact of a dozen pairs of eyes watching them, Lacy quickly resumed her koala-bear clutch on Michael Echevarria's body. She was practically riding his left hip and jeans-covered leg as she hobbled toward a back booth.

"I don't like places like this," Lacy hissed as he propped her against the table edge and tried to shift her leg out from between his thighs. Lacy clung even more tightly, her fingers grabbing his belt where the leather front of his jacket swung open. The last time she'd been in a place like this was four years ago in Scranton, Pennsylvania, on a shoot for a Young and Rubicam ad for Ford pickup trucks. She remembered perfectly well how traumatic it had been. Bar and grill clientele were almost abnormally interested, she'd found, in tall, willowy smoky-blondes with show-stopping figures.

"Two draft beers," the tall hunk she was clinging to said over the deafening noise. He held up his big right hand with his fingers in a V as the bartender came over to their booth.

"That's my kind of woman, Mick," the beefy man in the white apron said appreciatively, his eyes roaming over Lacy as he wiped off the Formica surface of their table. "You going to drink standing up or sitting down?"

"We're going to have dinner," Michael Echevarria said. "Bring us a menu, Freddie."

"They have menus in this place?" Lacy wanted to know. Michael's hands patiently forced her down in the seat. "I don't believe it! What are they written on—old truck bodies?"

"I ate here when I worked on the docks," he said, sliding in next to her. "I spent six years getting a degree in business administration in night school. When I graduated, the only people who came to see me get my diploma were Otto Posniaski, Pier Thirty-seven unit boss, and Freddie, the bartender here."

"Mickey?" Lacy said, staring at him. "That's what he called you, didn't he?" She would never have believed it. He was really someone known to the Seven Seas Bar and Grill on the Brooklyn docks as Mickey Evans? Lacy suddenly began to feel better. "Mickey Evans? You mean you're using an alias? Mickey? *Mick*?"

"I got tired of having my name mispronounced," he said evenly, handing her a menu as Freddie the bartender reappeared. "It never got spelled right on the payroll, either. So I shortened it to something my supervisors could handle."

"Mickey?" Lacy hooted, shoving the menu back at him. "*Mickey*?"

"Bring us two steaks," the president and chairman of the board said in a grim voice. "Medium rare."

Their thick, superb steaks arrived two draft beers later on wooden platters with a stack of sliced tomatoes and a mountain of French fries. Michael lifted his black, tangled lashes to look at her and say, "Do you take ketchup?"

"Yes," Lacy breathed, looking down at her gigantic char-broiled two-pound New York strip. Before she could say another word, his large hand up-ended the Heinz-ketchup bottle, and he gave it a smart smack with his palm. A splatter of bright red goo inundated her plate, burying everything.

"Steak and French fries, Lacy," he said very slowly and deliberately, his clear gray eyes watching her. "Not *chateaubriand aux pommes frites*. Right?"

"I thought you brought me here to show me something," Lacy muttered, parting the red sea with her knife and dunking a large fry into it delicately.

"I brought you here," he said, still staring at her, "to tell you, among other things, that I'm appointing you *Fad*'s new managing editor."

"Oh, no," Lacy choked, suddenly not able to make a mouthful of French fries go down. "Listen," she gulped, reaching for her beer, "will you lay off?" She took a big swallow and gagged again. "If you're going to do this to me, why don't you wait until I've finished eating? Or is this some plot to kill me while I strangle in front of your eyes? Good grief—isn't *marrying* me enough?"

He kept staring at her. "The stuff you've written has a light, trendy touch, a style like *New York* magazine's when it first started. An approach like that might work for a worn-out publication like *Fad*. That flake managing editor's got to go. She's not only incompetent, she's destroying morale."

"I don't have any technical know-how," Lacy wheezed, gulping her beer furiously. "Are you crazy? Being a managing editor takes years of experience! Why me?" she cried with tears in her eyes. "Why not—why not Jamie Hatworth?"

"Experience I can buy any time," he told her. He was cutting his steak now with sure, authoritative strokes. "The magazine is overloaded with experience and not enough fresh, smart ideas. Hatworth is good, but it wouldn't be wise to promote her out of her current level of effectiveness."

"You can have," he said, chomping a piece of steak decisively with fine white teeth, "two technical assistants to start with. You supply the ideas."

"But I'm supposed to be marrying you," Lacy gasped, finally managing an unobstructed breath. "Or have you forgotten about tomorrow?"

"I want you at *Fad* during regular business hours," he said with iron deliberation. He slashed at his sliced tomatoes. "I've just bought Houston-Maracaibo Refineries—I won't have a lot of time to put into the magazine from now on."

"Time? Technical assistants?" Lacy finally managed to yell. "Is this how you do business, putting kooks like me—without any experience whatsoever—in charge?"

"It's worked before, yes," he said, studying his

fork packed with speared tomatoes and dripping mayonnaise. "You underestimate yourself. You did a good job with the Zebra Lounge mess—you kept your head when the place caught fire, kept down panic and got a major press break in the bargain. That's not bad."

"You couldn't know about the Zebra Lounge," Lacy breathed, her mouth dropping open in dismay. "You couldn't."

The gray eyes lifted to bore into her. "I have a complete dossier on you, Lacy. Private detectives do more than follow you around, or didn't you know?" He looked rather smug. "I never said you were stupid. Just that I didn't like your sense of . . . humor."

It was a moment before Lacy could get enough breath, or wits about her, to say anything. Her lips, too, seemed frozen. She could hardly move them enough to say, "Peter Dorsey?"

"He deserved what he got," he said with his mouth full. "I read the court transcripts, and I believe your side of the story. Which was substantiated"—he dabbed his chin with a paper napkin and threw it into his plate as he finished—"by the reports of other models since then."

Deserved what he got, her mind repeated. Court transcripts. Followed and investigated the whole time.

"Bobby Sullivan?" she whispered, almost afraid to say the name.

He shot her a quick look from under dark brows. "Who the hell's he?"

Ah, the president and chairman had missed that one, Lacy thought, vastly relieved. She said in a small voice, "Did Alex van—I mean did I—if Alex has connections with some other business, will it hurt your company? My father brought it up," she added quickly. "He said it would."

"I don't want to discuss it with you, Lacy," he said, studying the check. "Your father's a nice guy—I like him. I'd say there's hope for your family yet. But if I ever see van Renssalaer with you again, I'm going to break him into little pieces and send him back to Ransom Tri-Star stuffed in his lawyer's briefcase. Is that clear enough?"

"You said you brought me here," Lacy reminded him, quickly changing the subject, "to show me something. Or have I already seen it?"

Strong, tanned fingers drew a familiar English-leather wallet from the inside pocket of his motorcycle jacket and took out several bills and laid them on the table beside the dinner check. "Lacy," the low, husky voice of the black panther said softly, "look at me."

She didn't want to. Not when he talked to her like that, in the low voice that could hold her mesmerized. She didn't want to lift her eyes to that gray gaze gone suddenly slate colored and urgent. The same sensation, like running headlong into a speeding bulldozer, was still there.

"This is where I come from, places like this," he said softly. "This was my life before I started on the way up. I want you to take a good look, Lacy—you don't know anything about me unless you understand this.

"Tomorrow," he added huskily, "will be different."

Tomorrow, she thought shuddering, tearing her

eyes away. She had to keep remembering what a farce getting married to Michael Echevarria was and resist everything else—what he was telling her, the appeal to her traitorous emotions, the fire in those gray eyes.

"Hey, Mick," the hard hats at the Seven Seas bar chorused as they got up from their booth, "don't be such a stranger. Bring your lady around some night."

"Yeah, come back, kid," Freddie, the bartender, called. "She's my kind of woman."

"I'll keep that in mind," Michael Echevarria said lifting a big hand and waving it as they made for the door. "We're getting married tomorrow."

Lacy whirled on him. Amid whistles, catcalls and the sound of beer mugs being slammed enthusiastically on the bar, she cried, "Oh, no we're not! I mean—"

In the sudden silence that fell, the towering hulk in black motorcycle leathers turned to her. "First," Michael Echevarria said softly, "it seems I have some homework to do."

"No," Lacy squeaked, "not in front of all these—"

"C'mere, babe," the chairman of the board growled, hooking one powerful arm around her waist and drawing her easily to his broad chest covered with a picture of a Harley-Davidson Electra-Glide on the front.

Lacy tried to struggle, even gave a little shriek. A helpless rush of shivering swept through her as his arms enveloped her, crushing her to him.

"Go for it, Mick," the stamping, whistling, applauding audience encouraged from the bar.

"You *are* going to marry me, Lacy." She felt his warm breath against her mouth before his lips closed over hers. "But I warn you, just don't try to do anything . . . funny."

At the door to her apartment, Lacy took out her keys and said determinedly, "You didn't have to see me up, and you're not coming in. Actually a groom shouldn't see the bride at all the night before the wedding. I still have to," she said, rapidly unlocking the door and practically jumping inside, "shampoo my hair and—"

He shouldered his way in right behind her. "Lacy, you don't think I'm going to let you out of my sight tonight, do you? Hell, I can't wait to get married and get this over with."

"Now you listen," she told him, following him as he sauntered into the living room. "Just marrying me doesn't mean you're going to know where I am all the time. Get out, Michael, do you hear me? I don't need a watchdog!"

"I don't know about that," he said, his back to her. "After springing van Renssalaer on me with a federal complaint, I'm beginning to think you need more than a keeper.

"Edward brought my clothes," he went on, switching on a table lamp in the living room, "so I've got everything with me.

"You've made this place very pretty," he said, taking off his leather jacket. He ran his fingers through his hair several times and stood looking around at the green hanging plants, mirrors and white-painted furniture. He surveyed the mountain of cartons in the middle of the living room containing blenders and microwave ovens that Lacy had yet to send back. Then he checked out his Louis Vuitton suiter, shoe case and overnight bag, which the chauffeur had carefully laid on top of the pile, along with several large white boxes. Finally he put his big body down carefully on a white-painted café chair and bent to pull off the motorcycle boots.

"You're not, repeat, *not*," Lacy cried, fleeing to the bedroom, "going to spend the night! If you think you're going to sleep with me, you're crazy. You can sleep in the living room!"

"I'm not going to sleep in the living room, Lacy." He pushed open the bedroom door easily, even though she had braced her body against it to hold it shut. Once inside, he looked around with the same careful interest. "This is pretty, too," he observed. He looked with interest at the off-white panels at the windows, the deep-blue rug and Lacy's round queen-size bed with its red velveteen and white canvas-stripe spread.

"Then *I'll* sleep in the living room," Lacy announced, sweeping past him haughtily.

He caught her arm. "Don't let's play kid games," he growled, "I don't like it, and I'm tired."

"Ah, God, you smell so good," he said in an entirely different tone of voice. He pulled her into his arms even as Lacy squirmed and tried to slide under them.

As he buried his face in her glistening, fragrant hair he murmured, "I've been through hell these past few weeks. I keep waking up at night thinking something is going to happen, like something jumping out at me in the dark or falling on my head when I'm not looking. I'm developing a damned twitch in my right eyelid that won't go away." His searching lips hungrily traced her cheekbone, her hairline and then nuzzled the gentle curve of her ear lobe. "I need you with me, Lacy," he breathed into her ear, "if only to be sure some new brainstorm of yours isn't going to take me by surprise. Sweetheart, I can't tell you how much I've learned to hate surprises since I met you. I'm as jumpy as a damned cat."

"Let go of me, Michael," she gritted. "I know all about how much you complain that you need to marry me to get a good night's sleep! That was really nasty, what you told your lawyer."

"I'm not going to bother to explain that." He traced her eyelid with the tip of his tongue, his gray-eyed gaze full of a quicksilver light. His big hand cupped the back of her head so she couldn't pull away. "This is not the time for one of our famous arguments."

"Oh, don't," Lacy moaned. His mouth touched the tip of her nose in a feather kiss and then moved slightly lower to graze her upper lip. "Don't kiss me like this, Michael," she told him. "You know I can't stand it. That's the way this whole thing got started— with those crazy, irresistible kisses!"

Even as she spoke, Lacy knew it was too late. The familiar slow-moving heat was swelling in her veins, settling in her inner body with a decided ache.

"I can't spend all night making love," she wailed. "You're going to make me get married tomorrow, remember?"

"Mmmhmm," he breathed softly. "Give me your lips, sweet Lacy, that lovely mouth that I feel in my dreams. That is, when I can sleep and don't expect something to hit me.

"Oh, love," he said, tugging up her fire-engine-red

cashmere to get rid of it, "you—" He stiffened. "Good, God, you haven't got anything on under this!"

"Let's not start that," Lacy cried. She struggled as he seized the bright-red cashmere and stripped it over her head. "I'm not going to sit up all night discussing underwear with you, Michael, or any of your other hang-ups!" But she gave a large gasp as the tips of his fingers found the soft undercurve of her breasts and began stroking the straining pink nipples in slow, sensuous circles that left her body quivering.

"Ah, Lacy, you're so beautiful," he murmured raggedly. "You're just so lovely and warm and trembling when I touch you. I just can't get enough of you." He pulled her close, his big, hard hand spread against the bare skin of her back to hold her while his other hand rhythmically stroked her rosy nipples into tight, rigid points. "I can't wait to see you in the clothes I've brought for you to wear tomorrow, darling."

"That's it!" Lacy said, shoving him away. "OK, Michael, that's definitely it!" She went around the corner of the bed at a run. "If you give me any more junk, I'll—I'll throw it out the window! You're not going to force me to wear any more of your freaky custom-made clothes. You're a compulsive, materialistic . . . *gift nut!*"

"Oh, God, that's lovely," he muttered. He stood back to admire her slender body, bare from the waist up, her satiny breasts swaying, her pale-blond hair falling over her naked shoulders as she warily climbed onto the bed and to the other side to escape him.

"You give me the creeps, Michael," she cried, unable to keep from trembling as his silvery eyes raked her desirously. "You're trying to crush me, dominate me, with expensive presents! I reject them—*reject* them, do you hear? I don't want anything from you!"

"I know that, darling," he said huskily. "You don't have to tell me." He came around the corner of the bed after her, pulling off his Harley-Davidson T-shirt and tossing it on the floor. The muscles of his shoulders rippled as he lifted his hands and pulled open the brass buckle of his wide leather belt.

"Lacy, you're the only woman I've ever met who doesn't want anything from me, doesn't like expensive presents, turns down promotions at work—I'm damned if I understand it. I have been called," he said softly, "stingy as hell, a cold-hearted bastard and a calculating son of a bitch in a lot of bedrooms but never a nutty gift giver before.

"Sweetheart," he murmured, reaching out for her as she climbed down the far side of the bed, "do you know how many women have wanted to marry me? How many of them I've had to chase out of my life? Out of my bed? Sweet darling, what the hell's the matter with you?"

"Nothing's the matter with me, Michael—uh, don't do that," Lacy cried as he peeled down his tight black jeans, exposing the corded, symmetrical length of his legs. He wore Jim Palmer-style Elance briefs in red, bulging with tiny silhouetted motorcycles. Lacy gave a quick, very audible gasp. "Goodnight, Michael, do you stay that way all the time? I'm just realizing I've almost never seen you—"

"Lacy, don't slide down in the corner like that," he murmured, stretching out on the bed and reaching for her with both hands. He pulled her up and drew her across the bedspread to lie against him. "I'm going to give you everything tonight, darling," he soothed her. "Everything you can think of, starting with this."

"Oh, drat, I don't know," Lacy whispered helplessly. Her hands moved down the clenching muscles under the silky skin of his arms. The face bending over her was that of the tough, handsome brute of a biker and the chairman of the board at his commanding, glittering best. Without wanting to, Lacy sighed. Her fingers rose to touch his thick, curling hair.

"Michael," she murmured, knowing that she was slipping into surrender, ensnared in his beauty and in his erotic power over her. Rocket sparks of pleasure shot through her with the feel of his mouth, hot and demanding, tugging at her breasts. "You always make me do what you want me to do," she moaned. "And I hate it!"

"You can't hate it, precious," he murmured against her fiery skin. "Not when you feel like this. I dream of you like this, beautiful Lacy. Holding you like this. Kissing you everywhere.

"What little sleep I've been getting lately," he said, kissing the curve of her hipbone as he lowered the zipper of her jeans, "is full of dreams about kissing you like this, giving you the one thing you can't use as a missile or send back to me in the damned United States mail."

"No, no," Lacy moaned, writhing under the scalding heat of his mouth. "Oh, Michael, you're, uh—good heavens, what are we doing?" She raised both knees to help him slide off her boots and then the Levi's jeans.

"I'm kissing you, darling," his low, husky voice said as he pulled her little silk and lace bikini panties down her legs and leaned over her to press his lips against the *V* of her fleecy softness. "Didn't you say you liked my kisses? I'm going to give you everything, sweet, lovely Lacy, every gift you can think of, and you're going to take them all."

"Eeek," Lacy gasped.

The *zap! bam! powie!* had, incredibly enough, ignited a charge of sheer dynamite. He pulled his big, shaking body over her and entered her. "Darling, look at me, open your eyes," he told her hoarsely as he eased into her. "Say you love me again, Lacy. I want to hear it."

"I can't," Lacy shuddered weakly. "I can't, Michael—I think I've lost my mind."

She heard him laugh, a wonderful sound. He stroked into her slowly, filling her up with his heavy presence, claiming her possessively. "Darling, look at me," he whispered. "Come with me, I want to give you this."

Dazed, overwhelmed, Lacy clutched him. His eyes were silver lights, making her acknowledge that he was her lover, claiming her, his body moving into her with gentle power. For once, Lacy could not fight what she felt.

"Michael," she murmured, touching his mouth with the tips of her fingers tenderly, "there was only one time before. In the front seat of a Buick with a boy named Bobby Sullivan when I was seventeen. We drank a whole six-pack of beer, and it was awful," she quavered, glad to get it out at last. "I never wanted to, uh, have sex again until—until I met you."

"I know, my love." His ardent mouth bestowed kisses along the delicate line of her chin and into her throat. "Your father told me."

"Daddy told you?" she gasped. "Michael, how did *he* know?"

"One of your sisters told your mother. Oh, God, sweetheart, can we have this conversation later? This is driving me crazy!"

Even as his mouth covered hers, even as they spiraled out of time and consciousness to the never-ending limits of the dark universe, wound together deeply and seeking each other, Lacy breathed the words that she loved him and waited for his words in return. Whatever his answer, it was lost in the glorious, shattering celebration of the very first time they had made love. At the peak of it her own cries were muffled by Michael's husky roar of perfect, ecstatic possession.

Later, when her lover lay resting peacefully in what was, he had murmured before closing his eyes, his first good night's sleep in days, Lacy stared wakefully into the dark of her bedroom. Her fingers played wistfully with the links of his gold neck chain and stroked the outline of his heavy arm down to his wrist. All his carefully stated power, his virile passion, his arrogant authority, was wrapped around her, holding her tightly, to keep her.

Oh, what have you done now, Lacy Kingston? the terrible inner voice rose up to say. It reminded her of all the things she had planned for tomorrow, which were already set in motion to destroy Michael Echevarria forever.

Cut and run, the small devilish voice answered. Sneak out now while the going is good, the way you did in Tulsa. Never come back. *That's* one sure way out of this mess!

Lacy was tempted to do as the devilish voice said. But heavy arms held her. Michael's big, powerful frame pressed her down in her bed, holding her there, his legs twined around and between hers, even his feet tucked under her own.

When she stirred, he only gripped her tighter in his sleep. His mouth, pressed against the satiny dampness of her breast growled, "Mine."

And nothing more.

22

Michael Echevarria's Silver Ghost Rolls Royce purred
quietly into a NO PARKING space directly in front of
the municipal-Greek-style edifice of the New York
Supreme Court at 60 Center Street, in lower Manhattan, promptly at five minutes before noon.

Edward, the chauffeur, smart in his dove-gray
uniform, slid out from behind the wheel to open the
doors for the limousine's passengers. But not before
Lacy, her fingers ready on the door handle, had shot
from the back seat and onto the sidewalk, closely
followed by the tall, broad-shouldered figure of the
president and chairman of the board of Echevarria
Enterprises in a splendid Savile Row charcoal three-
piece business suit and elegant homburg, carrying a
cream-colored woman's coat, jewel case and a delectable frothy confection of a hat bundled in his arms.

"Lacy, come back here," the chairman of the board barked as his bride-to-be ran for the entrance.

Former fashion model Lacy Kingston had only reached the first steps of the courthouse before a young woman carrying a microphone with the letters WWOR-TV and a power pack on a strap from her shoulder, two television cameramen and a photographer from the *New York Daily News*, converged on her.

The young television newswoman got there first. "Miss Kingston?" she cried, sticking the microphone in Lacy's face as Lacy took the long flight of gray marble steps two at a time. "Is it true that you're going to make a statement to the press that you are being forced to marry Mr. Echevarria, whose intention is to keep you from filing a complaint of sexual harassment against him with the EEOC?"

"No, go away," Lacy groaned. As she ran, she was trying to grab the zipper on the back of an ivory silk dress with dainty cap sleeves and a swirl of short, pleated skirt. "It's been canceled, the whole thing!" She lunged for the revolving doors at the courthouse entrance.

"Lacy!" The authoritative voice of the chairman of the board came from behind the television cameramen as he bounded up the courthouse steps, somewhat encumbered by the coat in his arms and the tulle-draped hat with seed pearls in one hand. "Put these on!"

"I don't want you to touch me," Lacy yelled.

She was still shaking from the struggle in the Rolls Royce to get her to wear the princess-style coat and the little Dior wedding hat. They had almost come to blows earlier in her apartment over the white satin garter belt and the silk stockings embroidered with tiny ivory-on-cream daisies that Michael had finally yanked on her himself.

"Leave me alone," Lacy cried, shoving the *New York Daily News* photographer out of her way. The WWOR-TV newswoman was right behind her and managed to cram herself, her microphone and power pack in as the doors began to turn.

"Isn't it true, Miss Kingston," the WWOR-TV news reporter panted as she stuck the microphone up between them, "that you've hired Harrison Potts Promotions, of Boston, to handle your wedding arrangements in Judge Markowitz's office? And that the Peptic Ulcers punk-rock band is going to provide incidental music for the ceremony?"

Lacy gave a little distracted gasp as the door caught against the heel of her Capezio strappy sandals. There had to be some way out of what was going to happen, she was telling herself, but she couldn't think of it. She had only herself to blame. What had seemed like a great, fantastic scheme for vengeance was now, in the light of what she knew she would always feel for Michael, a total catastrophe. Not funny, not smart, not a triumph of one-upmanship—just disaster!

"Listen," she told the woman crammed into the revolving door with her, "let's go around again and I'll hold your microphone while you zip me up."

"Right," the reporter agreed.

They could both see Michael Echevarria wrestling with the WPIX-TV cameraman for a place in the slowly rotating doors. The chairman of the board waggled a tulle-veiled hat at his bride threateningly as he, too, began to revolve, a scowl on his hard, good-looking face under the elegant black homburg.

"Hot damn," the WWOR-TV staffer gaped, watching the tall figure pounding on the glass before him with a handful of custom-made cream wool princess coat, "is that mad hunk Echevarria Enterprises, Incorporated? What's he trying to do?"

"This has to be the absolute pits, this whole idea," Lacy moaned. "Oh, why couldn't I be in some other place today. Like the Republic of Outer Mongolia?" She knew when they got to the fifth floor of the Supreme Court Building and Judge Markowitz's chambers, what they would find if Pottsy had done his work.

"It's a great dress," the newswoman said as she pulled up the long zipper in back. "Is Mr. Echevarria still assaulting you? Was he trying to tear you out of your clothes? Can't you make contact with some women's support group that can help?"

"Don't be silly—he's trying to make me put them *on*," Lacy shivered. "I'm a nervous wreck—I haven't even had time to shampoo and set my hair. He took so long in the shower I couldn't get in the bathroom. When I did, he'd used up all the hot water. I'm a mess, just look at me!"

"You look great to me," the news reporter said, staring. "Did I hear you right? You mean you spent the night with Mr. Echevarria? Wow! And you mean you're still going to denounce him today as a menace to American working women?"

The revolving doors spilled them abruptly out into the lobby before Lacy could think of an answer. As she broke into a run, a *New York Daily News* photographer darted in front of her, snapping blinding white photoflash shots.

"Hey, Miss Kingston," the newswoman shouted as Lacy sprinted for the doors closing on an up elevator. "Is it true that you met Mr. Echevarria under rather unusual circumstances in a bar in Lincoln, Nebraska?"

"No," Lacy cried, diving inside just as the elevator doors were closing. She fell back against the tight-packed passengers inside with a gasp of relief.

The relief was premature. Michael Echevarria, still encumbered by the woman's coat and hat, recklessly inserted his hands into the doors and held them open to the accompaniment of tripped alarm bells and warning cries from those inside. Then he squeezed himself into the elevator.

"Don't let him touch me!" Lacy cried. She burrowed her way through the court clerks, bailiffs, legal secretaries and municipal judiciary toward the back.

"Damn it," Michael Echevarria growled. His big hands pried two superior-court judges apart to seize her. "Put your hat on, Lacy. And stop yelling."

"Leave me alone," she protested. She tried to fight him off as he settled the Dior creation of pale-ivory silk and seed pearls on her head firmly. "I hate hats with veils—I learned my lesson last time!" Her hair tumbled over her face as she glared at him. "You're harassing me, Michael—you've been doing this right from the beginning. Ever since you thought I was a hooker in Tulsa!"

He held the ivory wool coat crushed under his elbow as he worked to open a maroon leather Cartier jewel case. "If you could," he said to a motherly looking court reporter jammed against his side, "just steady this for me—it would help."

"We see a lot of wedding nerves," the court stenographer murmured helpfully. She gasped as Michael Echevarria's fingers extracted a double strand of matched pearls, each gleaming globe the size of a large hummingbird egg, from the ruby velvet-lined Cartier case.

"Don't let him give me anything!" Lacy cried. "He's only marrying me because he has to! It's all his lawyer's idea!"

"Sweetheart, stand still," the chairman of the board ordered as he fastened the pearls around her throat.

"My God, what lovely pearls," a secretary breathed. "They must be worth a fortune."

"He has to marry me because—mmmmmfff," Lacy moaned as Michael lowered his dark head and seized her mouth in a smothering kiss.

At that moment the doors opened, and still kissing her, the chairman of the board pushed her outside.

He lifted ardent lips from her mouth to find chaos waiting for them in the corridors of the fifth floor.

"Don't look, Michael," Lacy cried, clutching the lapels of his suit jacket. "I can explain everything!"

Her voice was lost in the noise. As she stared up at Michael Echevarria's face, she saw his eyes widen with shock, then the skin of his face go so taut that his features seemed to flatten perceptibly. He swiveled his head as a battery of CBS- and ABC-television cameramen turned on their blinding portable lights. Flashbulbs popped. "You going to make your statement now, Miss Kingston?" someone shouted.

The fifth-floor corridor of the New York Supreme Court was mobbed from wall to wall. Lunch-bound Supreme-Court staffers struggled against a delegation of dapper tiny men with the unmistakable miniature *machismo* look of race-track jockeys, mixed in with the press and the electronic media and equipment. The Peptic Ulcers rock band from the Zebra Lounge were playing on a small portable stage, and in the crowd bunched around them could be seen the unmistakable red head of one of the Leonard Thornton agency's most beautiful models, Candy O'Neill. Stuck in the sea of bodies were the Fishman Brothers, Irving and his silent partner, Morton, and two elegantly dressed ladies, obviously their wives. And as though they had been waiting by the elevator doors, Jamie Hatworth and her two little boys and Mike, the layout artist, pushed forward.

"Lacy," the assistant editor yelled over the racket, waving her free hand.

If Lacy had been able to, she would have put both hands over her face to hide from what was before her, but her arms were pinned to her sides. She couldn't even bat away a photographer's camera that had just grazed her nose. Pottsy had done his job too well. This wasn't just retribution; this wasn't a setup to drive Michael Echevarria to the wall for humiliating her. This was total, irrevocable overkill of nuclear proportions!

Two burly bodies in electric-blue tuxedos with ruffled pink nylon shirts materialized in the hallway as the Peptic Ulcers struck up an ear-splitting reggae version of the wedding processional from *Lohengrin*. The crowd gave a few scattered cheers.

"Jeez, Mickey," the transformed figure of Freddie the bartender from the Seven Seas Bar and Grill rasped, "Otto and me came dressed for a wedding. What the hell's happening?"

"There's going to be a wedding," the president and chairman of the board growled. He held Lacy to his side tightly. "You can bet on it."

"Please," Lacy cried, her voice lost in the noise, "I want everybody to go home. This is all a big mistake! I'll take full responsibility."

"Lacy," Jamie Hatworth yelled, "room five-oh-one—" The assistant editor tried to point.

"Heah, dahling girl," the unmistakably Back Bay tones of Harrison Salstonstall Potts IV trumpeted as he plowed through the jam toward them. "Let me rescue you from this ovahly enthusiastic assemblage and welcome you, deah dreamboat, to yoah wedding." Boston's public-relations genius lunged for Lacy and planted a large kiss on her lips. "This is mah masterpiece, deah girl," he beamed at her. "Marital mayhem—just as you ordered."

"Statement," the television-news crews were shouting. "Make your statement, Miss Kingston."

"Do that again and I'll deck you," the black panther snarled, dealing Harrison Salstonstall Potts IV a shove that sent him back into the rock-band amplifiers.

"Mr. Michael Echevarria, I presume?" Harrison Salstonstall Potts IV boomed, prying himself out of a stack of woofers and tweeters. "I understand you're to be shafted today, deah boy. Don't forget to make a statement to *The New York Times*, will you, about molesting beautiful women?"

"Oh, no," Lacy whispered, her knees buckling. Cameramen, faces, bodies, even the glaring television lights were growing dim. A grim deity, looking down from heaven on the worst media event in history was delivering terrible justice. But for *her*, not for

Michael Echevarria. "Pottsy," she cried feebly, "it's all a big mistake. I'm not going to denounce anybody. I just want to go home! I've changed my mind!"

No one could hear her as the Peptic Ulcers segued into a version of "Oh, Promise Me" with a driving rock beat and drum solo.

"Stop," Lacy moaned. She felt sick. But she was swept nonetheless toward the doors of room 501 and Judge Markowitz's chambers, the chairman of the board on one side and Freddie, the bartender, on the other. A squad of uniformed New York Supreme Court bailiffs were clearing the area in front of the ladies' room and the familiar choked snarls of Sicky-Poo could be heard, trying to attack them.

"Daddy!" Lacy cried, catching a glimpse of a familiar figure.

"Mother," she gasped as the surging pressure of the crowd swept her forward. She felt something warm against her leg and then the cold slither of a metal chain and nearly went down on her knees as Sicky-Poo lunged past her, dragging Candy O'Neill, in a chartreuse gold-embroidered caftan, with him.

Judge Markowitz, impressive in his black official robes, stood in a siege position behind his receptionist's desk as the wedding party, the groomsmen in electric-blue tuxedos, assorted guests and a delegation of race-track jockeys stumbled through the door. The judge slammed down the telephone receiver, looking displeased.

"Great snakes, Mickey, what the hell's going on?" Judge Markowitz demanded. The president and chairman of the board of Echevarria Enterprises, Inc., fumbled vainly to retrieve his homburg hat as it disappeared over his shoulder into the hallway. The judge's administrative assistant slammed the door quickly before more race-track jockeys could slide their small bodies inside.

"Some kook's staged a circus in the hallway," the judge went on, reaching under his black skirts to produce a handkerchief and mop his face. "And the press has been calling here all morning about some woman who's going to denounce you as a rapist."

"Just marry us, Sam," Michael Echevarria told him grimly, bending to untangle Sicky-Poo's chain from his leg. "I'll explain everything later."

"I'll hold the dog," Jamie Hatworth's oldest boy volunteered as the Doberman lunged for him, slathering. "Mama, can I hold the dog?

"Gee," he said, bending down to examine his shoes, "guess what he just did?"

"Quick, grab her arm," Lacy heard someone cry. Then her mother's voice seemed to come sweetly out from an enveloping grayness.

"Lacy," her mother was saying, "you're not going to faint on us, dearest, are you?"

But she did.

23

"I guess I'll have to go ahead and marry Michael Echevarria," Lacy said as her mother wiped off her pale face with a wet paper towel in Judge Markowitz's private restroom. "Oh, Mother, I'm sorry nothing turned out the way I thought it would!"

A few minutes before, Lacy had gotten rid of the glass of orange juice and piece of unbuttered toast she'd had for breakfast. She'd been in a near faint for two or three horrifying minutes in the anteroom, and then after that, when her mother and Jamie Hatworth had steered her into the judge's own restroom, she'd thrown up.

Now, she saw, peering critically at herself in the mirror over the wash basin, she looked better than she really had any right to, considering that she'd both passed out in the hallway and then tossed her breakfast. She was pale, but her lack of color gave her a rather interesting, ethereal look that was a new variation on the standard Lacy Kingston pizazz. It certainly helped to finally have time to do something with her hair. Now all she needed was a little lip gloss, she thought wearily.

Jamie Hatworth leaned against the door of a booth and turned the Dior hat in her hands, tucking portions of the tulle veiling into the crown to hide the holes. "Frankly, kid, if you were mine," the assistant editor said, "I'd turn you over my knee and whale your tush until it blistered. Honestly, Lacy, you had no right to turn that lunatic from Boston loose on the New York Supreme Court! There was total panic outside there for a while, and the bailiffs are still cleaning up the mess. If the judges on this floor ever find out who was responsible, they'll arraign you on charges of trying to overthrow the municipal government."

"We don't believe in spanking," Lacy's tall, beautiful mother said firmly, "we never have. Lacy's father and I have always believed that violence is not the answer to disciplining children. We followed Dr. Spock's guidelines on that very closely.

"Dear," she said to her daughter, opening a blue velvet Cartier jewel case with exquisite pearl solitaire earrings and handing it to her, "the best man—isn't he the bartender from Brooklyn? He passed these in to us for you to wear for the ceremony, darling—they match your beautiful necklace. There was too much going on before you fainted to give you your engagement ring, but I saw it, and it's perfectly lovely.

"Twenty-two carats may be a little too big," she added thoughtfully, ignoring her daughter's loud groan, "for my baby's slender hand, but it's a perfectly magnificent diamond."

Lacy attached the pearl earrings to her ear lobes and stood back to view them in the wash-basin mirror. Their color, and that of the fabulous pearl necklace, was several luminous shades paler than the ivory tissue silk afternoon dress she wore. But the effect, as usual with the things Michael Echevarria chose for her, was incomparably tasteful. She squinted at herself doubtfully, hating to attempt a new hairdo but knowing she needed to wear her hair up. It was impossible to have the seed-pearl coronet of the Dior hat and its bridal cloud of shoulder-length veiling look right with her hair down and considerably disheveled.

"I wish Candy was here," Lacy sighed. "Candy really wanted to be my maid of honor. I hope she's making out all right at the jail.

"Of course," she added quickly, for the assistant editor's benefit, "I'm glad you could fill in, Jamie, I really appreciate it, and so does my family."

"Glad to do it, kid," the other woman responded. "I agree with your mother, my Macy's brown corduroy really goes better with that arsenic-blue tux the best man is wearing, anyway." Jamie shook out the tulle veil and handed the little Dior hat to Candy. "I certainly hope your girlfriend makes out all right down at the police station with the guy in the trench coat. That was some fight when he jumped that Harvard P.R. kook who set up this extravaganza. I told her not to worry, to go on over to the precinct station with him. Then she could go over to the emergency room at Bellevue and see if they had patched up the Boston nut case."

"I have a lot to thank you for," Lacy said, genuinely grateful. "And Mr. Fishman and his brother for getting permission for the band to stay after the SWAT team left." Lacy settled the Dior at the back of her head, where it fit nicely over her upswept French twist and lowered the transparent, shoulder-length tulle veil. Even she was somewhat startled at the transformation. Was that pale, glowing vision with jewel-green eyes and the seraphic face behind the tulle's mysterious mist really she? "Good grief," Lacy murmured, "I really do look like a bride." She couldn't stop staring.

"You look gorgeous," Jamie Hatworth agreed. She sighed, too. "I don't know how you do it, kid. You always come up looking so good it takes people's breath away. Lacy, for Pete's sake," the assistant editor said suddenly, "why don't you let up?

"I mean," she continued quickly when she saw Lacy's startled look, "why don't you stop battling with the big boss and give him a break? I know, I *know*—personally I couldn't cope with a ferocious-looking stud like Michael Echevarria. He's too much for any one woman to handle. But don't you realize you've got him bent all out of shape? Instead of murder one today, which would have been any man's normal reaction, he looked like he was going to pass out himself when you fainted. It took both those crazy longshoremen and Judge Markowitz to keep him from charging in here while you were throwing up." Jamie sighed. "Now they tell me he's sort of catatonic—he can't even talk or speak to anybody until you come out."

"But he doesn't love me," Lacy protested. "Remember, it took the threat of a federal suit to get him to offer to marry me!

"I really haven't got time to discuss it now," she

said, squaring her shoulders determinedly, "but all Michael Echevarria's ever offered me was expensive jewelry and the Ferrari and a sable coat and a lot of sleazy, humiliating propositions."

"Lacy—" Jamie began.

"It's all right, I've made up my mind," Lacy said, looking brave. "Although it's going to be a loveless marriage, I feel I owe Michael something. I'm really very sorry for zapping him today with Potts Promotions and a media event where they had to call the riot police. I really had no idea Walter Moretti was going to show up when he wasn't supposed to and attack Pottsy, just because Walter thought Candy was going to try to date Pottsy behind his back. From what I heard, nobody gave Walter a chance to explain that he has a permit to carry his gun because he's a private eye. What happened after that certainly wasn't my fault, but you've got to agree it *is* my fault that all the television cameras were here and that the riot is going to be on all three networks tonight. I did hire Pottsy to stage the media promotion, but I never intended to do all this to Echevarria Enterprises and *Fad* magazine, believe me."

Lacy settled the pearl strands at the boat neckline of the ivory silk dress and viewed them critically.

"Lacy, what I was trying to say was—" Jamie began again.

"It doesn't matter," Lacy said firmly. "I don't care what Michael Echevarria thinks—I didn't want to totally put him out of business. I'm going to have to patch things up as best I can."

"OK," the assistant editor said, a rather puzzled look on her pretty face, "it makes sense, sort of. At least I think so. Anyway, I get the impression none of your wedding guests outside want a perfectly good marriage ceremony to go to waste. Not after what they've been through in the last hour and a half." Jamie took a quick look at her wristwatch. "Which reminds me, they've been into the champagne for quite a while now. They were getting pretty happy the last time I looked."

"How's your tummy, dearest?" Lacy's mother asked, kissing her daughter fondly on her pale cheek. "No more upchuckie feeling?" The slightly darker pair of emerald eyes looked into the other green ones questioningly. "How long, Lacy, dear," she wanted to know, "have you been having these symptoms?"

Lacy looked from her friend the assistant editor to her mother and back again. "Well, actually," she said, frowning, "I really hadn't thought about it until today."

"Oh, baby," her mother said, smiling tenderly, "are you sure, or are you just guessing? Have you bought one of those nice little kits they sell in the drugstore so you can find out?"

"No, not actually," Lacy said, clutching her lower lip between her teeth and looking thoughtful. "But now that I've had time to think about it, I believe that's just what's going to happen."

"Wait a minute," Jamie Hatworth cried. "I'm not following this. Are you two discussing what I think you're discussing? Just standing there calmly, discussing it?" She clutched her hair with both hands in mock despair. "I mean, is this the same obvious conclusion that people obviously conclude when they're discussing such things?"

"Oh, darling," Lacy's mother rebuked her softly, "you really should keep track of these little items.

Especially right before a wedding, when you want to look and feel your best. I could have brought some smelling salts, you know, or some soda crackers for your tummy.''

"Well," Lacy said somewhat defensively, "there's no need for panic. I still don't *have* to get married, Mother. I could always be a single parent. I think I'd make a good one. I am definitely not marrying Michael for that reason, I want to get that much straight.

"And don't tell me what Dr. Spock says about single parenthood," she added a little crossly. "I don't want to hear it right now. I've got enough on my mind marrying a man who's wonderful but who only does what his lawyers tell him to do."

Lacy took a deep breath. "All I can think of is that it must have been that first night in Tu—that first night when I wasn't expecting anything to happen. My goodness," she said heatedly, "everything's been so confused lately with my major career changes and a new job as a fashion writer, and then getting involved with Michael Echevarria, and then Alex van Renssalaer. I certainly couldn't keep track of everything, could I?"

"We're not discussing *not* getting married now, are we?" the assistant editor cried incredulously. "Dear heaven, is this the Echevarria conglomerate's baby, or what? It must be, if I'm following this crazy logic." She shuddered. "Oh, my God, does this mean nobody's gotten around to telling big, mean Michael yet? You mean he doesn't *know*?"

"That's another thing, dear," Lacy's mother said. "Do you really think you ought to go ahead and marry Michael just because you feel you owe him that much? Or should we have your father speak to him and give him a choice? Under the circumstances, don't you want to be as considerate as possible?

"I mean," she murmured, "if you think the bridegroom should be in on any decision making, your father would be glad to help. He could tell the best man very confidentially and then have Freddie— that's his name, isn't it?—relay the message to your bridegroom. I believe that's what your grandfather did at your Aunt Prudence's wedding."

"The whole family's crazy," Jamie Hatworth breathed, staring at them. "But, by God, it explains a lot."

"Oh, mother," Lacy said testily, "it's not the same thing at all. Aunt Pru never did want to tell Uncle John whether Norman was his or not, that's what that was all about. And Norman turned out to look just like Uncle John—Aunt Pru was just being bitchy."

"Mama," an urgent juvenile voice said at the bathroom door, "the dog just ate part of a law book, the lady out here said. Now he's hiding under the desk."

"Not now, Philip," Jamie Hatworth yelled, "we're busy.

"Well, what have we decided?" she asked. "Are we pregnant or aren't we? We are? Probably? Yes, I know, as soon as you buy the cute, little test in the drugstore or see a doctor, whichever comes first, but yes.

"Almost yes," she said, taking a consensus. "Now, do we have a bridegroom, or don't we? Just nod your heads, please. Yes, definitely. We have a big, mad one waiting outside." The assistant editor took a deep breath. "OK, that brings us to item three, the wedding. I hate to ask this, ladies, but do we have a wedding, or don't we?"

"For heaven's sake, Jamie," Lacy said, frowning, "I've done Michael and his company so much damage today I have to make some sort of gesture, don't I? Just maybe the public won't believe everything they see on television and in the newspapers about those darned harassment charges and the riot if they know that at least I went ahead and married him."

"That sounds reasonable, dear," her mother said, giving her a last affectionate pat on the cheek. "Don't forget to keep your veil down, bunnykins, until the groom lifts it to kiss you at the end of the ceremony."

"On the other hand, who knows?" Jamie Hatworth muttered, opening the door to the restroom to let them pass. "Maybe this is all a fantasy trip. Maybe I'm really Princess Leia, and I'm going to the wrong kind of shrink if I ever hope to find Luke Skywalker."

"Oh, rats," Lacy murmured under her breath, "why couldn't Pottsy have used a little more . . . restraint? Then I wouldn't have to be doing all this."

"I usually," Judge Samuel Markowitz said, "read a few appropriate selections from famous poets to the happy couple before I begin the marriage ceremony."

His Honor bent his head slightly and looked over his glasses at the large and varied wedding party crowded into his inner chambers. The party that included the bride's handsome mother and father, Irving and Morton Fishman and their wives, Jamie

Hatworth's sons with Mike the layout artist, the judge's executive assistant and legal staff, two New York City policemen, Edward, the Echevarria chauffeur, and a delegation of small men from Belmont race track holding a large floral horseshoe rescued from the SWAT team's sweep and decorated with a large gold ribbon that read, GOOD LUCK, MICK. In the distance the bridal party could hear the driving beat of the Peptic Ulcers rock band playing assorted selections from *The King and I*.

Lacy held her bridal bouquet of rare cattleya orchids in pale tones of gold and ivory, which Jamie Hatworth had handed her rather stiffly. *Michael*, her mind kept repeating, with a note of wonder. It seemed incredible that before all these people in the judge's chambers in the New York Supreme Court Building, she was really marrying him.

From behind her veil, Lacy shot a look at the tall man standing next to her, stony faced and ramrod straight in his elegant, dark Savile Row suit, St. Laurent shirt and gray-on-pearl silk tie. Almost reluctantly she allowed her eyes to travel from Michael Echevarria's dark, curly head to his thick eyelashes, which tended to look even longer in profile, his straight, handsome nose and the sternly flattened curve of his lips, where she knew dimpled indents could flash when he spoke. As always, she felt her breath catch with unwilling emotion. Just looking at him always had the same effect on her, but this time the familiar breathless feeling was accompanied by a pained heaviness in the vicinity of her heart. Not a good feeling. A terrible feeling, actually, to have when one was gazing at one's husband-to-be. Not once had Michael looked at her, even when she took her place beside him; he kept his eyes straight ahead. Lacy noticed a small muscle that jumped almost spasmodically in the angle of his tight jaw. In fact, she thought, peering through the double layer of ivory tulle, there was a pronounced twitch in his right eyelid as well.

"Now, Adelaide Lacy and Michael Sean," Judge Markowitz began in a deep, judicial voice. "Before we begin, let us take a few moments to consider some beautiful thoughts on the joining of two happy people in the bonds of matrimony. Let us dedicate ourselves to the meaning of love as I read the famous poem 'How do I love thee?' by Elizabeth Barrett Browning." He opened the book of poetry his legal secretary handed him. "It speaks of the most sublime forms of love that all of us should remember as we tread life's sometimes stormy roadways that cannot but lead to the happy rainbow with our loved one beside us.

"Married, that is," His Honor added by way of clarification. He cleared his throat. " 'How do I love thee? Let me count the ways. I love thee to the depth and breadth of my being and height My soul can reach—' "

"Michael," Lacy murmured impulsively, feeling that she had to say something, "I'm really sorry you have to marry me." She saw him stiffen, but he kept his eyes fixed on the judge. She hadn't noticed it before, but there was a small stream of perspiration that ran down the side of his handsome face and into his shirt collar. "Michael," she whispered a little more loudly, "I really wish things had turned out better today. I *did* have Pottsy plan a media event so I could denounce you, but I didn't arrange for a *riot*. I just thought you'd want to know.''

For a long moment there was no reaction. Then she saw his eyelid twitch so fiercely that it brought an answering tremor in the muscles in his cheek. The matron of honor gave the bride a discreet poke in the side with her elbow and frowned.

Without turning his head the chairman of the board said in a low, uneven voice, "Lacy, I admit I've had to make some hard moves. I can see now I forced you into . . . some hard countermoves. You don't have to apologize.''

" '—when feeling out of sight,' '' Judge Markowitz was saying with deep emotion, " 'For the ends of Being and ideal Grace—' ''

"But I do have to apologize." Impatiently, Lacy blew the tulle veil away from her mouth. "Oh, Michael, I could have turned you down in the bar that night," she whispered, "but subconsciously I don't think I wanted to! I hate to tell you that, but it's the truth.''

"Shhh," the matron of honor hissed, bending forward to glare at the groom.

But he was staring straight ahead. "I don't mind admitting I wanted you any way I could get you, Lacy," Michael Echevarria's voice murmured rather rustily, "after that first night in Tu—after the first time we met. I've been a damned fool, that's all.''

" 'I love thee to the level of every day's most quiet need,' '' Judge Markowitz said, frowning a little over the disruptions, " 'By sun and candle-light—' ''

Lacy couldn't drag her eyes away from the tall man beside her who had just confessed that he, too, had made a mistake. "You make it sound as if—" Her voice broke. "As if it's all over."

Now Michael Echevarria turned to her, his molten silver eyes full of an expression she had never seen before. Regret? she thought, startled. Torment? Something else?

"Well, isn't it?" he grated.

"Oh, Michael," Lacy said, pressing the tulle veiling against her nose distractedly to see him more clearly. "I don't want you to hate me! I think you *did* break the law just like Alex van Renssalaer said by threatening to fire me if I didn't date you, but I still love you. I just wanted you to know I was sorry you have to marry me, that's all."

"Lacy," the matron of honor muttered, lifting her eyebrows and wagging her head sidewise to indicate that other people were listening. "Can you two knock it off?"

" 'I love thee freely, as men strive for right,' " Judge Markowitz was saying. " 'I love thee Purely, as they turn from Praise. I love thee with the passion—' "

"I don't hate you," the chairman of the board said huskily. The twitch in his carved right eyelid was very pronounced. "On the contrary, Lacy, I've found that I can't live without you. You've taken over my life. I'm not normally an insomniac, and it's really getting to me."

"But you don't *love* me," Lacy whispered. "It's just not the same as wanting a little peace and quiet! Or a good night's sleep!"

"I'd like," Judge Markowitz said, raising his voice slightly, "to go on to a few selections from the Rubaiyat of Omar Khayyam. Unless the participants would like to retire—'' He looked around the crowded room. ''Well, the participants could go out into the hallway and talk this over.''

''I'm crazy about you, Lacy,'' the chairman of the board said firmly, his gray eyes gleaming. ''I wouldn't be standing here getting married to you, sweetheart, if I didn't love you.''

His words were almost drowned out by a peculiarly doleful noise from under Judge Markowitz's desk, where Sicky-Poo lay alternately moaning and snarling.

''You do?'' Lacy screamed. She would have thrown herself into Michael Echevarria's arms at that moment, but the judge put out his hand to restrain her. ''Darling, I never knew you loved me! You haven't said a thing all these weeks—''

''I have another selection, from Dante's *Inferno*,'' the judge said sternly, looking over his glasses. ''But I won't go on unless we really want this. Mick, is there something we should talk over?''

''Of course, I love you, Lacy. I have to love you—to keep you from demolishing not only my company but my life.'' Michael Echevarria reached over the judge's arm to catch his bride's hand and close his fingers around it. ''Darling, I need you. I need things I never thought I needed before. Like someone to argue with me, and tell me when I'm wrong, and keep me from being a ruthless bastard.

''I need to hold you in my arms, sweetheart,'' he said softly, shoving the judge's arm away to draw her to him, ''to find you in my bed with me when I wake up in the middle of the night and want to talk to you. God, it will be good to wake up in the middle of the night for a change, instead of trying to watch the Late, Late Show and going nuts.''

Judge Markowitz was listening intently as he studied the faces of the bride and groom. ''I think while we're getting this cleared up,'' he said, readjusting his glasses, ''we might as well move on with more beautiful thoughts. How about a nice Shakespearean sonnet? I used to have one that begins—'' He pushed his glasses back on his nose and recited, '' 'Shall I compare thee to a summer's day? Thou art more lovely and more temperate. Rough winds do shake the darling buds of May—' ''

''Oh, darling,'' the bride said, ''you tear my heart out when you look at me like that.'' She grabbed for the white silk handkerchief in the groom's pocket and used it to dab at the perspiration-wet curls at his temples. ''Your poor eye.

''There,'' she told him, touching her finger tip lightly at the corner of his lid, ''does that make it feel better?''

''It helps,'' the black panther said softly, kissing the tips of her captive fingers. ''Everything helps, precious. I just didn't know it before.''

'' '—But thy eternal summer shall not fade,' te-dum, te-dum, something. I haven't used this one in years,'' the judge said. ''Ah—'Nor lose possession of that fair thou ow'st—' ''

''I don't believe this,'' the matron of honor muttered, staring at Freddie, the bartender. ''Are you *crying*?''

'' '—So long as men can breathe or eyes can see, So long lives this, and this gives life to thee,' '' the judge finished triumphantly. ''What about,'' he suggested, "the utility version of nuptials I reserve for weddings aboard sightseeing boats and on the observation platform of the Empire State Building?"

"There's just one thing, darling, if you're going to marry me," Lacy murmured. She stuck the white silk handkerchief back into the groom's breast pocket. "I don't want to argue with you, but I can't move up to Gloria Farnham's job without some sort of training. I'm going to have to keep short hours, anyway, because—"

"Go for it, Sam," the president and chairman of the board ordered. He grabbed his bride to him and kissed her through the veil on her nose. "Before we lose it."

Judge Markowitz nodded. "Adelaide Lacy, do you take this man," His Honor said at machine-gun speed, "to be your lawfully wedded husband?"

"Wait a minute," the bridegroom interrupted. He took the bride's hands from the back of his neck gently. "Darling, see if you can just turn around for a moment, and say, 'I do.' "

"Of course," Lacy said, her eyes shining like emerald stars. "I do, I do, I do."

"Once is enough," the judge said. "Michael Sean, do you—"

"You bet I do," he growled. "Look, honey." He held out his hand so the best man could place two golden wedding rings in it. "One for you, one for me. Plain, no frills—solid gold from Kay's Jewelers. I sent Freddie over to Atlantic Avenue this morning to get them."

"Under the powers vested in me," Judge Markowitz shot ahead, "by the state of New York, I now pronounce you husband and wife." He twitched the edge of his robe and looked down, feeling a suspicious dampness around his ankles. "Great guns," His Honor exclaimed, staring. "Some damned thing's eaten the hem off my robe!"

"Darn, Michael, I've underestimated you," the bride said smiling. She was admiring her solid-gold wedding band glistening on her slender white hand. "You do have a sense of humor, after all, you rat."

"Only with you, dearest, only with you," he murmured, pulling her into his arms again. "You've reformed me."

"The veil," Lacy screamed. "Watch the veil, Michael!"

"To hell with it," her husband muttered, the *zap*! *bam*! and *powie*! of his burning kisses searing through two layers of silk tulle.

"I came up to kiss the bride," Otto Posniaski, the other groomsman said, looking around. "Have I missed anything?"

Judge Markowitz closed his book of poetry with a sigh. "This was just one of those weddings. You get them every once in a while. I wouldn't hang around if I were you," he said to the longshoreman best man, who was watching the bridegroom kiss the bride. "Why don't you come and have some more champagne? The crowd seems to be going that way."

"Lacy, you can throw your bouquet now," the matron of honor offered hopefully. "Lacy—the bridal-bouquet toss for the next bride, remember?"

"When Mickey concentrates, he don't hear a thing," Freddie, the bartender, told her. His admiring eyes swept over Jamie Hatworth's petite figure as she tried, more or less, to gently kick the bride in the ankle to get her attention. "Listen, you beautiful, little doll, have you got a date for the reception?"

"Oh, Michael," Lacy murmured when she could get her breath. "You really have the most fantastic kisses—did I ever tell you that? I guess I would have followed you to the ends of the earth, anyway. Oh, good grief, that reminds me," she said, pulling back to smile up at him mistily. "I've got a really great surprise for you. Michael—don't look at me like that!"

"I don't know," Jamie Hatworth told the best man. She reached over and jerked the magnificent shower of ivory and gold orchids out of the bride's oblivious grasp and hugged it to her nicely rounded bosom. "Actually, I'm spoken for at the moment. But I'm reconsidering big, strong, *macho* types, believe me," she murmured, turning to look him over. "I never saw one cry all down the front of his tux before."

The judge examined the hem of his robe, frowning. "I'm hoping," he told his legal secretary, "we don't have to call the exterminator for something as big as I think this is."

"Don't look like that, Michael," Lacy cried. "You don't have to look like that, just because I said I have a surprise for you! It's something good, don't you believe me?"

"Angel, I can't help it, I have some conditioned reflexes I have to work on, that's all. Can we wait," he said, looking at the bridal party milling around the champagne bottles in the judge's outer office, "until the reception at the Pierre?"

"Well, we certainly can't talk very well here," Lacy agreed. The sound of champagne corks popping in the reception area was accompanied by a snarling salvo indicative of a Doberman attacking. "We need some place where we can be alone."

"I know just the place, dearest," Michael murmured, kissing her. "In fact, I've made reservations for a great suite on the penthouse floor. Although there's a nice little bar downstairs we can drop in on any time we want."

"Michael," Lacy breathed, "oh, for heaven's sake, you're a sentimental fool. I can't believe it!"

"Only for you, dearest," he murmured. "The place has great food, even if you do have to call room service for it."

"Don't tell me," she cried. "Wait—does it have music, like selections from the movie *Dr. Zhivago*? In quadraphonic sound?"

"And a great view of the city at night," he confirmed, kissing her ear. "The Lear jet's standing by for us at La Guardia—we can make Tulsa in less than three hours."

His hands lifted the veil slowly, and at last he regarded her beautiful face full of love. "My own dearest wife," he told her softly, "I may still be a roughneck, but I do love you. Whatever happens, now I've got you where I can keep an eye on you.

"All right, angel," he said, bracing himself perceptibly. "I can't stand the suspense—what's this big surprise you've got for me?"

"Well, Michael," Lacy began, thinking of the room in Connecticut with the rainbow painted on the walls, "this time you're really going to love it."

* * * * *

FREE!!
BOOKS BY MAIL
CATALOGUE

BOOKS BY MAIL will share with you our current bestselling books as well as hard to find specialty titles in areas that will match your interests. You will be updated on what's new in books at no cost to you. Just fill in the coupon below and discover the convenience of having books delivered to your home.

PLEASE ADD $1.00 TO COVER THE COST OF POSTAGE & HANDLING.